Cold Shadows

Bland P.I.R – Book One

by

KA Richardson

To Ange
Much love as always ♡
Hope you enjoy!

Copyright © KA Richardson, 2021

The right of KA Richardson to be identified as the author of this work has been asserted in accordance with the Copyright, Designs and Patents Act 1998

All rights reserved. No part of this publication may be reproduced, stored in a retrieval system, or transmitted in any form or by any means, electronic, mechanical, photocopying, scanning, recording or otherwise, without the prior permission of the publisher.

This is a work of fiction. Any resemblance to real persons, living or dead is coincidental. Names, characters, places and occurrences are products of the author's imagination or used fictitiously.

Published by KA Richardson – 2021
www.kerryannrichardson.co.uk

Cover design by
Emmy Ellis of studioenp

Cover design copyright © studioenp

For everyone who believes in romance, in whatever form that may take…

Acknowledgements

Having previously written crime novels set in the UK, I was a little nervous about writing romantic suspense set in the USA – but as I wrote, I found I loved the freedom it gives me as much as I love doing the research! These stories are all works of fiction, but the characters have felt real to me throughout – hopefully you will enjoy meeting them as much as I have!

There are so many people I need to give thanks to – Kate Noble of Noble Owl Proofreading – the wonderfully talented Emmy Ellis from studioenp who has done the amazing cover designs, the fabulous formatting, and has gone totally above and beyond with her amazing service. Both have been just brilliant to deal with throughout the publication process.

My whole family are so supportive – my husband, Peter, who makes the best coffee even if I let it go cold when I'm 'in the zone'. My lovely mam, Jeannet, who whisks me away from the laptop for much-needed downtime. My dad, Derek, who encourages me to get the books finished so I can become rich and buy him his Aston Martin. The support and patience my family provide is unwavering and constant. They all make me so proud every single day.

My close friends are my rocks – constant support through good and bad, and not being too shy to tell me when I'm doing something I shouldn't be! You know who you are – but to mention a few names (by no means all) Claire, Angela, Dionne, Rachel, Vicky, Eileen, Michelle, and Char. Keep reaching for the stars – even if you miss, your dreams will be within your grasp.

I would be nothing without those who love me and whom I love in return.

Finally, I'd like to thank *YOU*, the reader. Writing really wouldn't be as pleasurable without each and every one of you, and, whether I know you or not, you make my dreams a reality. It makes me proud to admit I'm a member of so many book clubs online, and get to meet wonderful people on an almost daily basis.

Bland P.I.R

Bland: Protection. Investigation. Recovery.

When Gabriel Bland first thought up the name for his company, it manifested as Bland Protection – it was based off everything he wanted to be in a man, everything he'd learned from his parents, and his life in general – a protector. But it evolved with every mission they undertook, every team member he selected.

Rapidly, the term 'protection' wasn't enough to cover everything they did.

And it was also really obvious to those looking in what the company did. Gabe hadn't really considered the implications prior to its instigation – so before the ink had even dried on the original company name, it had changed to Bland P.I.R, and the original buried under as much cover as the company tech guy, and Gabe's best friend, Dave Sowerby, could find.

Dave made sure that only the bare-bones basics about the company were available on any internet searches – he built their website and in-house security system from the ground up – and even the most hardened hackers would have issues getting through it.

The business was built on trust – Gabe handpicked every single member of his team. Some were ex-forces, though they'd all attest that once in the forces, you never really leave. All were unique – all were invaluable – and all were *family*.

The reputation for the company was built on word of mouth – Gabe didn't need to advertise. He was highly decorated as a Navy SEAL, and his reputation alone opened doors across most nations of the world. He had a direct line to the President's office, not that he'd ever had reason to use it yet, and often took on missions that the alphabet agencies had no cause dealing with. His team were adept at undercover, they all came with their own unique histories and skill sets. He had the money to buy the latest tech, ensure that the training for the team was consistently above par, and kept his eyes peeled for anything that would improve the work environment for his team.

The business will be here for years to come – instilling its values into all team members. Truth above all else, and working with integrity and morals to Protect the innocent, Investigate all cases, and Recover whatever is required.

The stories in this series cover various missions undertaken by Bland P.I.R – as a reader, you'll get to know Gabe and each member of his team individually. I'm sure Gabe would echo me when I say, welcome to the Bland P.I.R. family.

Chapter One

Rhododendron Cemetery, Rhododendron

The funeral had been hard – it was always going to be that way. Losing one of their own was never easy.

Gabriel Bland sighed and rubbed his hand over his eyes for the hundredth time that afternoon. The rivulets of rain running down his forehead were removed for all of a second before they returned.

He was the last one in the cemetery. It was the same with any mission. First one in, last one out, like an unwritten rule. He knew no other way; it was just what he did. Always had and always would.

Gabe placed his hand on the mound of freshly dug dirt. A single tear melded with the rain, indistinguishable to anyone else, but he knew it was there. And he didn't care.

Terence Aldershot, or Shotgun as he had been affectionately called by the team, had been shot and killed during a mission in the Kabul province a few weeks before. It was the first loss for the team, though not the first for Gabe himself. He'd been occupied getting a woman and two children to safety when it had happened. He hadn't even needed to be told. The dread had settled in his stomach like a hard ball the moment the shot had ricocheted around the small village. He'd hidden the woman and children away and ran around the corner to where Shotgun had been standing. Deacon Marshall, another member of the team, had already yanked Shotgun from view and behind their armored vehicle. Deacon had been pumping Shotgun's chest up and down rhythmically, but it was already too late. Shotgun was gone.

Gabe sighed, pulling himself back from the sights his mind refused to forget. Checking his watch, he stared for a minute. It was later than he thought. And it was time to go. The last thing he wanted to do was attend the wake – he hated them. Would usually do anything he could to avoid them. But it was his duty, and he'd never been one to run from duty.

Darkness was starting to claw at the light. Even through the heavy rain, Gabe could see the sun's light fading. He removed the tissue from his top pocket and wiped the mud from his hand carefully, turned and walked back across to the path and up to the entrance where his car was parked.

His senses suddenly prickled – someone else was here. His stride didn't falter. He reached the halfway point of the path – the cross-junction ahead meant access to the whole cemetery was possible, and subtly, he glanced from side to side. Seeing nothing, he continued.

The sound of pounding feet against the tarmac was sudden, and he tensed, ready for an attack. What he didn't expect as he spun to meet the oncoming runner was being nearly knocked off his feet by someone barreling into him.

'Oh god, I'm sorry, I …' The woman checked over her shoulder, looking the way she'd come from.

Looking for whom? Interesting.

'Are you okay?' Gabe kept his voice quiet, his hands resting on the woman's arms. He quickly ran his gaze up and down her body, checking for injuries. The only things he saw were utter fear in her eyes and the way her deep-auburn hair shone in the oncoming dusk. *How can it shine like that in the rain?* He was drawn from his mental examination of her hair by her voice – softly spoken, but the fear she obviously felt gave it an edge.

'I'm fine, sorry. I didn't mean to run into you. Are you okay? I didn't hurt you, did I?'

'It'd take a lot more than that to hurt me,' he said wryly, flashing her a grin. 'What're you running from?'

'Running? No, nothing, I mean I was running but not from anything other than the rain. I'll be on my way as long as you're okay?'

She shot another quick peek down the path toward a dark copse of trees at the end. The whole area was in shadow, the dusk already plunging the area into darkness. He doubted she could see anything, but he did. He was trained to see those hidden in the shadows, and he squinted almost imperceptibly. *A man* – he was sure of it. He needed to get the woman out of the cemetery safely. Whoever was after her would grab her the second he left if he didn't.

How do I do that? She plainly doesn't want to ask for help despite being terrified. Finds it hard to trust? You and the rest of us, darlin'.

He stopped the knowing grin appearing on his face as a plan unfolded.

Shuffling a little, Gabe let out a gasp. Completely fake, but she wouldn't know that.

'Oh my god, you are injured. What did I hurt?'

'Not hurt – just tweaked my ankle a little. It'll be fine, I'm sure.' Testing the water, he took a step forward and winced visibly. He could act when he wanted to.

He didn't anticipate her moving to his side and shrugging his shoulder and arm over her much smaller one. 'Lean on me, I'll help you to your car.' Her voice was shaking, even as she 'helped' him farther up the path. She kept swinging frantic glimpses behind them to the copse of trees.

They reached the gates in no time, and Gabe stumbled, using the motion to peer behind them also. The trees hadn't changed – and the shadow hadn't moved. That at least was good news.

They approached his pickup truck, and it unlocked, the sensor activated by proximity to the key in his pocket. He loved this truck; it had everything he could possibly want. Including a gun safe in the central console.

'Ouch, it's my right foot. I'm not certain I can …'

The rustle behind him was quiet. Any normal person wouldn't have even noticed it as being out of place. The shadow had moved from his position in the trees. He was now near the gate to the cemetery. Mere meters away from him and the damsel in distress beside him.

No more charades. It's time for action.

Without saying anything, he tightened his grip on her waist and threw her in the passenger seat. Ignoring the shocked gasp, he hopped in the driver's seat, hit the start button, and eased out of the cemetery car park.

All business now, Gabe said, 'Does he have a car with him?'

'What the hell are you doing? Stop the car this instant. You can't just throw someone in your car like that. Who the hell do you think you are?'

Two hells in quick succession. She's feisty. 'Answer the question – does he have a car with him?'

She turned in her seat, glaring at him. 'I don't know. I didn't even know he was there until it was too late. You didn't jar your ankle at all, did you? Stop the car, right now.

I'm getting out.' Her hand strayed to the passenger door handle.

Momentarily, he wondered if she would actually try and open it while the vehicle was in motion.

She thought better of it and put her hand back in her lap.

'Who is he?'

'I don't know,' she said quietly.

'What's he after you for?'

'What is this? *Jeopardy*? Even if I did know, why on earth would I tell you? I don't know you. You've all but kidnapped me and won't stop the car to let me out.' Her lip jutted out; she was obviously annoyed and terrified.

But what was he supposed to do? Leave her to the shadow man's clutches?

'Would you rather I let him get hold of you and whisk you off to wherever?' His tone was blunt, but maybe that's what she needed.

She turned her face away from him, not realizing he could see her reflection in the window. Her expression went from anger to shock to acceptance in the blink of an eye, and she moved her head back toward him. 'No, I am grateful you helped, but you could've just said you'd seen him. I probably would have gone with you.'

'No, you wouldn't. You'd have thought I was with him if I'd said anything. Anyway, enough said. We're not being followed. Is he likely to know where you live?'

'I'm not from around here. I was visiting a grave. My car is parked a block away from the cemetery.'

Gabe wasn't even aware he'd narrowed his eyes until she called him on it.

'Don't look at me like I'm lying – the car park was full, there was a funeral late this afternoon.'

'Sorry, so where to? Your car can stay where it is until later. I'll get the details off you and make sure it's picked up.'

'Why are you doing this?' Her voice was filled with emotion. Almost as if no one had ever helped her before.

Which he knew couldn't be true. Everyone needed help sometimes. *Maybe she'd just never accepted it?*

'Because I thought you were in danger – it's kind of what I do. I'm Gabe by the way.'

There was a momentary pause before she responded. 'Paige Matthews. I'll get my car tomorrow. I don't need it right now. And just dropping me at a hotel would be great. I've not booked in anywhere. Was intending to once I'd been to the cemetery.' The words fell from her lips easily.

But Gabe could see she was either lying or holding something back. He didn't call her on it, however, she'd tell him when she was ready. If he pushed now, she'd never trust him.

Chapter Two

Rhododendron Inn – Rhododendron

Gabe pulled the pickup into the parking bays outside a small inn – not a name she recognized. The building was beautiful. Paige assessed it carefully. Large rhododendron bushes were spread throughout the front garden, and there was a metal arch at the base of the porch. The building itself was like a picture postcard, all subtle curves within strict lines of architecture. Whoever had designed it had an eye for making stone look pretty.

How the heck do I get out of this?

To stay here had to be so far out of her price range it was silly. That said, everything was out of her price range currently. Besides, she had a place to stay. She just didn't want *him* to know of it.

If she'd known the town a little better, she'd have just given a random street and asked him to drop her off there.

'Gabe? Is that you? It's been a while. Tough day today. How you doing?' As Gabe got out of the truck, a woman ran down the steps. He swept her into a warm hug, planting a kiss on her cheek.

And a flare of jealousy swept over Paige. *What the hell? I don't even know him – I've no right to be jealous of anything.*

'I'm okay, darlin'. Yes, it was a tough day, everyone else is at the bar for the wake. I've come across a stray who needs a room tonight. Do you have room?'

'Always room for you and yours, Gabe.' She smiled past him at Paige. Stepping out of Gabe's arms gracefully, the woman opened the passenger door.

'Hi, I'm Alice. I own this place. You have any bags?'

'Um, no. I'll only be here one night. Heading back home in the morning.'

Paige got out of the truck reluctantly. *Another fine mess you've landed yourself in. You should've just done what Mags said to do – gone straight to the office and spoken to the boss at the protection company. Instead of getting waylaid in the cemetery and almost accosted.* Instant guilt flashed through her – she'd been at the cemetery for a reason. Not to visit a grave like she'd said, but to pay respects at the nearest cemetery she could. It was a reason she definitely did not want to discuss but she shouldn't diminish or betray the memories by making excuses.

'Come on in – let's get you settled.'

'Put the room on my tab, Alice. Paige has had quite a scare – she needs a place to unwind and de-stress before she heads back tomorrow.'

'I can talk for myself, you know,' Paige grumbled as she followed Alice up the steps. 'And I'm perfectly capable of paying for my own room.' *Is it that obvious I don't have any money?* Paige sighed softly and walked into the hallway behind Alice and Gabe.

Her eyes widened, flicking around and taking in the interior. The hall had a hardwood floor that almost moved due to the sparkles from the chandelier mounted above on the high ceiling. The décor was warm and inviting, soft cream and pale pink. A huge vase of rhododendron flowers sat on the small table in the center of the hallway. Heavy oak doors led off to other rooms, and the pictures mounted on the walls were all well-painted landscapes. Squinting, she tried to see the signature. They were paintings but they were done so well they could have passed for photographs.

'Wow, this is spectacular. Did you decorate this yourself?'

'I did. I inherited it about eighteen months ago. I've turned it into home – glad you like it.'

Forgetting her troubles for a minute, Paige paused in front of the picture directly to her left. It was a mountain scene, with a large lake at the base. The water was painted so skillfully that the ripples looked as if they were moving. Her fingers touched the canvas gently.

'That's one someone I know painted a long time ago – his cabin is at the base of that mountain near the lake. Beautiful, isn't it?'

'Amazing. It draws you in; you can almost feel the water.'

'All of the paintings in the inn are done by the same artist. Feel free to have a browse around, but let's get you settled in first, okay?'

Paige nodded. *How am I going to get out of here?* Part of her wanted to stay – the inn was lovely. But she couldn't stay. And she definitely couldn't pay for a room. The best thing was to slip away as soon as they weren't paying attention. She didn't even know where she was but she knew she'd be able to find her car once she found the cemetery.

Alice led the way through the hall and down a short corridor. 'I'll pop you in the first-floor room, it's nice and quiet, and you won't be disturbed. I expect you'd like to freshen up and maybe have some coffee. I'll put a pot on.

There's a robe hanging on the bathroom door and fresh towels on the bed.'

'Thank you.' What else could she say? She watched Gabe and Alice head back down the hallway and turned left – presumably to the kitchen. Paige frowned. Gabe following meant he intended to stay while they had coffee. That could potentially make it harder for her to leave – he seemed to be very switched on to his surroundings. A rush of warmth flooded her cheeks. *Unusual reaction to thinking about Gabe. It's probably just because he got me out of the cemetery.* She nodded once and pushed the bedroom door open, trying to ignore the other voice in her head arguing back. *Yeah right, more like because his arms wrapped round you like they were made to. Those huge, muscular arms and chiseled chest. You'd have to be dead not to notice how nicely you fit when he caught you. And his eyes – storm-cloud gray, the same as the ones in that picture you liked so much.*

Paige wrapped her arms round herself and suddenly shivered, remembering the reason she was here in the first place. All thoughts of Gabe faded and were replaced by a menacing shadow – it held the face of someone from her past. She shivered again, this time from fear rather than desire.

Who was the man in the shadows today? Was he linked to my past or was this random? She gave one sharp nod – whoever he was, he had to be linked to *him*. Alan Graham, or Al as he was known to everyone. He'd always hated his Sunday name. Al was the one person on earth who had the power and the money to hunt her down wherever she went. If this was linked to Al, she couldn't put anyone else in danger. Leaving today to go to the cemetery had been a mistake – a mistake she knew she had to fix.

She moved to the large window, opening the latches and carefully swinging it outward. Happily, she realized it hadn't made a sound – maybe the watchful Gabe wouldn't even know she'd gone until it was too late. She had about enough change in her purse to pay a cab – she'd call one once she found out where she was. Paige had some experience being quiet – *years of practice*. She slipped out of the window effortlessly and used the side of the house to navigate her way back to the front before picking up the pace and racing down the side of a shop opposite the inn. At the end was a one-pump gas station. The sign above gave her the location she needed, and she pulled out her cell phone and Googled the cab number.

Within minutes, she was seated inside, telling the driver to take her back to the cemetery.

Dread settled in her stomach – hopefully the man who'd been following her had left.

Gabe loved seeing Alice, they all did. She was like a sister to almost everyone on the team. Some of his employees lived out of town, and Alice was always ready with rooms when they needed one. When Alice started speaking animatedly about an encounter with a hedgehog, he smiled.

Glancing at his watch, he realized that twenty minutes had passed and there was still no sign of Paige coming into the kitchen for the coffee.

'Sorry to interrupt, darlin'. I think I'll go check on our guest. She's been a while.'

'She's exhausted, you could see by the shadows under her eyes. I bet she's fallen asleep on the bed.'

'I'll check quietly.'

Alice nodded and stood, removing the tray of whatever it was she was baking from the stove. Gabe made his way back down the hallway leading to the room Alice had allocated to Paige.

He placed his ear to the door, listening intently.

When he couldn't hear any movement, he pressed the handle down and swung the door open, expecting to see Paige asleep. The towels were still where he knew Alice would have left them, the bed linens were still smooth and not even sat on, let alone slept on. Even the door to the en suite was ajar.

The only thing out of place was the open window.

Realization dawned quickly, and Gabe dashed from the room to the front door. Flinging it open, he stepped outside, half expecting to see Paige in the yard.

But the driveway was clear but for his truck.

Paige had gone.

If I know women, and I'm pretty sure I do, she's headed to get her car from wherever she parked it.

Sticking his head back into the house, he shouted for Alice. 'Paige has done a runner. I need to go. Catch you later.'

Alice bobbed her head, and he turned tail and hopped back into his truck, gunning the engine and driving back to the cemetery. Approaching the junction, a cab drove past him the opposite way. Not unusual, but he knew instantly she'd found a base location and taken a cab there – it made perfect sense. What she didn't know was the shadow man was likely still lying in wait to see if she returned. He might even know her car. *Hell, he might've found her already.*

Gabe pressed his foot firmly on the accelerator. He increased his speed again, screeching into the car park, eyes scanning around rapidly. The place was empty. Darkness had fallen fully while he was at Alice's inn, and the rain was still falling steadily – wherever she was, she'd be soaked through, no doubt.

Not knowing where Paige had parked her car was a problem – there were several streets around the cemetery. All she'd said was she'd parked a block away. He drove around for half an hour before finally accepting the knowledge she was gone. *Damn it.*

There was only one other thing he could do, and that was to head to the office and do some searches to see if he could locate her through other means.

Paige made it to her car and back to the house without difficulty. She parked several streets over and walked the familiar route to the shelter where she now lived. She entered the secure code into the gate lock, slipped inside then made sure the gate closed firmly behind her. Non-residents weren't allowed in after dark, and the secure code was changed weekly so no one uninvited could use it to get in.

It was the security that helped Paige feel safe – that and knowing Mags was inside. Mags Brannigan didn't judge – she was there for all the residents in the shelter, most of whom had fled domestic abuse with their children. It was a small shelter – everyone helped out, but Mags owned and ran the place.

Paige punched in the password to the house and waited mere seconds for her friend to arrive at the door from the kitchen. Mags swept through and pulled Paige into a tight hug.

'Child, where on earth have you been? You know I like the place locked down well before now. What happened?'

'I didn't go to the Bland offices. I'm sorry, Mags. I took a detour and went to the local cemetery. There was a funeral this afternoon, and I parked a few streets over. I needed to go – I can't explain it any other way. But someone was there, they watched me and followed me. A man named Gabe helped me. He drove me to an inn. I didn't want to tell a stranger about the shelter so I went with him. I just got a cab over to my car from the garage in Rhododendron. I should've just gone straight to the office. I'm sorry, Mags.'

'Gabe you say?' Her eyes narrowed in thought, but before Paige could ask anything, Mags continued. 'I'm glad he helped you. Are you sure you weren't followed back here by whoever was in the cemetery?'

'Yes – I drove back like you taught me. Didn't see another car behind me the whole journey.'

'Okay – go freshen up. The others have already eaten – there's some leftovers, though.'

'Can I just have some toast, please? I feel a bit nauseous.'

'Sure – I'll bring it up. You go get yourself settled.'

Mags turned and strode purposefully into the kitchen, leaving Paige to head upstairs to her room. Tears pricked her eyes. Each step felt like her feet had lead weights inside. *Why was I so stupid? I shouldn't have left here at all today. What if he finds me?*

The tears spilled over and trickled down her cheeks. Reaching her bedroom door, she escaped inside her sanctuary. She wouldn't be leaving the shelter for a good while. Of that she was certain.

Chapter Three

Six weeks later – Main Street, Rhododendron

Paige gently laid her hand on the grass beneath the large oak tree she was sitting under. Only she knew what lay beneath that soil – something so valuable its owner was willing to kill to get it back.

The ground felt cold beneath her bottom, but she could sit for a moment longer.

A solitary tear rolled down her cheek and dropped from her chin onto the bobbled, woolen sweater she wore over the well-loved pair of denim jeans. Even the thick wool didn't keep the fall chill from her bones today. *And no wonder with you sitting on the cold ground like this.* She wasn't quite ready to get up yet, however.

She traced her hand over the slight difference in the grass – a difference so small that if a person didn't know it was there, they'd never see it. Paige knew its location for one reason and one reason alone – she had stolen the item and buried it there.

It was her insurance policy – the only thing left of her old life. The thing that Al Graham coveted more than anything else.

Everything else in her life had changed. Even herself. Never again would she be the young, carefree woman she'd been back then. The two years since she'd left him the first time felt like a lifetime. Her hair was the most recent change. Gone were the stunning auburn curls she'd been born with, the dark-brown tendrils now hanging down. Redying regularly and straightening every day was essential or the telltale curls would reappear. From looking in the mirror earlier, she saw the stress lines around her blue eyes. Blue eyes that had once held hope and wonder but were now filled with fear and despair. Her once porcelain skin was pasty and pale. She'd dropped weight – the curvy figure she'd once had verged on being too skinny. Stress did that to a person. She felt like the happiest part of her was the part she'd left behind.

There had been a time when Paige had loved walking in the woods or along a pretty beachfront – these days it took all her energy to make it back to her home without having a panic attack or complete meltdown. It had taken more strength than she thought she had to leave the shelter today. Mags had practically kicked her out of the door, desperate for her to get the help Mags knew she so needed.

Another tear fell from her eyes.

The anger hit her suddenly. Coming from nowhere and slamming into her like a steam train. One minute she was fine remembering, and the next she could happily scream and shout.

She drew in a deep breath, steadying herself. Again.

Five more long breaths in and slow breaths out, and she felt a little calmer. A little less ready to kill anyone crossing her path at any rate.

Paige got to her feet and started walking down the main street to the park she knew was there – she needed help. She knew she did. No way could anyone face this on their own.

But how could she explain what *this* was. She stared at the front window to the Bland P.I.R office, and her frown deepened.

I can't do this – no one will believe me anyway. What's the point in asking for help? No one can help me. It's not like he knows where I am at the minute. I've been here for months and haven't seen hide nor hair of him. Just that one incident in the cemetery weeks ago, and that might not have even been linked to him. It was probably just my own paranoia. Maybe he's given up looking.

Dread settled in her stomach – deep down that wasn't the case. It never would be. What she'd taken was far too precious for him just to give up.

She moved her hand toward the doorknob, utter panic settling in once more. Paige turned from the door and made her way to the bench in the park.

Bland P.I.R Office – Main Street, Rhododendron

Gabe's desk faced the window and the street outside. He'd positioned it that way on purpose way back when they'd commissioned the office. He liked to be able to gaze out and see the people walking past, or rushing past, as was the general rule of thumb nowadays. It didn't matter what happened where, people always seemed to feel the need to rush through life and not enjoy the moments. He was one of them. It was all too easy to get wrapped up in the humdrum of life and let the moments pass a man by.

His keen eyes homed in on the woman sitting on the bench opposite. She seemed familiar, but he couldn't place her face. From his desk, she was about average. Average height, average build. Brown hair fastened in a bun. Nothing about her stood out. But she held his attention. It could be to do with the fact he'd watched her approach the office door four times so far today without coming inside. The last time she'd actually reached for the door handle then retreated and sat on the bench.

She would speak to him before the day was out, though.

Of this he was certain. Something was bothering her, and it was his job to find out what.

'Dave, I'm heading over to Bella's for some coffee. Do you want anything getting?'

'Coffee?' asked Dave, his voice a little disbelieving. 'You're going to Bella's for coffee when we have the best coffee machine known to man and all the flavors you could possibly want?' He shook his head, staring at Gabriel in confusion, but then a grin spread rapidly. 'That said, though, Bella's does have the best donuts this side of the county, and we are about to have a debrief session. I'm sure the team wouldn't mind a snack, as long as there's a cinnamon drizzle with my name on it.'

'A dozen donuts. Check. That it?'

Dave nodded and gestured to the door.

Gabe smiled, turning away; Dave was easy pickings. He could never resist the sugar high that Bella's donuts gave. Dave had no idea that Gabe knew about the candy stash in his desk drawer either. Shotgun was another one who'd had a sweet tooth. His hand had been permanently buried in a pack of Twizzlers. Didn't matter where he'd been in the world, those damn Twizzlers had gone with him. Gabe sighed at the slicing pain. Shotgun shouldn't have died that day. None of them should. He banished the thoughts from his mind, opened the main entrance door to the office, and stepped out into the cool, fall sunshine.

Walking across the road, his tummy grumbled and, glancing at his watch, he knew he'd missed lunch. Again. Another thing that happened all too regularly. Him actually being in the office all day like he had been today was a rarity, missing lunch again not so much. He strolled leisurely along the path that cut through the park to the other side of Main Street. Knowing she would see him coming, he pulled his phone from his pocket and pretended to be concentrating on giving the appearance he was texting.

Nearing her he saw she was fiddling, her thumbs bashing against each other as though each was jostling the other for center stage. Whatever was up with her, she was nervous or afraid, possibly both. His face showed no reaction, though, his mind was working overtime. Her face and eyes were cast downward, hiding her features, but he couldn't shake the feeling that he knew her from somewhere. She hadn't even noticed him approaching. He hoped she would glance up, giving him the opportunity to smile and make eye contact. But she didn't even move when he passed her by.

I could just talk to her... but that would make her bolt. Just get what you want from Bella's – she'll approach the office in her own time.

He got the things he wanted from Bella's and was back out heading toward the office within five minutes.

He scanned the area ahead, checking bench to bench, but the woman was nowhere to be seen.

'Shit,' he cursed, speeding up.

Striding in through the front door caused it to slam loudly against the filing cabinet, something that happened around ten times every day, if not from him then from one of the team.

'This is the last straw. That bloody cabinet needs moving. Now.' Gabe's voice echoed off the walls.

It was then he saw the woman from the park bench, who was now standing in front of the counter, looking both shocked and terrified. *Who is she? I know her from somewhere.*

Gabe could come across as intimidating at the best of times – his sheer height made him more so than the average man. He stood at six foot four inches in his socks, and he had broad shoulders and muscular arms to widen his appearance even more. Anyone who knew him knew he was a softy when it counted, but this woman didn't know him.

Doesn't she? His mind still niggled, trying to place where he'd seen her before. Whoever she was, all she'd see now was a huge man who'd smashed a door off a cabinet.

He flashed a quick glance toward Dave who gave an almost imperceptible nod.

The woman's gaze darted from Gabe back toward Dave who was still sitting behind his desk, an exasperated expression on his face. 'How many times have I told you not to barrel into the office like that? Gabe, head back to the meeting room and set up for the debrief. We'll be having words later about your outburst.'

Gabe nodded curtly at Dave and made his way to the room behind Dave's desk. The meeting room was a vague term – it was more an information hub. There was a huge round table where the team sat and debriefed after each case. But there was also CCTV set up, fully wired up with sound. It recorded everything from the front part of the office, and other cameras positioned around the building, and saved the data as encrypted files. Those files were then downloaded and backed up in a central server room in the basement of a nearby building every twenty-four hours. Working in the security business was tough. He had to make sure his team were protected as well as those they were hired to keep safe.

And yes, he meant *his* team. Gabriel Bland was the mastermind behind Bland P.I.R. He alone picked the team members, every one of them had rigorous background checks and went through specific training to become an employee. Except Dave – Dave had been there since day dot. His friend and comrade in arms through years on the same SEAL team. Dave was more than a friend. He was family. Lord knew family wasn't just made up of blood. Dave knew all of Gabe's deepest and darkest secrets. *Almost all, anyway.*

Dave also knew Gabe came across as an ignorant ass at times. He knew he spoke without thinking and sometimes walked around with his eyes shut. And Dave knew when to step up and 'be the boss' in order to put a customer at ease.

Which was what he was doing now. Gabe watched Dave who rested back in his chair, his body language open and believable. Dave was one of those 'what you see is what you get' kind of men, and he could put just about anyone at ease.

Turning the sound on, Gabe leaned his backside onto the edge of the table and listened.

'Sorry about that, miss. Gabe ... well, Gabe forgets how loud he is at times. How can we help?'

The woman's gaze was steady as she faced Dave.

If I didn't know better, I'd say she was adept at not giving her emotions away. But I saw her in the park. Her heart had been breaking. So why was she hiding it now?

He was about to stand and go back out. Dave's job was more doing the tech stuff. Could he cope if she suddenly burst into tears or whatever? But he stilled himself. He trusted Dave. There was never a problem with that. He probably couldn't cope with tears very well himself if that's what was going to happen.

Her bottom lip dropped down – she was considering speaking. And suddenly Gabe remembered where he knew her from. It was *her* – the woman from the cemetery. He knew instantly she'd recognized him from the worry now shadowing her features– it hadn't been at the noise from the door slamming the cabinet, it had been shock at seeing him again! *No way will she hang around now.*

In his eagerness to get to the door and back out to the front, he tripped over the leg of the table and tumbled into one of the office chairs. A loud bang sounded from the office outside, and he knew his team had just arrived. By the time he picked himself back up and sped into the front of the office, the woman was gone and the rest of his team filled the small space.

'Where is she?' he barked at Dave.

'She bolted the second the door opened.' Dave's response was quick.

Gabe ran for the door, and his team parted.

'Paige?' he shouted, urgently scanning up and down the street, then across to the park. But she was nowhere to be seen. No car pulled speedily away, the only people milling around were locals. Squinting, he scanned the street a second time, both left and right.

Gabe didn't bother hiding his annoyance, stepping back inside the office.

His team fell silent, picking up on the thunder emanating from him.

The door banged off the filing cabinet again.

Without speaking, he flexed his muscles and lifted the full filing cabinet from its spot by the door as if it weighed nothing. He kicked his chair out of the way and plonked the cabinet in the corner of the room.

'Debrief. Now.' Gabe's voice was sharper than it needed to be.

But his team didn't comment, they headed into the meeting room quietly, each grabbing some coffee and a donut and sitting at the round table.

'Where are we on the Santino case?' he asked, pouring his own coffee, doing his best to control himself. His team didn't need him to be angry. They were all still reeling after Shotgun's death. They needed him to be their boss. To be in control.

The slight tic of the muscles in his neck was the only thing that betrayed his newfound control. *How the hell can I have lost her twice? Idiot.*

Paige had run from the office and all but fallen into the back of her car, crouching in the backseat, swearing at herself for being such a dumbass. She'd been plucking up the courage all day to go and see someone at the protection company – Mags had been gently pushing her since the last 'incident' as they liked to call it. It had taken her almost six weeks to build up the nerve again, and then she'd walked into the office and been confronted by *him*. Her knight in shining armor from the cemetery. He'd stared at her in the front of the office but hadn't recognized her, all thanks to the dye she'd administered several times over the previous weeks to change her hair from bright auburn to dark brown, no doubt.

Mags had said that Bland P.I.R were best in the business.

That was what Paige needed.

The best.

The mess she'd managed to get herself into would not be handled by the mediocre. So why had she left without asking for help? *Because you're an ass, that's why. You saw him after dreaming of nothing but him for weeks and everything else faded away.*

When he'd followed her into the office, Paige had held her breath, taking in the thick, muscular arms that no woman on earth couldn't help but feel safe wrapped inside of. She'd even noted the shadowing beneath the shirt on his arms. *Tattoos maybe?* The rough five o' clock shadow of stubble on his chin, and his eyes, gray and smoldering, like the darkest cloud in a thunderstorm.

But he was also really tall, and his shadow had filled the office. And for just a moment, she'd seen *him* in her mind. Gabe stood at near enough the same height as *him*. The whole reason she was where she was searching for help at this very moment in time.

Al Graham. Even his name sent a shudder of fear spiking down her spine.

She didn't know where Al was now – she could guess – it wasn't likely he'd ever leave his empire behind. But she didn't know for sure. He'd done the unspeakable. It was so raw she couldn't bear to let her mind go there. Not yet. Not ever, if she had her way. She knew in her heart of hearts he'd have killed her back then. That last time she'd seen him – six months ago – was etched in her mind. A memory so vivid she still woke every night with that terror coursing through her veins.

And it would again if she didn't get help. Paige knew it as surely as she knew the sun rose every morning. He'd never stop until he found her.

She'd meant to tell the man behind the desk what she needed – his presence was calm; Paige figured he was the boss. She'd even opened her mouth to say the words. But they wouldn't fall from her lips. Her skin had turned clammy, the words caught in her throat. And then all those people had burst into the office and she had run. Because it was the only thing she could do. Because saying the words made everything so much more real.

And if Al ever found out ...

Well, she'd need more than protection, that was for sure. He had spies and contacts in pretty much every corner of the country. She shuddered again, Al's face popping into her mind, twisted in a grimace. She felt his hands round her throat, her breath caught, and without her noticing straightaway, her own hands flew to her neck to try and dislodge Al's. It took more than a minute of her scrabbling with her fingers to pull her focus back to the car seats in front of her. She stared at the patterns, the blue swirls inside dark-gray coarse material. Her breathing returned to normal, and her hands dropped from her neck. *I hate Al Graham – all of this is his fault. If he hadn't ...* She drew in another shaky breath, and another, then another until she felt herself again.

Paige had been huddled into the backseat of her car for so long now that her bones had stiffened. It didn't take much for her to get stiff nowadays. She'd have put it down to age if she hadn't known better.

With a deep sigh, she stretched as gracefully as she could without showing herself above the back of the seat. She didn't even know if the guy on the desk had come outside to see where she'd gone. He might not have. She raised her head and peeped over the parcel shelf at the door to their office. Not one person was in her view.

She sighed, confused between wanting someone to be there looking for her and accepting that they weren't. Her clamber into the front seat wasn't easy – her knees protested the most, but she didn't want to risk getting out of the car. Her fingers shook as she put the key in the ignition. The engine burst to life with a soft rumble and, checking her mirrors, she drove away. *You're a coward, Paige Matthews.*

Making her way back to the shelter, no further forward in her predicament, was one of the toughest things she'd ever done. Mags had been so lovely this morning. She'd given her gas money and pushed her out of the door with a firm hand at her back.

'Just go and speak to him, child. Mr. Bland is one of the nicest people I've ever met. He's the only one I know who'll be able to help you. He will understand, and it's his kind of help you need.'

Paige had let herself be ushered, knowing that now was the time to seek help. She worried over how much to tell. Was there a right amount, without giving all of her secrets away? Because it was those secrets that kept her alive, and those secrets were the reason Al wanted her dead.

She parked up near the shelter, and a pang of regret hit her – she wanted to tell Mags everything, she really did. *Maybe it's time?*

Mags was amazing – she was Paige's hero. So strong and able. Nothing at all like how Paige saw herself. Despite this, though, Paige had never been able to tell Mags her story. It was just too much. Waves of emotion threatened her composure, and the walls started closing in. She did her best to push them back, like she always did. Burying her head in the sand and ignoring what was happening never did work. Not really. But it was instinctive to her. Surviving and opening up was so much harder – because it made everything real. She staggered at the sudden rush of pain, her composure slipping. She used the wall for balance and drew in a slow, deep breath.

The kitchen door opened as she made her way down the hall, and Mags stepped out. She looked relaxed in her comfy jogging bottoms and sweater, her blonde hair short and spiked at the top, tinged with a little pink dye. Mags was a law unto herself – Paige didn't know any other fifty-something women who would dye their hair such a funky color, but the pink definitely suited Mags.

Paige sighed and readied herself for an onslaught – but it never came. Mags put her arm round Paige's shoulder and led her into the kitchen, sat her at the table, and handed her a hot cup of coffee.

'Not to worry, child. There's always tomorrow.'

Chapter Four

Brannigan's Shelter for Women – King Street, Sherburn

Paige concentrated on the task at hand. The storybook she was holding was familiar, she'd read this tale a thousand times. She focused on the title, running a finger over the smooth cover of *The Shmoogly Boo* by Eileen Wharton, and she had to fight not to give her feelings away. The book was all about facing challenges, perfect for the scared kids she read to in the shelter. And for her too. *Oh, my baby ... what happened?* Her heart cracked, and the pain in her chest was intense. Remembering where she was, though, she tried to draw in a deep breath.

A sob hiccupped in her throat, and she paused, stricken. The kids sitting in front of her hadn't noticed anything amiss. They all hung on her every word. This book was always one of their favorites. And they loved Paige reading it because she did all the different voices. Even when the Shmoogly Boo roared in the book, she roared right along with the story.

There were four children today. And she turned her attention to each one as she spoke the words in the book from memory.

Little Andy was five. He worried Paige every day. He and his mom, Wendy, had been through so much in his short life. It had taken Wendy every penny she had to come here, to this particular shelter, where Mags made problems disappear. Andy was a quiet, solemn child, far older than five in his mind. Five going on fifty, his mother joked. He rarely played, didn't speak very often due to the stutter he'd developed since learning to speak. But he adored story time. Paige understood that – it gave him another world to escape into for a while.

Carly and Willow were twins, three years old and full of beans. Their mother, Sarah, was at work – she'd found a job and was dedicated to earning the money she needed so she could get them a home after her husband had frittered away every penny on a bad gambling habit. She'd known when the loan sharks came knocking that she had to protect her girls. Sarah had fled with nothing more than the clothes on their backs.

Jason was the oldest – he was twelve now but had the mental age of a four-year-old due to his disabilities. He'd been born on the autism spectrum and had cystic fibrosis. A lot of things freaked him out, but he loved story time. Even now the pleasure twinkled in his eyes. His mom, Frankie, just couldn't cope on her own. She'd been at the shelter for four years – and Mags would never kick her out. Frankie helped out with the people coming and going and did babysitting for the kids.

Since Paige had arrived at the shelter, story time had been her favorite time of the day. She loved being able to entertain the kids, even if it did break her heart a little more every day. It was part of her routine. And routine was important to her. She had become a bit of a control freak, and reading stories made her feel free, like doing this meant she could be whoever she wanted to be.

She refocused her attention on the book and turned to page six.

Bland P.I.R office – Main Street, Rhododendron

Gabe had been in the office now for two hours, and his staff were filtering through the door. The strong scent of coffee hung in the air, the machine whirring to life for about the twentieth time that morning. He frowned at the computer screen on his desk, scanning the image before him. He was tired. He'd spent a good portion of the night checking the CCTV feeds from the street cameras, looking for Paige. Somehow, though, she'd managed to avoid pretty much every angle. *Had she done it on purpose? Did she know where the cameras were?* He couldn't even get a facial that was strong enough to be run through the database and he knew from his previous searches that he hadn't managed to locate anything pertinent to finding her.

Why was she here?

The question hung in his mind unanswered. 2 a.m. had come and gone, and he'd made it home for a few hours' shut-eye before waking and hitting the gym. Then he'd gone to Bella's for a hearty breakfast, finally making into the office at 6 a.m.

He liked the solitude of mornings – it gave him the space to plan and read over everything he needed for the day. And let him plan the staff schedule. That's what he'd been focusing on, using it to avert his attention from *her*. He wondered for a moment why he was so drawn to her. He'd never really met the woman, not for long anyway, and he didn't know anything about her, yet he felt an inane sense of responsibility to find her and help her. It was fast becoming his most important case. And that pissed him off a little. He had plenty of cases he could be working on, but the sense that he had to help her was almost overwhelming.

Gabe grunted, flicking to the roster screen. Daydreams were for those who had the time to waste. And time was something he always ran out of.

He put the finishing touches to the roster, a different color for each staff member. They all knew what they had to do. Or would as soon as the roster hit their inbox.

He finished assigning the four active cases – it left just one. The case of the missing Paige. He smiled grimly. It sounded like one of the old Perry Mason movies his grandpa made him watch when he was younger. Gabe knew he wasn't assigning that one, though, he was handling it himself.

Thinking about Paige had his cheeks reddening. *How can someone I don't even know have this effect on me?* He'd been staring at snippets of her face for hours on CCTV, and she'd drawn him in. He now knew with absolute certainty there was nothing average about her – her appearance had changed since he'd seen her in the cemetery. Her hair color was different, the curls gone. She'd slimmed down – he frowned at that. It was obvious she was afraid. *So why didn't she come inside and talk?* Her bright-blue eyes had been filled with fear and worry again – the same as the first time he'd seen her. He knew he needed to ease that fear. His thoughts drifted to the way her oversized sweater had pulled slightly in front of her breasts.

His breath whooshed out of his lungs.

Enough already. You're being a perv. You don't even know the woman. What the hell is wrong with you? She's a case. Pure and simple.

He tore his gaze away from the computer screen and used the Alt+Tab keys to change the screen.

No wonder you're imagining her that way, you've done nothing but stare for an hour. Get over yourself already.

He brought up his email and sent the roster out team wide. Those who weren't due in would get it to their inboxes – all had the latest smartphone technology courtesy of the business. He believed in having the best tools for the job. It cost plenty but it was worth it.

Gabe focused on putting the woman to the back of his mind and stood, flexing his muscles and stretching. It was time for more coffee. And then he would head out and start making inquiries.

See ... just a case. Like any other.

Brannigan's Shelter for Women

Story time well and truly over, it was time to head out. She couldn't put it off any longer. It was time to face her nightmares. It's what her dad had always taught her. The only monsters under the bed were the ones she invented herself. And Lord knew, she'd been dealing with those monsters on her own for long enough now.

She needed help.

Her heart twinged, thinking about her dad. He'd been dead for years, but it was amazing the things she remembered as if it were yesterday. The smell of his aftershave, always the same one. It was woody and reminded her of the open air. His dimple when he smiled. Something he'd done a lot. The glint in his eye when he laughed – something else he did often. He'd been a good dad.

Even now, she sometimes had trouble believing he was gone. She missed him – and she knew that feeling would never go away. In the rare moments of complete honesty, she didn't want it to. Missing him meant he was still with her. In spirit at least.

She stared at her reflection in the mirror, almost surprised at the person staring back. Her dad wouldn't have approved of her new look. She used to be so carefree, content to be wrapped up in her bubble world. Then she'd started seeing Al, and her bubbles had slowly but surely been popped. The first time he'd hit her, she'd accepted his apology, certain it was a mistake and he'd never do it again. The next time she blamed it on the drink. Then the time after that ... well, needless to say, a broken collarbone had forced her to see sense, but she still hadn't felt like she could leave. Even back then she'd known if she left, he'd find her and kill her.

Then she'd fallen pregnant. And he had changed. Or she'd thought he had. He hadn't laid a hand on her for nine months – telling her over and over that his son was going to be just like him. Except the baby had been a girl. He'd pulled away instantly after the birth, going so far as to fill in the birth certificate without her present. Barely two days after she'd gotten home from the hospital, he'd reverted back to beating her. And then there was a baby involved. She'd fully realized her predicament at that point – knowing she should have left before falling pregnant. If she'd thought he'd kill her back then, now she was even more certain of that fact, and she had a child to consider.

She shook her head at her reflection. *Don't go there. Keep it locked down.*

Taking in a deep breath, she sighed and adjusted the scarf over her hair. The hair she now hated. The curls were all her – it didn't matter how much she used straighteners, her hair reverted to curls throughout the day. The only way to truly hide them was to tie it back in the tight bun she favored. It was the color she hated the most. That bland shade of boring dark brown – so dark and dreary compared to her deep auburn. Her jeans hung loosely on her waist, and a minimizer bra pushed her ample breasts back and hid them as best she could. She felt as boring as her hair.

She stepped outside, and the chill in the air had her fastening the zipper on her jacket. Fall was definitely here – the freshness in the air was crisp as she made her way to her car. She always parked a couple of blocks from the shelter. Always afraid that someone would find her, recognize her.

After the incident at the cemetery, she was even more paranoid.

It had been six months since she'd last escaped from Al. He had to know she wasn't coming back. That she wouldn't tell. *He wants it back, though. He'll never stop until he gets it.*

It was easier than she'd thought to alter her appearance. Yes, she missed her natural hair color, but she hadn't been comfortable as the person she'd been before Paige. Al had always made her feel like she was putting on an act or living someone else's life. She'd found her new name when wandering through a graveyard not long after. A few hundred in the pocket of a bad lad she'd known from her youth had secured her new identity. From there she'd never looked back.

Except she had –every single day. Whether from worry that someone would recognize her, or fear that someone had found her. There was never any forward. Never would be for Paige. She'd lost too much just to keep living. But she would make him pay. He thought she'd never tell. He thought he could control her even now. She'd prove him wrong, though.

Then she'd do what she felt she needed to do.

Paige had proof of Al's crimes. Proof she'd hidden somewhere no one else knew about. Seeing that old oak tree the first day she'd visited Rhododendron had been like a sign. She'd returned that night and buried it. That sturdy box hidden away from the light of day containing Al's secrets, and the things that meant the most to her. It had taken days to gather it all together, weeks before she'd had the opportunity to run with the mother lode. She'd known she couldn't go forward all cock-a-hoop and trip herself up or give Al chance to cover his tracks. He had friends in the police force; it was why she'd never stepped out of the darkness.

With a little manipulation, though, she was sure Bland P.I.R would be able to do the job for her. As long as she never had to face Al again it was all good. Even his name was like poison in her brain. Hate was a strong word, but she knew with every fiber of her being that she hated Al Graham.

And what about the promises you made. They don't just disappear. Just because you're someone else now doesn't mean they don't still count.

The sob caught in her throat, and she stumbled into the wall surrounding the corner house. 'Can't. Won't go there.' She muttered the words while swallowing the sob back down – she couldn't lose control. Not here and not now.

Not ever.

Paige rounded the corner and finally reached the street her car was parked on. Or had been parked on. Nervously she scanned the street in case she'd parked it farther down, but part of her already knew it wasn't there. Broken glass lay on the curb where her car had been. Nothing else. Just broken glass.

Tears filled her eyes. It had taken everything she had to get that car. It was her one bit of freedom. And now someone had stolen it.

A sudden newfound determination swept over her. *I'll speak to Bland P.I.R today if I have to walk the fifteen miles to get there.*

She set off, one foot in front of the other. Not able to do anything else.

Joey Mendino glanced up from his newspaper as the woman he'd been waiting for strode past his car. *Is it her?* He wasn't sure, not yet. She resembled the person he was searching for, but he couldn't be certain until he confronted her.

He wouldn't give up. Not until all the money was in his bank. He'd heard on the rumor mill Al Graham was after his ex, Beth – and Joey had put obstacles in the way of the other investigators. Whoever thought there was honor among thieves was dead wrong. It was a cutthroat, ruthless business.

Knowing he would be called on eventually, he'd waited. The cash that Al had given him was already deposited and moved to a separate bank account, and there'd be more where that came from. Al was nothing if not rich. Joey had no problem taking money from anyone.

He'd come close to grabbing the woman that day in the cemetery. If that giant of a man hadn't intervened, she would have been back with Al Graham and the money would be in his bank waiting to be spent. He wasn't a hundred percent sure the woman he'd been tracking now was the same one. There were similarities – her build, her height, but she didn't look the same. He needed to be sure before he progressed.

Stealing her car had been a genius move on his part. He'd been watching her for days. Now meeting her would seem like the most natural thing in the world. He waited until she turned left at the top end of the street, folded the newspaper, and placed it over the gun on the passenger seat, then turned the key and followed slowly.

Paige had been walking for about fifteen minutes when the hairs rose on the back of her neck. She slowed her gait, glancing over her shoulder. Nothing seemed out of place.

If nothing was there, though, why did she feel as though a snail was crawling down her back? Had he found her?

Panic clawed at her, and she fought for control. The last thing she needed now was to lose it completely.

She sped up, almost running, and tried to breathe to calm herself down. The rumble of a bus growled behind her, and a couple of people flagged it down at the bus stop ahead. She hated public transport, it always made her feel exposed. The whole world seeping in through the windows. It was impossible to hide on a bus.

More impossible than hiding on an open street?

Biting her bottom lip, she checked her purse for change.

'Where ya headed?' the bus driver's voice was to the point and efficient.

'Umm, how far do you go?'

His expression gentled.

'Fourteen miles over to Rhododendron then back around and over to Perkinsville. That far enough?'

'How much to Rhododendron?'

The driver lowered his voice. 'Just give me what you can afford, I'll make sure you get to where you need to go.'

Tears pricked her eyes at his kindness. He didn't even know her. Silently, she handed over all the change from her purse. He didn't count it, just popped it in his money tray and motioned for her to sit.

Paige huddled herself as close to the side of the bus as she could. She was shaking and couldn't stop. Whatever had been out there had been enough to send her into a tailspin. Not that it took much these days. Anything could tip her over the edge. It was all she could do to maintain control when she was with other people. In her own room, however, her pillow had seen more than its fair share of tears. Tears for the children in the shelter, tears for the homeless man on the street, tears for her. And tears for … *Stop. Don't go there.*

She listened to her conscience, focusing on the buildings passing her by in a blur.

Before she knew it, the driver was telling her she was in Rhododendron.

She paused at the door, turning to face him. 'You're a good man …' she leaned over to check his name badge, 'Bert. Thank you.'

'Anytime you need a ride, my bus is the X10. It's the only one I drive. You sure you want to be in Rhododendron?'

Paige nodded and stepped off the bus, watching it pull away, and wondering if she was doing the right thing.

Even traveling hadn't abated the anxiety, though. If anything, she now felt even more anxious. *What if it all goes wrong? What if Bland P.I.R can't help me? Gabe seemed nice enough, but he has to listen to his boss – if the boss didn't want to help then what will I do?* Her chest hurt when she breathed, and her eyes were darting all over the place; everyone knew the monsters hid in the shadows. She needed to calm down. The panic attacks were becoming more prevalent, and it was because she'd been putting off asking for help and allowing the situation to control her, rather than taking that control back.

Spotting Bella's over the road, Paige made a beeline for it. She had no money left for coffee, but even a glass of water would help. Her spit had all but vanished from her mouth.

She felt rather than saw the car crawling behind her. Every sense she had flew into overdrive, and she took off at a run, straight up the path that led to the café. A door slammed behind her, but she didn't dare turn to look.

The alley that ran alongside Bella's was narrow, but she ran into it at full pelt, searching urgently for somewhere to hide. Empty cardboard boxes and large rubbish bins were the only things strewn around, though – the only door in the alley was locked tight.

A six-foot wall stood at the back of the alley.

She was boxed in.

A shadow filled the alley entrance, and she ducked behind the big blue bin.

Paige held her breath. Her heart was pounding, and fear clawed at her – she was already panicking when shiny black shoes appeared in front of her; she couldn't hold it back anymore. Her breath held in her chest, lights danced in front of her eyes, and her mind took her to a place far away from the terror in the alleyway.

Chapter Five

Main Street, Rhododendron

Gabe had happened to glance up and saw Paige, the woman he'd been staring at virtually all night, fly through the park as though the very hounds of hell were on her tail. He was up and out of the office in the blink of an eye, motioning at Dave to stay where he was. He was halfway through the park when she ran into the alley, and a grim expression set across his face. The alley was a dead end.

The man following her was carrying a gun – Gabe had seen the bulge under his jacket as it flew backward in time with his step. Pausing at the alley entrance, Gabe drew his own weapon from the holster under his jacket. Whoever that guy was, he meant business.

A voice drifted on the wind to Gabe's ears, the accent not local to Rhododendron. 'What's the problem? I just want to talk.'

He raised his gun and took a step into the alley, aiming it at the back of the creep in front of him. His view of the woman was obscured, but he noted that she didn't reply to the man's words.

Gabe moved forward, his shoes silent on the cobblestones of the alley. He'd learned stealth a long time ago. The man wouldn't know he was there until Gabe wanted him to.

'I know who you are. Al wants me to bring you home. I'm not here to hurt you. Just come with me and this will all be over.'

A whimper sounded from in front of the man. Gabe caught a glimpse of the woman, her knees tucked up to her chest, and he was punched in the gut by the utter terror on her face. *No way is that dick taking her.*

'Back away, now.' Gabe's voice was sharp and commanding.

The man in front of him stilled, and Gabe knew he was contemplating his options.

'Trust me, my bullet will send you spinning before you even pull your gun from that shoulder holster. I won't say this a third time. Back. The. Hell. Away.'

He complied, turning to face Gabe, maneuvering until he rested against the wall.

'You don't know what you're doing. If I don't take her, Al won't just be sending an investigator – she won't survive the asshole he'll send. You're putting a target on her back. You know that, right?'

The man was wiry. His eyes were set close together, and it gave him a sly look. Gabe didn't like sly. He kept his gun raised and aimed at the man's heart while putting his hand down toward the woman.

She didn't take it.

Glancing down, he realized she hadn't even seen it. She was wrapped up in panic and fear.

'You need to take my hand. Come on,' he said firmly.

Not even blinking, she didn't move. He doubted she'd even heard him.

'What the hell have you done to her?' he snarled, turning his attention to the man against the wall.

But the man had prepared for Gabe's attention lapse. His foot connected with Gabe's arm, and he powered into Gabe with more strength than Gabe would have thought possible. It almost knocked him off balance. The man forced Gabe's hand into the wall, trying to make him to drop his gun. A powerful uppercut connected with his chin.

Gabe chose that moment to fight rather than try and control the situation. His gun skittered across the cobbles, and he pulled back from the man and punched him to the jaw. His left arm blocked a further punch, and he used the right again to smash into the man's nose. A bleeding nose always inhibited vision, and the man stepped away to recoup.

Gabe's knee rose hard, connecting with the man's stomach and leaving him gasping for breath while his eyes bulged in shock. One swift kick with his size twelves, and the man collapsed to the ground, unconscious.

He turned to Paige. She hadn't moved a muscle, her eyes still directed downward.

Kneeling to make himself smaller, he spoke, his tone soft. 'We really need to go. Let me help you.'

Still, she didn't look up. She didn't even know he was there. He needed to get her away from here and somewhere safe. She wouldn't like it, but he didn't have a choice. He reached down, took hold of her, and picked her up as though she weighed nothing. The contact brought her back to the present, and she screamed long and loud, kicking out and struggling against him. Her fist caught his eye, and he blinked, his eye watering from the harsh contact. Gabe tightened his grip; letting her go now would be a mistake.

She'd end up hurting herself in the panic-stricken mode she was in.

Her struggle turned feeble, and her screams abated.

'Boss?' Dave's voice came from the alley entrance, his eyes widening as he took in the woman squirming under Gabe's grasp.

'Go and open the truck. I need to get her away from here. And get one of the guys over to this alley. There's a guy in there we need to have a chat with.'

Paige's head thrashed side to side; she didn't like being restrained. He felt guilty for holding on to her so tightly, but he knew if he let her go, she'd bolt. She obviously needed help. The man with a gun had made that very clear.

Shit, my gun. What kind of professional leaves his gun?

He hoisted the woman into the passenger seat of the truck, clicking the seat belt in place to secure her. Catching the keys that Dave tossed in his direction, he yelled over, 'My gun is in the alley. Can you make sure it's retrieved?'

Dave nodded, and Gabe got into the driver's seat and sped off in a squeal of rubber on tarmac.

He knew just the place to take her.

Paige felt herself coming out of the utter terror that had gripped her, and she noticed things again. The faint smell of diesel from the engine, the soft hum from the man in the front seat – in time with the country music on the radio. *Where am I? It's him, he's taking me to Al.*

Glancing up, she slowly registered that it was Gabe and not the attacker sitting in the seat beside her. She tried to recall exactly how she'd come to be here, speeding along a country lane with soft music playing. But her mind drew a blank. The last thing she remembered was … the alley. The wall in the alley. That feeling of despair knowing Al had found her.

'You're safe. Please don't do anything stupid, Paige, like jumping out of a moving vehicle or whatever. I don't have the time to scrape you off the road, okay?'

His voice was soothing, friendly even. Her anxiety ebbed a little.

'Wanna tell me what happened back there?'

'I … don't remember.' Her voice had dropped to a whisper, and tears threatened to fall. 'I was on a bus. I got off and was going for a glass of water at the café.' Her eyes widened, and she tried to focus. 'Someone was behind me. I ran into the alley. And then … then I was here with you.'

'Okay, don't try and force it. We'll be at the house in fifteen minutes. Until then, just breathe, try and relax.'

You need to tell him everything.
But I can't – not everything. Al will find out.
So what if he does? He can't hurt you anymore, can he?

Paige stared out of the window, her mind arguing with itself, barely even noticing the trees and change in scenery from town to country. *What the hell am I gonna do now?*

A lump filled Paige's throat, and two tears fell from her eyes.

Alley behind Bella's café

Dave stepped back into the alley with his own weapon drawn. Gabe had a cut to his mouth and bruising round his cheek. Dave had noticed it when he'd waved him off. Whoever was in the alley could fight. It took a lot to land a punch on the boss. And he should know. He'd seen enough people try.

Not one sound came from the cobbled alley. Scanning up and down it, he saw no one. He'd been watching the entrance since Gabe left, and no one had come out.

Which meant the man Dave was looking for had jumped the wall.

Behind the wall was a wood. Dave needed Mitch Lockley.

Mitch, one of the other Bland employees, was a tracker. He'd never met a person he couldn't find even in the harshest of environments. But Mitch was undercover. Just the act of Dave ringing him could blow that cover, and that was more than his hide was worth. He'd have to depend on his own skills.

He quickly scoured the alley for Gabe's gun. Even moving the bins and cardboard in case it had slid underneath. There was no sign of it.

That rat-bastard who'd jumped the wall must have taken it with him.

Dave groaned. Gabe was going to be a nightmare when he found out.

And if he didn't catch the guy who'd jumped the wall, it would be Dave's ass on the line too. It didn't take a lot to piss Gabe off, especially since Shotgun had died. Gabe blamed himself, but this would be a monumental-sized pissed. Not that Gabe scared Dave, it wasn't that at all. Dave was his friend, his brother. He hated seeing Gabe hurting and blaming himself for something that wasn't anyone's fault except the guy who'd fired his weapon at Shotgun.

He checked his watch quickly. It would take Gabe twenty minutes to reach the cabin, and the signal was nonexistent there. Dave had to wait until he arrived so he could call him on the landline.

That gave him ten minutes now to hop the wall himself and see if he could find the guy from the alley.

Dave was fitter than he gave the appearance of – with black-rimmed glasses and a slightly receding hairline – he knew when people saw at him, they saw a geek or a nerd, and he couldn't really blame them. But at least it meant they didn't expect him to be … him.

They didn't know he had a husband at home: Paul; a trusting, safe man who knew exactly what Dave did for a living and let him do it. No arguments, no hissy fits. Just support. Paul always knew when he needed to be hugged and understood when to leave him to his thoughts. The ones seeing Dave didn't know he was an expert in two martial arts. They didn't know because Dave didn't need them to know that. It was enough that they always underestimated him.

Expect the unexpected. That was his mantra. And he went day-to-day using that same one. Dave pulled himself up and over the wall with ease. Gabe wasn't the only one who hit the gym every day. He glanced down at the undergrowth on the other side and spotted a couple of broken stems.

He paused and cocked his head in the direction the man had taken. A branch cracked farther into the trees – so far in he couldn't see any movement.

Dave quickly activated the GPS on his watch – it would send an alert to the office computer which relayed the location to the Wi-Fi at Gabe's cabin. Just in case anything happened.

That done, he advanced on the location through the trees. His gun was raised, and he swept side to side slowly, searching for anything out of place.

Something was off. Every hair on his body stood at attention, and he paused, scanning the area ahead. He listened to his gut and moved behind a thick oak tree. A dull thud sounded as a bullet hit a tree somewhere in front of him.

He yanked his cell phone from his pocket and used his thumbprint to open the main screen. Then touched the only app on the front page. Gabe had arranged for the app design – it was on all their phones. It meant 'get your asses here now, I'm in trouble.' It was designed to show their unique code name and provide the longitude and latitude of the location. It worked using satellites, so even if there was no service, the alert would reach the targets with no problems at all.

Another bullet thudded, this time off the tree he was using as a shield. A large piece of debris flicked off the trunk and lodged in his shoulder. Dave didn't curse or react in any way.

Another thud – a bullet hit another tree nearby.

That was good. The shooter was trying to draw him out. *Not a chance, buddy.*

Gabe's cabin – base of Crookhill Mountain

Gabe reversed the truck in the clearing that led to the front of his cabin so that it faced the exit to the driveway. He liked to be prepared, and having to turn a vehicle when he was in a hurry was a pain. His phone buzzed twice in quick succession in his pocket – the signal here was crap. It was the only downside to living in the sticks. He knew it would have connected to the Wi-Fi the second he pulled up the driveway.

He got out, stood, and flexed his back, grabbing the phone. Seeing the red alert flash on it had him jumping back into the truck and revving the engine.

Before he drove off, though, he paused.

Paige. He couldn't very well take her back there, could he?

'Paige, sorry, darlin', but you're going to have to get out and make yourself at home. I promise you will be safe here. No one knows this cabin is here outside of my team. There is a key in the panel under the pot with the pink geraniums in it. Let yourself in, lock the door behind you. I'll be back as quickly as I can.'

Paige stared at him from the passenger seat, then nodded and got out. She stood beside the car, looking scared.

He opened the window, leaning out to talk.

'I'm sorry. The man from the office, Dave? He's in danger. I need to leave. I promise I will be back, though, okay? Please just go inside. Like I said, I'll be as quick as I can.'

Paige gave him one nod. It was all he needed. Gabe hit the gas and headed back down the driveway, gravel spurting from his back wheels.

He felt instantly guilty. *What the hell else could I do, though? I can't take her back there. Not with that dick running loose. Unless Dave has him detained, but I can't know that.* He was going to help her. She probably didn't realize that, however – to her mind he'd just picked her up and dumped her at a cabin in the middle of nowhere. Gritting his teeth, he gunned the engine – the sooner he got this whole mess squared away, the sooner he'd be back to hear her story.

Paige stood for a moment, watching the truck disappear round a bend. She didn't quite know what to feel. She knew Gabe had to leave, but now she was here, alone, at the place he lived. *At least I think he lives here.*

It only took seconds for the fear to seep back in and make her feel vulnerable. All a person would have to do was stand in the trees – they provided perfect cover for someone to hide behind.

She took a couple of deep breaths – panicking wouldn't do any good. *What did he say about the key?* Pots were scattered all over the decking that surrounded the cabin. On any other day it would have looked picture-perfect. But all she wanted now was to get inside. She felt exposed on the porch – anyone could happen along and see her. Or worse still, take her. Her heart was pounding; panic threatened to take over her mind. She struggled to draw breath. *Oh god, no, not a panic attack. Not now.*

Her vision blurred, and she stumbled, falling onto the wooden rocking chair on the porch. The panic and anxiety roared, and suddenly, she was too weak to resist. Her brain filled with images. Like photos moving at lightning speed. A gun. A dead man. A smiling child who drifted away on the wind. She tried in vain to claw her way out of the array of images. They weren't allowed in. They were never allowed in. It was the only way to cope, pretend they weren't real.

Paige was sure her lips turned blue; she was trying to force air into her lungs, but it wouldn't work. They wouldn't expand no matter how much she begged them to. Spots danced in front of her eyes, then thick black curtains closed in. Tears streamed down her cheeks. And then – darkness.

Her body slipped from the chair and onto the deck with a thud.

Woods behind Bella's café

The drive back to Rhododendron felt like it had taken forever. Gabe parked at the track on the outer edge of the town. The signal restored itself on his phone, and he glanced down to check the location, ignoring the feeling of dread settling in his stomach.

Dave hadn't called in. His position hadn't moved since Gabe had left the cabin, making the drive in just seven minutes instead of the normal fifteen to twenty. He unlocked the gun safe concealed between the two front seats and drew out his .45 along with a couple of spare magazines. Practically throwing his thin Kevlar vest over his shirt, he secured the safe and the car, and made his way toward the location flashing on his phone.

I'm coming, brother. Just hang on.

The trees grew thicker the farther into the woods he got. His feet fell softly, not cracking a single twig.

Five hundred feet.

Four hundred.

Three hundred.

He was alert; every sensor on his whole body was primed and ready to react. Movement flicked through the trees at the beacon location. There was short flash – barely even a second; it was one of his men. That was their signal. Gabe flashed back quickly.

Gabe edged forward, his ears straining for anything out of place. He cocked his head, listening to the noise. It went silent again, and he advanced.

One hundred feet.

Fifty.

Twenty.

That's when he saw him.

Dave was propped up against a tree, blood spreading across the chest of his once pristine white shirt.

Then all hell broke loose.

Gunfire sounded ahead – loud bangs from the .45s his team carried, and pops from a smaller caliber weapon. *Probably a 9mm.*

He ran toward his friend and hoisted him over his shoulder. Gabe retreated, and Dave groaned against his back, his head bouncing off Gabe's waist. His team would handle the shooter. He was more concerned about his friend right now.

He stopped as soon as he could and gently placed Dave on the ground. His skin was gray. A quick check of his pulse told Gabe he was tachycardic – his heart was beating too fast. His body was trying to compensate for the blood loss and trauma. Gabe ripped open Dave's shirt and turned him on his side, checking for the exit wound. There wasn't one. Which meant the bullet was still buried inside Dave's chest.

He put pressure on the wound, pushing down harder than he wanted to; it was his best shot at slowing the bleeding.

'He came out of nowhere. Some move I've not seen before. One minute he was behind me and the next … he's like a ghost. Oh god, the guys …' Dave's voice was raspy, and he tried to sit, and then flapped at Gabe's arm. 'You need to get them out. Please …'

Dave's head lolled to one side, and he passed out.

'Dave, don't you go leaving me, brother. Not after all we've been through. Not after Shotgun. We can't take another loss. I can't take another loss. Not you, Dave. Come on now, stay with me. I'm here. I'm right here.'

Swallowing his pride, he yelled out for help. He couldn't keep force on the wound and carry Dave at the same time.

Becca appeared from the trees, running at breakneck speed toward him.

'Boss,' she gasped, drawing in a deep breath and kneeling beside him.

'Press the wound, hard. You know the drill. Is anyone else coming?'

Gabe let go, and Becca positioned her knee above the hole in Dave's chest and leant her weight forward. 'Jacko was heading up my six, he'll be here any minute.'

As if he'd heard her, Jacko appeared from the tree line and was by their side in seconds.

'Stretcher?' he asked Gabe who nodded in response.

He'd already gathered two straight logs to use for supports. Jacko dipped into his backpack, pulling out a tarp from one of the pouches – it took only moments for them to secure it to the supports and lift Dave onto it.

Becca kept her knee on his wound, knowing the other two would take her weight as well as Dave's.

'Who else is out there?' Gabe was short, barely holding his anger in check.

But Becca and Jacko both knew it wasn't aimed at them.

'Mitch, Deacon, and Grayson. They arrived the same time we did.'

Gabe nodded. If anyone could corner and catch the shooter it was those three. All brought different skills to the team, but they were all invaluable.

Once Dave was secured in the back of the truck, Gabe revved the engine and sped off toward the hospital.

Gabe's mouth was set in a grim line, and he knew one thing for certain, when he got back to the cabin, Paige had some serious explaining to do.

Chapter Six

Gabe's cabin

As soon as Dave had gone down to surgery, Gabe had jumped into his truck and sped back over to the cabin. Dave would never have forgiven him if he hadn't gone to see to Paige. He was trying to calm himself down – he really was – but it was tough. If Paige had just gone into the office the day before and told them what was going on, then Dave wouldn't be in the operating room having a bullet removed from his chest right now.

You know he'd tell you to calm down – and he's right. You go in like this, all guns blazing, and she will run. All of this will have been for nothing.

Gabe knew his conscience was right. Hell, he knew Dave was right – Dave was always his voice of reason. Worry etched lines into Gabe's normally smooth brow. *What if …*

Don't even go there. Dave's strong, he'll be okay. Dying is not an option. Dave is not Shotgun!

The gravel spurted as he pulled into the clearing, and for once, Gabe didn't turn the truck around.

All was quiet at the cabin. No curtains twitched – there wasn't any sign that Paige was worried someone else had arrived. Gabe frowned – that wasn't normal. Not by a long shot. If he'd been her, he'd have been on high alert.

He made his way to the steps that led to his door, the gravel crunching under his feet.

And that's when he saw Paige slumped on the deck.

'Shit!'

He was on his knees turning her over in less than a second. Running his fingers gently down the side of her face caused her to groan softly. Gabe couldn't see any blood. Nothing obvious to say she'd been hit by anything or anyone.

'Take it easy. Nice and slow. Open your eyes, Paige.'

Her eyelids fluttered, and she moaned again. Slowly, her eyes opened, blue with flashes of silver threading through them.

'What happened? Are you okay?' His tone was short, but he couldn't help it.

'I … I think so. Why am I on the floor?'

'How the hell would I know?' he growled.

She stiffened in response, her expression fearful.

'Sorry, I didn't mean to snap. Let me help you up and we'll try to figure out how you ended up on the deck.' He pushed her into a sitting position and stood, unlocked the door, and held a hand out for her to grab.

Gabe applied too much pressure, and she stumbled, face-planting into his chest. He steadied her, about to apologize again, and found for a second he didn't want to let her go.

What the … nope, that is not happening. Get your mind out of whichever gutter it just visited. She's a case. Nothing more.

He put his hands on both of her arms and steadied her properly, giving her a quick nod to make sure she was okay. If nothing else, Gabe could always be professional. And it never paid to mix business with pleasure. He'd found that out the hard way.

Paige's heart was going ten to the dozen. She didn't expect to feel anything when he helped her up, let alone the explosion of lust from a moment's contact with that massive chest. Again. How could the same thing happen to the same woman twice? It had been a long time since she'd found comfort in a man's arms. A very long time. It definitely wasn't something she'd sought from Al at any point. And not something she wanted now. She took a step back, her hand finding the rail of the deck fence behind her.

Al wouldn't have offered his help – he'd have kicked you in the gut while you were down. How could you have been so blind?

And just like that, the lust vanished and was replaced with a melee of other emotions. None of them pleasant. Her chest tightened; the animal response to fear was flight or fight – hers was no different. Al made her want to run.

Paige shuddered. After everything he'd done, she still couldn't fight. She wasn't strong enough. No matter what Mags said.

Mags! She'll be worried sick.

'Sorry to be a bother, but could I use the phone? I need to call my friend. She'll be worried.'

Gabe opened the door and guided Paige through to the kitchen, motioning toward the landline on the counter.

Paige picked up the receiver, plugging in the number from memory.

'Brannigan residence.'

'Mags? It's Paige. I just wanted …'

'Where the hell have you been, child? I've been going out of my mind. I even rang the Bland offices, but there was no reply. Have you even been there?'

Paige sighed. 'There's so much to tell you, but I can't right now. I'm with a man called Gabe. He works for Bland P.I.R.'

Mags chuckled down the phone, confusing Paige. 'Okay, well, keep in touch, child. Everything's fine here. We had another intake this morning, but I'll tell you about it later.'

'Oh, one thing, Mags, could you file a stolen report on my car? Some little shit nicked it. The details are in my room, in the desk drawer.'

'Stole your car? Where from? How did you get to Rhododendron? You know what, never mind – we'll discuss it when you call me tomorrow morning, okay?'

Paige got the hint and grinned. 'Yes, *Mom*.' She'd used that term jokingly with Mags since her second day in the shelter.

'Good. Now go and tell that man everything.'

Paige agreed again – though she didn't think she could tell him *everything*. Everything was too much.

She hung up the phone and glanced up to find Gabe staring at her intently. *What did he see? Did I give something away?*

'We need to go.'

They weren't the words she expected him to say. Puzzled, she said, 'Go? Go where?' It was then she noticed the blood on his arm and T-shirt. How could she have missed that? 'Oh crap, you're hurt. Let me see.' She stepped forward, her fingers on his arm, until he stopped her by taking hold of her wrist gently.

'It's not mine. My friend, Dave, was shot chasing after the guy who cornered you in the alley.'

Paige felt the blood drain from her face. *Shot? As in by a gun?* Her heart rate shot back up to lightning speed. She tried and failed not to panic. She darted her eyes around as if expecting to see the shooter in the same room. And a solitary tear fell down her cheek.

'Whoa, easy there. He's going to be okay. He's in surgery. I need to be there when he wakes up, though. Which means you coming with me. I could do without the panic of finding you passed out again.'

Paige nodded without speaking and walked out of the kitchen toward the truck.

What if he's there, though? At the hospital? Waiting ... for me.

You selfish cow – his friend is in hospital, and you're worried for yourself?

But Al ... he ... A sob forced out of her mouth as the not-allowed-to-enter thoughts crashed through every barrier in her mind. *Diana ...my beautiful Diana. With her toothy grin and gorgeous curly hair.* Her heart broke in two for the hundredth time, and Paige fell to her knees, all but oblivious to Gabe cursing behind her.

He didn't speak – he pulled her into his arms and held her. She shook, the tears coursing down her face soaking the front of his T-shirt.

They stayed like that for more than a few minutes, and slowly the tears subsided. She hiccupped, unfurling her fingers from the grip she had on the arm of his shirt. Vulnerable and hurting, Paige held his gaze, wanting in that moment for him to do something, anything to make all the pain go away. She was tired – holding it together and hiding it was hard work. And in that second, she wanted to tell him absolutely everything. Her mouth dropped open, the words formed, and the signals traveled from her brain to her mouth which was about to speak, when sanity crept back in. Worry crawled back inside, and finally, acceptance. No one could help her, not with everything. No one could take the past or the pain away. Not ever.

'Sorry,' she said, casting her eyes down. 'Stressful day.'

And just like that, her barriers were back up.

Perkinsville General Hospital

Gabe arrived with Paige to find all of the team now seated in the waiting room with Paul, Dave's husband. Everyone except Mitch. Gabe frowned.

'Where's Mitch?'

'Not responding to calls. He hasn't activated his GPS or his beacon. Simple answer, we don't know, boss.' Becca's voice was matter-of-fact and to the point. She stared at Paige momentarily.

Sizing her up? Gabe thought and replied, 'Jesus, is it that hard for him to check in? Do we even know if he's caught the shooter?'

Becca shook her head and then turned, sitting next to Jacko.

The whole team was worried. They probably hadn't eaten or drank anything in hours.

'Go get a coffee and some food. You all look like hell. I'll come and get you as soon as the doc comes out.'

Not one of them moved, all making out as though they hadn't even heard him. Gabe appreciated it – in their position he wouldn't have moved either. Dave was one of them. That was one of the things he valued about his team – they weren't just team members. They were family. What one went through, they all went through.

Worry etched the faces of each member of the team in the waiting area.

'This isn't the same as Shotgun. Dave will be okay. We got to him in time.' Gabe's voice sounded hollow even to his own ears, but it seemed to bolster the team. A few nods, a little more determination in their expressions than worry. They'd needed to hear it.

He made his way to where Paul was sitting, utter devastation on his face. Dried tears had left salt trails down his cheeks. Dave was Paul's world. Gabe didn't speak, just grabbed Paul's hand and pulled him to his feet and into a bear hug, silently letting him know he was right there with him. Paul was practically one of the team – he was always in the office seeing his husband and had helped them out on a consultancy basis more than once. He loved Dave. It was that simple. There was nothing else required.

'He'll be okay. He's made of strong stuff.' Gabe's voice was gruff as he comforted Paul. He didn't give a toss that it wasn't common practice for men to hug or cry. That shit was all bollocks anyway. Emotions were emotions – whether you were a man or a woman as far as he was concerned. Though it still broke his heart every time he saw a woman cry.

The team shifted behind him; the doctor was arriving.

'Are you all family?' The doctor plainly knew they weren't but accepted Gabe's nod regardless.

'Dave is out of surgery. We've removed the bullet, and it hasn't hit any major organs or arteries. It'll take a while and some rehab, but he'll be fine. Two of you can go in and see him when he's back from recovery.'

The relief on everyone's faces was obvious. Becca and Jacko fist-bumped. Paul grabbed hold of the doctor's hand and shook it hard. Blood ties were irrelevant. This team *were* family.

A wave of relief swamped Paige at the doctor's news. She couldn't cope with anyone else getting hurt because of her. She had to tell Gabe what was going on.

What if he doesn't believe me? What if he's pissed I got his friend shot? What if …

Grow a set of cajones, for god's sake, woman. You tell him as much as he needs to know.

She sighed, knowing her mind was right. She moved as if to stand, but Gabe stood huddled with one of his colleagues. They looked deep in conversation, and she didn't feel right interrupting.

Paige suddenly felt really weak. She'd barely eaten for almost three days now – longer really when she thought about it. Food had tasted like cardboard for weeks, possibly even months. Even Mags was worried – she kept trying to feed Paige, but she just couldn't face it. Maybe these people would appreciate some coffee and sandwiches. Then she remembered her purse was empty. She had no money, none to get them coffee or to pay for their services. Mags had told her it wouldn't be a problem, to send Mr. Bland her way and she'd sort it. But Paige didn't feel right doing that. Mags had already done so much for her. What she needed was to sort her life out and start paying her way properly instead of relying on other people.

A wave of dizziness passed over her. The sounds in the room suddenly faded, and the room spun. She pursed her lips, trying to breathe deeper to steady herself.

I need air.

Standing, she moved to leave the waiting room to step outside, but her feet wouldn't do as she wanted. She stumbled, her right knee connecting with the chair beside the one she'd been sitting in. The pain mingled with the darkness, and she tilted forward, falling to the floor in a dead faint.

Gabe just happened to glance up from his conversation with Becca in time to see Paige stand and then fall.

'Shit.' His expletive was loud and unexpected, and everyone turned to stare at him. He didn't care, though, it took him but a few seconds to reach Paige.

A nurse shouted for a gurney, and he stopped and knelt next to Paige. Gabe turned her gently, and she moaned softly without opening her eyes. Gabe noticed her sunken face, the dark circles beneath her eyes indicating little sleep in some time. Her skin was almost gray. *She looks… ill. How did I not see it before?*

The nurse pushed him out of the way and with the help of her colleagues, moved Paige onto a gurney and wheeled her through to a private room.

'What just happened, boss?' Becca's voice beside him sounded a little disbelieving.

'I have no idea. I saw her pitch forward then hit the deck. You know as much as I do.'

'Little convenient, though? She passes out before even telling you why she needs our help? You sure she's not going to do a runner?'

'She could've done that the minute we arrived at the hospital if she was going to. Maybe it is convenient. Maybe it's coincidence. I'll find out as soon as she wakes up.'

Becca narrowed her eyes and stared at him. 'If you say so, boss. I could question her instead if you like.'

Now it was Gabe who stared at her. 'This one's my case, Becca. By all means tell me if I'm not doing my job to your standard. Or if you aren't being kept busy enough on your own cases.' Gabe leaned back slightly and folded his arms across his chest.

Becca had the good grace to blush in embarrassment.

'Sorry, boss. Didn't mean to imply anything. I'll keep my gob shut.'

Gabe nodded curtly, knowing he was being a little harsh in his demeanor. He relaxed his arms and sat back down next to Paul, who was sitting staring at the floor in front of him.

'You okay?' Gabe asked Paul.

'Still in shock, I think. I can't believe he's been shot. I mean, I know what his job entails, but you tell yourself nothing like this would ever happen. Then it does. Twice. Were you with him when it happened?'

'No. I was at the cabin. Dave activated his emergency beacon. We had them installed on the new smartphones a few months ago – his idea really. He'd seen them advertised at one of those geek shows he likes to go to. It saved his life. It gives the location, and everyone drops all tools and heads straight to that location if one is activated. If we'd been any longer ... well, let's just say I'm glad we got there.'

Paul had gone pale. 'Does this sort of thing happen to your team often? I mean, first Shotgun, now Dave ...' His voice was guarded now.

Gabe could practically see the cogs turning, could picture in his head the shitstorm Dave would walk into when he was released if Gabe didn't answer properly.

'Shotgun was a different scenario. We were in a part of Afghanistan known for terrorist activity. I can't tell you much, as you know, but it was the first time anything like it had happened in the seven years we've been in business. Dave went above and beyond, he always does. I can't give you the promise it will never happen again, but I can promise I'll be doing my damnedest to make sure it doesn't.'

'That'll have to do then. That woman, the one who passed out. Is she the reason he got shot? You know I appreciate you being candid.'

Gabe couldn't give out details of the case – it would contravene everything he stood for – even to Paul. And Paul knew that too. But he still deserved an answer.

'Paige was chased into an alley by a man. We fought, and I knocked him out but had to get her out of the situation. Dave went to retrieve something of mine in the alley and must've been blindsided. I can't say for certain it was the same man until I speak to Dave, but it does seem likely.'

Paul nodded, knowing he wouldn't get any more of an explanation. Even Dave wouldn't tell him what had happened. Gabe knew that. Of all the people on the team, Dave had the tightest lips. He would never want to lie to Paul, so he purposely shielded him from the worst side of the stuff they dealt with.

The doctor approached at that moment, and they both turned to face him.

'Dave is in his room. Only two of you can go in, please. And only stay for a couple of minutes. He needs his rest. He's awake but pretty groggy.'

Paul stood and paused, then put his hand out toward Gabe. He didn't need the help, but Gabe took Paul's hand anyway, knowing enough to see when an olive branch was being offered.

Dave was pale – he had an oxygen mask over his face, and his breathing was steady. The blood pressure and heart monitor at his side beeped steadily. Gabe could just make out the bandage over his chest beneath the hospital gown.

Dave's eyes fluttered open, and Paul leaned in, giving his husband a gentle cuddle. Dave's arm snaked around Paul, pulling him in closer. These two were the perfect fit. Gabe had never seen a couple more in tune with each other. Except maybe his mom and dad. They'd been together going on forty years and were closer now than they'd ever been. Dave's fingers closed round Paul's T-shirt tightly, and Gabe knew in that moment how Dave felt. He was gripping his husband's top like that because it showed him that he was still alive, that he had something to hold on to. Gabe remembered the feeling all too well, and he knew without a doubt that Paul and Dave would be together as long as his parents had been.

Moving back, Paul kissed Dave on the cheek gently. He stood and nodded at Gabe, then left the room.

A lump rose in Gabe's throat. It took a lot for him to feel emotion this strongly, but his friend was lying in the hospital bed because Dave worked with him. That alone made this whole situation his responsibility.

'Hey, bro. You could've just asked if you wanted some time off.' Gabe curled his hand around Dave's arm and squeezed.

'I'm okay, Gabe. Or I will be. How much have you told Paul?'

'Just the basics. Didn't mention guns or anything. Said you'd gone into the alley after I'd knocked the guy out and that he must've taken you by surprise.' Moving the chair closer, he sat beside the bed.

'Pretty much what happened. Though it was in the woods. My fault – knew if I rang Mitch, I'd blow his cover so I figured just see where the guy had gone. My Spidey senses set off in the woods, and I hit the button. I felt the bullet hit me seconds later. He came over – stood above me grinning like the Cheshire fucking cat. The bastard shot me with your gun. Then he left.'

Gabe's composure slipped. 'He shot you with my gun? What the actual fuck? When I get my hands on him, I'll do more than fucking shoot him. Shit!'

Gabe leaped to his feet, and the chair he'd sat on went flying backward.

'Bro, chill. Seriously. Is the woman okay? Presume she's here somewhere. You didn't leave her at the cabin, did you?'

Gabe tried to rein his temper in. It wouldn't do to lose it right now. 'Yeah, she's here. I don't know is the honest answer. She passed out in the waiting room. When I came in here, she was still being seen to by the nurses.'

'She's terrified. I'm surprised she hasn't bolted again to be honest. Do we even know her name?'

'Paige Matthews. That's what she said when I met her a few weeks ago.'

'Weeks? How many weeks? And you didn't mention it? You didn't seem to recognize her today.'

'Six weeks – it was the day of Shotgun's funeral. And I didn't recognize her, not straightaway anyway. She dyed her hair, lost some weight. Too much weight. She's bordering on being too skinny now. It'll be the stress of whatever has her terrified, no doubt.'

'Okay. Tell Paul to bring my laptop in later, will you? I'm a little tired now, but later I'll …' Dave's eyes closed, and his head dropped to the side.

Gabe grinned – his friend had always been able to fall asleep at the drop of a hat. He had color back in his cheeks, though – that was a good sign.

Gabe moved the chair back to the side of the bed for Paul. He wouldn't tell him about the laptop request yet. If at all. Shaking his head, he already knew he'd be the one grabbing the laptop himself – and that he'd only bring it in when he felt Dave was feeling better. Leaving the room, Gabe held the door open for Paul to reenter just as the nurse came out of the door beside the waiting room.

'Are you here with the woman who passed out? I need some details on her, please.'

'I don't know much, but I can tell you what I do know. Is she okay?'

'She's still out for the count at the minute. We'll sit in the room with her in case she wakes while I'm getting her details.'

Gabe followed her into the room. Paige was still as white as a sheet and was breathing steadily. She was hooked up to a drip.

'Fluids? She's dehydrated?'

The nurse nodded with a smile. 'You're observant. What's her name?'

'Paige Matthews. I think. Hold on …' Gabe grabbed the bag off the small table beside the bed. Pushing the instant guilt aside, he quickly rooted through it to find her purse and cell phone. He flipped open the purse, searching for her ID.

It was virtually empty and pretty much brand-new. Cheap and cheerful – clearly from one of the discount stores and not a brand. It held a driver's license and a debit card. Nothing else. He frowned, then took the driver's license out and gave it to the nurse.

'Do you know if this address is valid?'

He glanced at it – and shook his head. 'I don't think so. She's a long way from home if it is. Just put my business address down – she's a … client.'

He handed one of his business cards over so he didn't have to recite it.

'Mind if I keep this?' The nurse smiled coyly at him and put it in her pocket without waiting for an answer.

When a groan sounded from the bed, Gabe turned to face Paige.

Paige's head was pounding. She struggled to drag herself out of the darkness and open her eyes. And then she smelled it. The cloying, sickly scent of disinfectant and that aroma that only hospitals have. Panic filled her mind – he was here. He had to be. He'd found her!

Her eyes opened quickly, too fast it appeared as another wave of dizziness spread over her. Her gaze darted around the room, searching for *him*. He had to be here. She was experiencing the worst bout of déjà vu.

The dark shadow of a man filled her view, and Paige's breath caught in her throat.

A nurse appeared at her side, checking her over. 'Take it easy, Paige. Do you know where you are?'

Paige was confused, then slowly she nodded, not trusting herself to speak. She glanced at the shadow. *He'll kill me. This is it.* Al wouldn't care if there was a nurse present.

Her eyes focused on him – and she realized it wasn't Al. It was Gabe. The man who'd brought her here. The one who'd rescued her from the alley when Al's henchman had found her. Her fear subsided.

'Hey,' he said.

She could tell he was saying it to put her at ease.

'What happened?' she asked, her voice quiet and gravelly.

'You passed out. They're running some tests to see why. How're you feeling?'

'I know why,' she said ruefully. 'I've not eaten in days. Just couldn't face food. I should've at least tried to have some toast or something.'

'We took some bloods,' said the nurse. 'You're hooked up to a saline drip, you're dehydrated. Are you allergic to any medications?'

'Temazepam. That's it.'

'Any known medical conditions?'

Paige shook her head. *No one needs to know. It's not relevant to the fainting.*

'We'd like to do a CT scan. It's possible you hit your head when you fell.'

'It's okay, I'm fine. I don't need a CT scan. Just some food, I think.'

'We'd like to be certain. Make sure there's nothing underlying that could've caused you to pass out.'

'No, really. I'm all right. I'd rather you didn't waste your time running a scan. I'm okay. Really.' Paige knew she sounded desperate. She also knew she didn't have medical insurance or the money to pay for any treatment. A fact which she couldn't come out and say with Gabe standing there or he'd never offer her his help with Al. Why would he if he knew she couldn't afford to pay?

'You can run the scan – all bills to be sent to my office, please.' Gabe's voice was smooth and the offer accepted by the nurse without question. It was like Paige hadn't even been heard saying she didn't want the scan.

The nurse flashed Gabe a smile, and she patted her pocket, sharing some secret that Paige wasn't aware of.

'I said I don't want the scan,' said Paige firmly. 'I meant it. It's up to me if I get scanned or not. I'm not some hopeless female who you need to control.'

Gabe appeared taken aback by the harshness of her tone.

'I never said you were. You had no money in your purse. I offered because the nurse believes you need the care.'

'You went through my purse? How dare you?' Paige pulled herself up to a sitting position, glaring daggers at Gabe.

'The nurse needed your info, and I didn't know it. It was merely to get the info from your driver's license. I haven't touched anything other than that.'

'You had no right. She could've waited until I woke up. I'm perfectly capable of handling my own affairs, thank you very much.'

'I never implied otherwise. I'd rather not do this. I've got a friend in recovery who's had surgery to remove a bullet. A bullet he caught trying to help you. So, cut the attitude and tell me what the hell is going on. Who is Al? And why does he want you back?'

Paige had to force back the tears threatening to fall. Had she mentioned Al? The last thing she needed was to blub – again. As angry as Gabe was, he was right. And she knew it. He deserved an explanation.

Gabe's temper was on a knife edge. He reined it back in before he blew his top completely. He'd always had a short fuse. Being angry at the situation that got his friend shot wasn't unreasonable, but he didn't need Paige to see the outburst and be afraid of him. That was the last thing he'd ever want. Gabe had never and would never raise his fist to a woman, but his outbursts tended to be loud and over fast. Like a firework his mom used to say. All bang and no buck. But anyone who didn't know him personally wouldn't realize that. People who didn't know him wouldn't know how much he hated violence against women. If there was one thing guaranteed to get his back up it was men demeaning and hurting the fairer of the species. It was plain wrong. And he got the feeling Paige had been on the receiving end of such treatment.

He drew in a deep breath and stared at her, waiting for her to start explaining.

'I was in a relationship with Al Graham for a few years. We were … together for a long time, but I was stupid. He was abusive. I ran, and he's been after me ever since.'

'And?' Gabe knew there was more than that to her explanation He needed more than just the abused ex-partner story. Men killed women. It happened more than people would think. The perp would travel the breadth of the country to find those they felt had wronged them too. But there had to be more to it than this. He waited, watching her body language silently.

If there was one thing Gabe did well, it was reading people. He'd picked the skill up when he was young, and it had been honed over many years. When her head slipped back an inch, he knew she was readying herself to tell him more.

'I saw Al do something – he thinks I'm going to tell. That's why he wants me dead.'

Paige's voice dropped to a whisper. There was something else she wasn't telling him, but he could also see she wasn't ready. She had to trust him before she would release whatever information she'd held back. And she didn't yet. She wanted to – he could see that – but the trust wasn't there. He relaxed his stance to put her at ease but also because his back was twinging. He was still in the denial phase after his injury eighteen months before. Even now he told himself it was age. The scars hidden away under his shirt said something else, though, but again he chose to ignore and instead pulled his shoulders back and stretched slowly, waiting for Paige to answer.

'He killed someone.'

'You saw him do that?'

Paige nodded.

'Did you tell the police?'

She shook her head.

'Why not?'

'Because he would have killed me. He beat me half to death as it was. I woke up in hospital – he was beside me. He swore he'd kill me if I told. I believed him. I still believe him.'

'That's why you need my help? To get justice for the man your ex killed? There's nothing else?'

He watched as something flashed in her eyes – something she masked quickly, obviously not wanting him to see. Then she nodded slowly.

'Yes, I need your help dealing with Al. Please.'

There was still something she wasn't telling him. As sure as he knew pushing now would result in her running at the first given opportunity. Leaning back in the chair, he was about to agree to help without asking any of the questions he'd normally ask before accepting a case, when his phone rang loudly and they both jumped.

'Gabriel Bland.' His answer was short and succinct.

Her eyes widened at his surname, but she stayed silent.

'Boss? It's Mitch. We need to talk. You at the hospital?'

'Yeah, I …'

'I'll be there in five. Meet me by the back entrance to the morgue.'

Mitch rang off before Gabe could reply.

'I need to pop out for a second; my team are outside the door in the waiting room. They all have their eyes open, and no one will get in here who isn't supposed to be. Okay?'

Paige nodded, and he got to his feet and closed the door behind him with a quiet click. He motioned Jacko over.

'I know we're all here for Dave, but she's a case, and I need someone to stay with her while I go and speak to Mitch. No one in or out unless they're medical personnel, okay?'

Jacko acknowledged his request with a grunt and took up position leaning against the wall beside the door to Paige's room. Gabe turned and made his way to the location requested by Mitch.

Chapter Seven

Perkinsville General Hospital

Gabe was more familiar with the hospital better than he'd like to admit, both from being a patient and visiting others. The door at the back of the morgue was obscured from view – whatever Mitch had to tell him, he knew Mitch planned on returning to the undercover case he was working as soon as they'd spoken.

He pushed the door open with ease and stepped out into the rear yard. Large overgrown bushes concealed the door – only a select few people other than the hospital staff would know that the door was there.

Gabe didn't speak, there was no need to. Mitch would have heard him coming out of the door from another two hundred feet away. As it was, he sidled from behind one of the bushes and stood shoulder to shoulder with Gabe.

'Followed the shooter back to his car. I've already input the registration into the system, and the details will be in your email. I was on foot so couldn't follow after he'd driven off. His name is Joey Mendino – he's known as The Fox. He's a lowlife scumbag who picks up high-paying jobs from assholes. Sometimes it's investigation work, sometimes it's that the people he works for need people bringing back to them. Kind of a take-the-money-and-ask-no-questions kinda guy. He has a rep for being reliable. I've had a quick glance over his rap sheet on the systems – he's tough. He's had some combat time that resulted in a dishonorable discharge. The records are sealed currently, but I'll find out some more information when I'm back in the office. He likes money, and rumor has it he's taken a liking to torturing information from people lately. We need to find out who he's working for – whoever it is will be paying top dollar for his services.'

'We already know – Al Graham – Paige named him and said he wants her for witnessing a murder. That he conducted. Paige said he runs a business called Graham Industries – import and export.'

'Paige?'

'The woman I was helping – this … Fox obviously found her, would've taken her too if I hadn't got there first. She's in the hospital with the team. Dave was shot. He's doing okay, bullet hasn't hit anything major.'

'Give him my best. I need to get to it. The gang will be suspicious if I'm not back in the next ten minutes.'

'Good. Go. Do what you need to and keep your head down. Check in at the scheduled times.'

Mitch nodded, and when Gabe blinked, he faded into the bushes. Gabe never heard a sound, and he smiled. Dave had mentioned The Fox acting like a ghost. He was pretty sure The Fox had nothing on Mitch.

Paige sighed deeply. The shadow lurking outside the door was obviously one of Gabe's men. Her cheeks flushed at the thought of Gabe. *Not the reaction I want to have when I think of any man at the minute.* Life was already far too complicated to want to get into … well, anything, with the head of Bland P.I.R.

She'd registered his surname the second he'd said it – he was the one Mags had told her to speak to. She also now understood Mags' chuckle on the phone earlier. What she didn't get, though, was why he would want to help her. He hadn't mentioned payment once – and she knew her medical bill wouldn't be cheap, especially not with the CT scan he'd insisted was tagged on for good measure.

Sighing again, she rubbed her hand over her head. The mother of all migraines was threatening to spring forth. She hated migraines. She'd suffered for years. It was a genetic inheritance from her mother who had spent days at a time in bed when Paige was a child. Her mother had passed away when Paige was younger – a sudden brain bleed resulting in her instant and shocking death. Paige had been seventeen at the time. It had been well before she'd ever met Al Graham. Her mother's death had left just her and her dad. Tears threatened again at the thought of her father. He'd have given every warning possible not to get involved with a man like Al. And he would have been right too. Al had been nothing but a bastard. Even now Paige wondered why she'd put up with it so long. *Cos you're a fool. No one but a fool would have stayed with an abusive dick like that.*

The door suddenly swung open, and she jumped violently, pulling her from her thoughts.

Paige did her best to slow her heartbeat down as Gabe strode into the room.

'Have you heard of someone called The Fox?' His voice was curt and to the point.

Confused, she thought for a moment and shook her head. *The Fox? Who has that kind of a name?*

'Okay. The nurse will be in shortly to take you for your CT scan. I need to pop back to the office, but Jacko, one of my team, will be outside the door at all times. If you need anything just holler.'

Panic threatened to overwhelm Paige – she didn't want to be left alone. She hated to admit it – even to herself – but being near Gabe made her feel safer than she had in forever. Whether that was some strange form of gratitude for him saving her from the alley, or because of the unwanted lust that filled her mind when he was close to her, she wasn't quite sure. *Definitely not the lust. I'm not going there. The last thing I need is another man complicating my life.*

Gabe's voice softened on seeing her reaction. 'It's okay, I'll be back in a bit. Jacko is more than capable of looking after you while I'm gone.'

Paige didn't trust herself to speak, so she nodded and lay her head back on the pillow, closing her eyes. Gabe left, the door clicking behind him. The pounding in her temples was increasing in tempo – she needed to relax. If she could, maybe the migraine would ease.

Bland P.I.R office – Main Street

Gabe's fingers clacked the keys on his keyboard loudly in the silent office. He'd left Jacko standing over Paige and told the rest of the team to either get on with their respective cases, or if they were done for the day to head back home.

He liked the solitude of the office when it was quiet like this.

Squinting at the screen, he let the face of The Fox become permanently etched onto his memory. Everything from the age lines on his head to the small silver scar beside his right eye. This guy was never going to get the drop on him again. It really stung that the man had stolen his gun – if

Gabe had still been a SEAL, he'd have been severely reprimanded for allowing his gun to fall into anyone's hands other than his own. Not to mention the ribbing he'd have got off his team.

Gabe hit print on the documents he had open and retrieved them from the printer beside him. He liked to be organized with a paper file as well as the digital version – old-fashioned, he knew – but if the electric ever went off he could still function. Momentarily, he wondered how many others would be able to do the same.

Pushing the papers into a file, he stood, grabbed Dave's laptop from his desk, and made his way back to the hospital.

The atmosphere was tense when he walked in, and he wasn't surprised to see Chief of Police, Kyle Barker, in a staring contest with Jacko outside Paige's room.

'Kyle. I was about to call you. Everything okay?'

Kyle spun around, one finger pointing at Gabe accusatorily. 'You are under agreement to report any shootings within this jurisdiction – you know how the mayor feels about the police being kept out of the loop in relation to your … investigations. Especially when it results in someone getting shot.'

'I just said I was going to call you – I meant it. Come on, Kyle, you know what it's like when you're chasing down leads. I wanted to be able to tell you something before I let you know. You know one of my core beliefs is transparency in relation to law enforcement. Hell, you know me. We grew up in the same damn area. A little trust wouldn't go amiss.'

Kyle sighed, running his hand through the mop of sandy-colored hair. His cheeks flushed, showing his embarrassment.

'You're right, of course I know that. The mayor heard before I did that one of your team had been shot. He heard it from his cousin, the anesthetist who worked on Dave. It looks bad when the mayor asks me for an update on something I never even knew happened.'

'Well, we all know Mayor Strangford is a pain in the ass. You could have just said I was working on something confidential.'

'Give me some credit, Gabe, I did say that. I also said I was fully aware of your investigation and that you were operating with my full discretion. Even told him your report would be with me by close of play today. Doesn't change the fact I know nothing about a shooting that happened in my own damn town now, does it?'

'Thanks, Kyle. I will submit the shooting paperwork later on today, but I can't go into a lot of detail. It is confidential and relating to an ongoing case. You know what that means. I could be putting someone at risk if I do.'

Kyle bowed his head marginally in acknowledgement, a slightly hurt expression marring his features. 'I know better than to ask for *too much* information. Just do me a favor and make sure no one else gets shot, okay?'

Gabe sighed at the sarcasm in Kyle's tone. 'I will. Trust me, that's the last thing I want.'

'And keep me updated. If there's something I need to know, you make sure I get the information, okay?'

'Absolutely.'

Kyle nodded curtly and strode purposefully away from Gabe.

'One thing you do need to know, Kyle,' said Gabe.

Kyle paused mid-step and stretched his neck back round to glare at Gabe.

Gabe continued. 'The shooter took my gun. I was trying to help a witness, and it fell to the ground during the scuffle with the offender. He picked it up without my knowledge. He shot Dave with my gun.'

'Jesus Christ,' muttered Kyle, clearly about to launch into a tirade until he saw the pain on Gabe's face. 'Send me the serial number and details as soon as you can. I'll get it logged on the system. Hopefully this prick won't become a pain in my ass. I trust you're hunting him down?'

'Too right we are.'

'Okay then, send it all on over.' Kyle's voice softened slightly. 'I'm sorry about Dave, keep me updated on his progress.'

'Will do,' said Gabe, watching Kyle turn the corner at the end of the corridor.

'He's a dick,' said Jacko

'He can be, but today he was right. I should've told him about what had happened before now. You get yourself off home, Jacko. Everyone else is long gone. Thanks for keeping an eye on Paige.'

Jacko turned and headed off, leaving Gabe in the corridor. He paused at the door, his ear pressed to the wood, listening to see if she was awake.

He pushed the door open. Paige turned to face him, and their eyes locked. Blue on gray – it was like a bolt of electricity passed between them, and he broke the eye contact by coughing and glancing at the floor.

'I've got a photo to show you, would you mind?'

Paige shook her head, and Gabe perched on the edge of the bed and opened the file in his hand.

'This is the guy who cornered you in the alley. Is he familiar to you?'

Paige scanned the photo then sat back, her expression almost relieved.

'No, I've never seen him before in my life.'

'You're sure? I think it's time you and me had a talk about why you were coming to Bland P.I.R yesterday, and why you ran off. Don't you?'

'I'm sure, and yes, I know you're right.' Paige shuddered.

Gabe placed his hand on her arm in reassurance. 'No one can touch you. You're safe.'

'I know, it's just knowing what's relevant and what isn't. And I've never told anyone about it before. Ever.' Paige drew in a deep breath and opened her mouth to speak when the door flew open suddenly and an orderly strode inside.

'Time for your CT scan. Excuse me,' he directed the last at Gabe who got to his feet and stepped back from the bed.

'She'll be back in about half an hour. You can wait here or go get yourself a coffee or whatever.'

'I'll come with you.'

'You can't – non-patients aren't allowed in the CT room, radiation exposure. As I said, you can wait here or you can go get a coffee.'

'And as I said, I'm coming with you. I'll wait outside the CT room if I have to. Though Anastacia always lets me into the room with one of those lead-lined aprons on.' Gabe referred to his sister's friend who was one of the radiographers for the hospital, and higher ranked than the bossy orderly currently standing in front of him.

'Fine, whatever,' he said, his gaze growing darker. He shot Gabe a look of pure venom.

His attitude continued as Gabe followed him from the hospital room down the corridor.

What the hell is this guy's problem? Gabe picked up his pace and took hold of the side bar of the trolley bed, walking alongside Paige at the same pace.

When the orderly made a wrong turn, Gabe frowned. They were now heading toward the morgue and not the X-ray and scan area.

'Think you've taken a wrong turn, bud. The CT scans are conducted just next to the X-ray department. Are you new?'

The man grunted from behind him but didn't alter his direction.

Gabe gripped the bed harder, his weight pulling the bed to a stop.

'Let go of the bed.' The man's voice was filled with poison, and his eyes moved around furtively before settling on Gabe with a glare.

'How about you let go of the bed. I'll take her to X-ray myself. Who's your supervisor?' Gabe readied himself, widening his stance slightly, staring the orderly down.

The man pushed the trolley hard at Gabe and turned and ran.

Now Gabe was stuck – did he go after him or stay with Paige?

'Go if you need to.' Her voice was small and quiet, her eyes shiny with unshed tears. She was plainly terrified.

'It's fine, he'll be on CCTV, so I'll grab his profile off there and run it through the database. Come on, let's get you to X-ray.'

'What did he want, do you think?'

'I've no idea, but he was taking you to the rear entrance. It's not known to everyone, so he must be familiar with the layout. He might even really work here. But if he does, he won't be for much longer. Not if I have any say on the matter.'

'He was going to kidnap me?' The little color Paige had regained from the fluid IV vanished, leaving her pale.

'Possibly. Don't worry, you're not being left alone until you've told us everything and we've sorted this whole mess out.'

'What if you can't? Sort it out, I mean?'

'We've never failed on a mission yet. I have to believe you won't be the first.'

'If he was taking me outside, does that mean someone would be waiting to pick me up?'

Gabe stopped the trolley and stared at her in astonishment – he'd been so focused on the orderly he'd never even considered that. *Which you bloody should have – rookie mistake, Bland.*

He was torn now – he needed to go outside and check but didn't want to leave Paige on her own.

'Stow me in a room along here somewhere. I can wait there for you to come back. Then at least you can do what you need to do. I'm okay, honest, I was terrified, but it's easing now. I will be okay.'

Gabe nodded and tried some of the door handles. One opened into a small office space. He quickly moved the table and chairs out of the way and pushed her inside. 'Here's my tablet. If anything happens and you need help, touch this button here in the middle. It'll alert everyone on the team to come running. Keep it under the sheet so no one can see it. The location updates every five seconds. Understand?'

Paige nodded silently, accepting the tablet he withdrew from his pocket.

Paige couldn't stop shaking. The second Gabe had shut the door it had started. *What on earth possessed you to tell him to stow you in a room and go after whoever is outside – it could be Al, for god's sake. You could've just gotten him killed!*

Her hand rested on the page of the tablet with a big red button in the middle. She kept moving a finger to the side of the button to keep the page open – she didn't know if it had a security lock like her cell but she didn't want to risk it.

I can't do this. Maybe I should just go. I already got his friend shot. What if he gets hurt trying to protect me? I can move again – find another name to live by. Then she thought of her extremely meager bank balance and the fact that she'd grown so close to Mags and knew she couldn't just uproot like she had before. Mags wouldn't let her for one. *But if I stay, I'll put her in danger. Her and everyone else in the shelter.*

A sudden sound outside the door caught her attention. What was it? A shuffle, a whisper maybe? Whatever it was, she felt like she was about to be caught. Panic settled in her stomach; she was nauseous and on the verge of throwing up. *Have I really gone through everything I have to be this weak woman? I need to man up. I'm terrified of my own shadow at the minute. Where did the woman I was before Al go? That woman would have kicked ass in this situation.*

She drew in a deep breath, grabbed the glass vase from the middle of the meeting room table, and steeled herself for someone potentially entering the room.

I can do this.

Gabe ran to the entrance at the back of the morgue. He paused at the door, pressing his ear to it and listened. Not hearing a peep, he pushed the button on the wall beside the door to unlock, pushed it slowly, and glanced around. There was one van in the small parking area reserved for the morgue vehicles. It was black, and the windows were tinted so he couldn't see inside.

Moving back slightly, he withdrew the trusty .45 he'd grabbed from the truck's lockbox before heading into the hospital from its holster. He took the safety off and held it in front of him, did a quick sweep to each side, then made his way cautiously toward the driver's door.

He held the gun in his dominant hand, reached for the door handle with his right hand, and pulled, not surprised to find it opened easily. There was no one inside, however. Placing his hand on the hood of the van, he knew they hadn't been there long. The engine was still warm.

Suddenly his phone buzzed in his pocket, and he checked the alert. It was from his tablet. *Shit!*

He knew as soon as he entered the corridor where he'd stashed Paige that something was off. The air felt different somehow. He turned the corner, and the office door stood wide open. Broken glass was strewn over the floor mingled with a few drops of blood. *Please don't be hers.*

Paige was nowhere to be seen.

He checked his phone again. The app cursor hadn't moved – the location was still the same. She was still in the hospital, but he couldn't say where yet. Not with only one movement point to compare to.

He sent a rapid text to his team, giving them a very quick overview of what had happened; he waited mere seconds for their replies. They were on their way. That's what he needed to hear. He paused outside the room in the corridor – silence reined. The hospital smell lingered in the air.

Knowing whoever had Paige hadn't passed him on the way to the morgue. Which meant they would be heading for the southern entrance as that was the next closest to the van.

There's no proof that van is even connected to this, though – if I go to the van and it's not connected then Paige will be gone and I won't even know where to start. If I go through the hospital then they might make it to their vehicle before I catch up.

'What kind of an idiot lets the whole team go home and doesn't expect something like this to kick off? Dave was shot, for goodness sake – it's not rocket science to understand whoever it is after her means business,' muttered Gabe. He raced toward the southern entrance of the hospital.

His phone pinged again with an updated location for his tablet – *still in the hospital.*

He sped forward, ignoring the stares of horror from the few people he passed. Someone would call Kyle and say there was a lunatic with a gun running around the hospital if he wasn't careful.

They wouldn't be far wrong at this stage …

He ran forward and came to a junction. *Should I go left or right?* His phone pinged again – showing the updated location as to his left. He turned the corner and caught sight of a man's back as he disappeared around the bend farther down. His stance made it look as though he was pushing something. Gabe all but flew to the corner, closing the distance rapidly.

Gabe reached the spot in seconds, and something hard connected with his jaw, sending him careening backward into the corner of the wall. He steadied himself and realized it was the orderly who'd first tried to push Paige out through the back entrance. He stabilized his footing and glared at the man in front of him.

'You shouldn't have let me leave,' sneered the man, taking a step forward.

Gabe took in the scar to his face, above his eyebrow, the darkness in his gaze, and the undertone of uncertainty. The way the man held himself indicated he'd fought before. Gabe stowed his gun back in its holster and took a step forward, glancing past the man to the gurney where Paige lay, her head back on the pillow and her eyes closed as if asleep. His anger surged at bruise spreading across her face, and he instinctively knew the orderly had physically knocked her out. *Probably to stop her shouting for help.* Violence against women was bang out of order.

'Punching her was a big mistake. Not the first one you made, but a big one nonetheless.' Gabe's voice cut through the tension.

'Am I supposed to ask what my first mistake was? I don't have time for stupid questions. Let's just get this over with so I can get her to my boss. Reckon you can take me, do you? An ass like you? I don't think so, big man,' the orderly snarled.

The orderly closed the distance and drew his fist back. *Another mistake.* The man had left himself wide open — was more of a bar fighter than formally trained. Gabe ducked forward, his shoulder hitting the orderly's torso with enough force to push him back into the wall with a loud thud. It allowed the incoming blow to glance off his shoulder. Gabe flattened his palm and drove it upward into the orderly's nose. Blood burst forth, and the man cried out, his hands working on autopilot and grasping at his nose. Tears fell from his eyes down his cheeks, and he stumbled sideways.

Gabe, ready for the movement, brought his left fist round and connected with the side of the man's head, and it slammed against the wall with a thud. This time the force was enough to crack the plaster a little, and the man slumped to the floor with a soft groan.

Knowing he'd knocked him out, Gabe ran to Paige's side.

'Paige, open your eyes, darlin'.' He spoke quietly, trailing his finger gently down the side of her face that wasn't bruised.

She groaned loudly, her eyes fluttering, fighting to drag herself from the blackness. She bolted up in the bed suddenly, her eyes darting from side to side and finally settling on Gabe.

'What happened?' she asked, laying her head back down.

He liked that instinctively she knew she was safe with him. He smiled down at her.

'A minor inconvenience. It's been taken care of.' He nodded to the side and watched her eyes widened when she saw the orderly's unconscious form.

'He came into the room you left me in. I tried to hit him with the vase, but he was too strong. He grabbed me and then … hmmm, then it went black. I'm guessing from the pain in my face he hit me?'

Gabe nodded. 'Yeah, you're gonna have a shiner for sure.'

Loud footsteps approached from around the corner, and Gabe turned, tensing in anticipation. He was relieved to see Becca Smith and Deacon Marshall heading in his direction with their guns raised.

'Boss. You okay? Your text said you needed assistance.' Becca's gaze was sharp, but when she rounded the bend, her expression softened. 'Under control then. Who's he?'

'Supposedly an orderly – he tried to kidnap Paige.'

'Well, trouble seems to be following her about, doesn't it. Do we know his name?'

'Haven't asked him yet,' said Gabe, doing his best not to react to her comment about Paige. *What is it with Paige? I shouldn't be feeling the need to defend her against my own team's comments. She's a case. Pure and simple.*

Liar. He sighed at the argument in his head. There'd be time for all that later.

He refocused his attention on the orderly who groaned loudly, seemingly in response to being talked about. Becca stepped forward and bent, positioning her gun so it would be the first thing he saw when he opened his eyes.

'What the …? I'm not getting paid enough for this shit. I'll tell you what you want to know. Don't shoot me.'

'Then speak. What's your name? What was the plan?' Gabe spoke from behind Becca.

'Martin Coldfield. I'm an orderly here. It pays the bills, but I've got debts and my ex-wife's alimony. He offered me two hundred bucks to take her out to the car park at the back. Said if I had to knock you out to do it, he'd pay me an extra hundred. I don't know nothing else.' His voice turned sullen, but his expression showed he was telling the truth.

'Who's *he*?'

'I don't know, I swear. Some guy came up to me outside when I was having a smoke. Gave me the two hundred there along with the room number for *her* and said to say I was taking her for a scan. I don't know his name.'

'Description?'

Martin's head cocked to one side as he considered the question. 'Truth be told, I was looking at the money in his hand, not him. He was white, short. Sly. Sorry, I'm no good at this sort of thing. I'm really sorry, I didn't know what he wanted with her but I shouldn't have tried to take her outside. I need this job, man, please don't grass me up.'

'Don't grass you up? You pathetic, sniveling little weasel! You punched me – you kidnapped me. You should be locked up and the key thrown away.' Paige had jumped off the gurney and was standing next to Becca with her hands on her hips, glaring at Martin on the floor.

'Kidnapped? I didn't kidnap you. I was just taking you outside … I didn't know what …' Realization dawned, and Martin's face paled instantly. 'Shit – I did kidnap you. Fuck – I'm sorry. I didn't think. I'm sorry I hit you – you went for me with the vase, and it was instinct to react. I shouldn't have done it, though, I shouldn't have done any of it.' He hung his head in shame.

For a millisecond, Gabe almost felt sorry for him. He pulled his cell phone from his pocket and dialed Kyle's office number.

'Kyle. I could use a police assist. One of the hospital workers just tried to kidnap Paige – he's assaulted her as well …. No, she's fine. We've got him detained … Yeah, no bother. See you in ten.' He hung up the phone and looked at Martin. Suddenly the man seemed much smaller than he had originally, and far less threatening.

'I'm done for.' His voice was weak, and he shook his head a little. 'Fucking prick.'

'Excuse me?' said Gabe, thinking Martin was referring to him.

'Not you. Me. My ex-wife will never let me see my son again now. I've fucked everything up. I get why you called the cops. Again, I'm sorry. I wasn't thinking straight.'

'The guy who paid you, was this him?' Gabe brought up the picture of The Fox from the gallery on his phone and held it in front of Martin's face.

Martin nodded then returned his gaze to the floor.

'Becca, Deacon, when Kyle gets here, hand this guy off and get yourselves home. I've already canceled the text – doubt anyone else will land now, but if they do, they can head back off. I'm taking Paige to my place. We'll sort everything else out tomorrow.'

Chapter Eight

Back road near Rhododendron

Joey Mendino put his car in park at the side of the road and hit dial on his cell phone.

'Graham Industries. How may I direct your call?' The woman's voice was irritating, and Joey's anger rose instantly.

'Joey Mendino. I need to speak with Al.'

'Mr. Graham is in a meeting at the minute. He asked not to be disturbed. Can I ask him to call you back?'

'No, you can most certainly not ask him to call me back. Get him on the phone right now. It's urgent.' Pure venom in his tone, Joey knew that Marcia, or Mercy, or whatever the heck the new girl was called, would be feeling it as he intended. He could practically see her shake in her seat.

Hold music grated on his ears as he awaited her return.

After less than thirty seconds, she was back on the line, her chirpy voice now cool to the point of being arctic.

'Mr. Graham said he is in a meeting and will call you when he is done. He has your number. Thank you for calling Graham Industries.'

Before he could even formulate a single word, in the receiver clicked in his ear and the dead tone of the line sounded.

Now the red mist descended fully – he hit the phone off the steering block hard, not even caring when a large crack appeared on the screen.

I'm the best in the business. If that dick can't make time to speak with me then maybe I shouldn't continue with the job. He frowned – his petty thoughts seemed reasonable only one second ago, but now … well, the reality of it was he wanted the money and he needed his reputation intact. If he canceled the job with Al Graham, he had no doubts the man would spread bad word. *Sometimes being the best means you have to take a hit every now and then.* His thoughts moved to the man in the alley. His punch to Joey's face had been the first time someone had connected skin on skin for he didn't know how long. He was good. And built like a mountain. There had been power behind those punches. He couldn't remember the last time he'd been knocked down by one.

I got his gun, though, arrogant prick. Must think he's some white knight on a mission to protect a maiden.

Joey would keep hold of the gun too – it'd bring a couple of hundred bucks on the black market, but it was also insurance in a way. No man liked it when someone took his gun – it was liked even less when the same gun was used to kill one of his friends. Joey was only assuming, of course, he had no way of knowing the man he'd shot was linked to the first guy, but it made sense he would have had someone standing by when he ran out of the alley carrying Paige Matthews.

He fucked that right up. He will pay for his interference. Whether it's on the books or not!

Joey's phone buzzed in his hand, and he was surprised to see Al Graham's name pop up on the screen.

'Mendino,' he said sharply once he'd swiped to accept the call.

'You rang?' Al's voice was just as short as his own.

You'd think the guy would be a little more pleased I was ringing with news.

'How long did you say it was since you last had a location for Beth?'

'Five months. Why?' Al's tone changed, his interest clearly piqued.

Joey considered whether to tell him outright that he'd found her and he knew the name she was going under, or whether to play him a little. Deciding on the latter, he quickly formulated a response – the longer the investigation took, the more he would get paid.

'I've got a lead. She's possibly using another identity. I'll be following up over the next couple of days. Make sure you're available to answer my call when I ring. I don't like being kept waiting.'

'Just do your job. Track Beth down and bring her back. I need what she stole from me. You're being paid well for your assistance. Do not give me cause to obtain assistance elsewhere.'

Joey rang off with a swipe and glanced at the thin line of blood appearing on his thumb. The crack in the screen had separated ever so slightly, just enough to cut the top dermal layers of his thumb as it passed over.

He slid his tongue along the cut, the small amount of blood transferring in the process. He tasted the metallic tang and smiled.

Al had said not to hurt Beth, that he would quiz her for information when he got her. Joey had never agreed to that part. Al presumed because he was being paid, that Joey would do as he was instructed. Unfortunately for Al, nothing was ever as it seemed. Joey had recently discovered a bit of torture provided a wealth of information. Information that he could retain for use at a later date if it wasn't needed straightaway. And he didn't care whether he hurt a man or a woman. They all screamed the same.

Joey might yet turn the situation around so that Al would be the one begging for help – he couldn't stand people who passed the buck, and that was something Al did without thinking. *Need an ex-partner found?* Call Joey. *Need a body disposing of?* Call Joey. Seemed like every time someone needed anything, the mantra was now 'call Joey.'

A loud sigh filled the car before Joey twisted the key once more and continued on his journey.

Gabe's cabin

The drive back hadn't taken long. Gabe had signed Paige out from the hospital and into his care, promising to return her in the morning for a checkup – and to have the CT scan completed if the doctor thought she needed it at that point.

The gravel crunched under the wheels of his truck as he pulled onto the drive and put it in park, glancing at Paige who had been sitting in silence the whole way back to the cabin. 'You okay?' he asked softly.

'Yeah, just thinking. Why are you helping me like this? You don't even know me. Or do you bring every case back to your home?'

'Helping people is my job. I've never brought a case home until you – you need somewhere safe to stay, and no one outside of my team knows this cabin exists. It makes sense to keep you with me here for your own safety. If you're uncomfortable, we can go to back to the inn, I can get two rooms there, no bother at all.'

'No, here is fine. Are you sure he won't find us here? Who is he anyway? Do you know?' The remnants of an earlier conversation in the hospital room burst forth in her mind, and she stared at Gabe. 'The Fox, that was what you said his name was? What does he want with me?'

'You tell me. In a minute when we're inside. I need coffee and food. In that order. You can explain while I rustle up some dinner.'

Within minutes he was chopping vegetables in the kitchen with a steaming mug of coffee beside him.

Paige stared at Gabe thoughtfully while he chopped. His skill with a knife told her he'd cooked before, maybe even enjoyed it. She'd always found cooking a chore – didn't really understand what she was doing with it. Al had always ordered in from his favorite restaurant, so it hadn't left much time for her to do any cooking. *He was always in control – wouldn't have let me anyway. I'd have chipped a nail or something.* Al liked his women to be what he considered a 'real woman' – boobs and ass with prettily styled hair and nails. She'd hated the weekly trips to the salon he insisted on paying for. The only thing she'd ever forced his hand on was working – but even that he'd controlled, inserting her into a role within his business.

'So … spill.' Gabe's voice was husky, and he took a long mouthful of coffee, maybe to help clear the gruffness in his throat.

Paige could almost taste the warm headiness on her tongue, and for a moment she wanted to taste him along with the coffee. It would start as a small kiss, then escalate rapidly into a hot, smoldering, 'don't ever want to leave' kind of kiss. She'd bet every penny she'd ever earned that he knew his way around a female body. She barely managed to disguise the shudder that burst through her. *Get a grip. He took a drink of coffee, it's not seductive and it's not enough to give you that reaction. Cold shower needed much!*

A small grin played on his lips, and suddenly she knew he realized what she'd been thinking about. Deep heat flushed her cheeks, and she looked down at her hands which she held tightly in her lap. *Oh Lordy – what the hell did you go and stare at him like that for?*

Gabe had moved closer, so when she glanced up from her hands, he was standing right in front of her, his gray eyes piercing as he stared at her.

'Not that I don't want to progress whatever the heck that look was, because trust me, I do, but we had agreed to talk about who is after you and why. I need to know what's going on so we can protect you.'

If ever there were words designed to act like a cold shower, it was the ones Gabe had just uttered.

'I don't know what to say or how much is relevant. You're right, though, I do need help. Mags told me you were the best in the business, that you're the only ones equipped to help me. I can't go to the police – he has too many on his payroll. I wouldn't know who to trust. You need to understand that this is … difficult. I've spent months purposely not talking about any of it, trying to protect myself from Al.'

'Mags being Mags Brannigan, perchance? She's good people. I'm glad she's in your corner.'

He seems to know Mags well, possibly even better than I do. That he knew she was good people just strengthened the knowledge that she could trust him. *Maybe I do need to tell him everything …*

Paige drew in a deep breath and spoke. 'I started seeing Al Graham about six years ago. He was suave, made it easy for me to want to be with him. I moved into his home after a few months.' She exhaled shakily, peeking up at Gabe.

His face had darkened – like thunderclouds on a summer day.

Drawing in a shaky breath, she continued. 'The first time he hit me, I thought it was a mistake. But the beatings kept happening, and I grew less and less like myself and more like some timid little shrew, always afraid and hiding from him. But I couldn't leave. At that point I was pregnant. And he changed, or I thought he had. He never hit me once during the pregnancy. But the day I brought Diana home, it started again. Small beatings at first. I was trapped. I didn't know how I could leave. He had all the money and power, and I had nothing.'

Gabe made a strangled noise; his face was flushed, and his eyes were sparking – lightning in storm clouds. She could see he wanted to comment but also wanted her to finish. So she carried on.

'Even his right-hand man, George, showed no mercy. If Al said to punch me, he did. If Al told George not to let me in to see Diana when she was crying, he wouldn't let me in. He used our daughter to control me and keep me at his side. I ended up doing some paperwork for the business – Al's in export and import. I didn't know anything was wrong until it was. I'd noticed some inconsistencies in the numbers – it looked minor but it needed sorting out. I was taking the paperwork to check it against the files held across the warehouse floor …'

Paige's voice broke slightly, her mind flashing back to the utter fear on the face of the man on his knees in front of Al.

'Al was standing near his office. There was a man on his knees in front of him. Fred Donnington – he was a lovely man. Wife, two kids – the whole white-picket-fence lifestyle. Al had a gun. He …' Paige drew in another shaky breath, steeling herself to say the words aloud that she'd never spoken once before.

'Al shot … Fred fell forward. There was blood. Al had shot Fred.'

Tears spilled over from her eyes; a sob caught in her throat. Paige kept shaking her head, as if shaking would rid her mind of the images that now overwhelmed her. When Gabe pulled her into his arms, gently pushing her head onto his chest, Paige let loose and sobbed. All the pent-up emotion escaped in rivers down her face, wetting Gabe's pristine shirt. She couldn't stop if she wanted to. It was like a dam had opened.

It seemed like forever before the crying finally ebbed. Momentarily confused when Gabe released her from his arms, she just stared at the tissue in his hand as he offered it to her. Then recognition kicked in, and she took it from him.

'I can't imagine you seeing him kill someone went down very well?'

'No,' she said somewhat wryly. 'He grabbed my hair, dragged me out to the car, and slammed my head off the car door when I didn't get in quick enough for him. I didn't wake up until we were at home. I tried to promise I wouldn't say anything to anyone. But he just looked at me with … empty eyes. He hit me. I don't really remember how much, but when I woke again, I was in hospital. He told the hospital staff I'd thrown myself down the marble stairs at home – they believed him. He said I'd had postnatal depression since having Diana – again they believed him. Put everything down to me having a psychotic break. They sent me home with him a few days later.'

'How much longer did you stay?' Gabe's hand found hers, his thumb drawing soft circles on the back of it.

It was calming, and Paige focused on that. Anything was better than the remainder of her story. The gentle rubbing of Gabe's thumb didn't stop the shaking, though. Tremors racked her body; it was hard to talk about the one thing she'd buried so deep she never wanted it to come out.

'I stayed for another three years, I couldn't get away. No matter how many times he hit me, no matter how much I wanted to leave and escape, I couldn't. He had my Diana. I couldn't leave her with that monster.'

'He used her to make you stay?'

'Not just used her like that. He hid her away, hired a nanny. Only ever let me see my daughter when supervised by him. He would grab her out of my arms when she came to me for comfort. I didn't know what to do, Gabe. He had my baby.'

Paige's heart broke in two, and she began to cry again. 'I can't do this. I can't tell you any more. It's breaking me apart. I just …'

'Shh, it's okay. You don't have to tell me anything else. Not yet. Not until you're ready. Just take some deep breaths and lock the memories back up, darlin'. You're safe, you're here. Nothing will happen to you. I give you my word we will protect you. We will stop Al Graham from ever getting his hands on you again.'

Paige cried onto his shirt again. Gabe couldn't let her go. He'd never been good with women crying, but this woman clearly needed a release. He was still trying to wrap his head around the fact that she'd endured another three years with the monster that was Al Graham. *One day me and him will meet; he'll be lucky if I don't rip his head off his shoulders. It's no more than he deserves.*

Paige's sobs slowed to hiccups, and eventually her body went lax against his. Without breaking a sweat, he picked her up gently and carried her through to the lounge. With great care, he laid her down on the oversized sofa, grabbing the throw off the back and putting it over the top of her. She looked peaceful – innocent. Her eyelids were wet with tears, and she had streaks down her cheeks – he leaned over and wiped the streaks away. *How can anyone do something like that to a woman? Any woman? We need to rescue her daughter. She must've reached the end of her tether and left – it'll be killing her not having Diana with her.*

Gabe left Paige to rest and quickly put the finishing touches to the pasta in the kitchen. There was plenty left for when she awoke, even after he'd piled a large dollop on his plate. Grabbing his laptop from the back room he used as an office, he set himself up in the chair next to the sofa. The first thing he did was bring up files on Al Graham. *The better one knows their enemy, the more equipped one is to defeat that enemy.*

He let Paige sleep while he did some research, but after a couple of hours, he needed to wake her. She could have concussion from being punched at the hospital, not to mention the fall on his porch which felt like a million years ago. She would also need food.

Gabe put the laptop on the small table to the side of the chair and knelt in front of Paige, gently touching her with his hand, trying to wake her slowly. It didn't work, though, and she bolted awake, her eyes showing her terror and darting around. It almost split his heart in two. He understood how it felt to be so terrified that every subtle change in the environment caused fear to rise.

'Easy, Paige. It's just me, Gabe. You're at my cabin. You're safe.'

Paige's fear ebbed, and she stared at him, vulnerable and open. Her tongue darted out, and she licked her bottom lip nervously, not speaking.

He understood the nerves too – being this close to her had set every sense he had on alert. Her tongue flicking over her lip, and his pulse pounded loudly in his ears. It took all of his control not to lean forward and capture her mouth with his, to show her that with him she could let her guard down, that he would protect her.

He refrained – barely – but it took everything he had. He could swear he heard her sigh in disappointment when he rocked back onto his heels, creating distance between them.

'You need food. I made pasta – hope that's okay?'

Paige nodded and went to pull herself up from the couch, wincing visibly.

'You're in pain. What's the matter?'

'Nothing, I'm just stiff. I just need to move a bit and it'll ease my creaky joints.'

'Liar.' Gabe was blunt with his one-word retort, but she plainly wasn't telling him the truth. He didn't need to be king of reading people to see that.

Paige stared at him, her eyes wide. Acceptance slowly passed over her face. 'Okay, you're right. I'm sorry. It's not something I tell people. Even Mags doesn't know. After the last hospital stay courtesy of Al, because of the stress and severity of my injuries, I contracted systemic lupus. Have you heard of it?'

Gabe nodded once. 'It's an autoimmune condition. Causes pain in the joints, fatigue, headaches and whatnot. I know someone who has it. Do you have medication?'

'No, not at the minute. I don't have health insurance. Can't afford to pay for them either. I was diagnosed a few years ago. Had medication at first but I ran out after I'd escaped from Al. I managed to get some from a free clinic I visited which covered me for a while after but since then I've never been able to renew it.'

'That puts you at massive risk. You must know the implications of not getting adequate medication?'

'I do, but there isn't really anything I can do about it. I didn't say anything at the hospital as I didn't want them tagging the medication onto the bill. You're already paying for the CT scan if I need it tomorrow. Which I don't think I do by the way. It had settled a bit, but when Al found me six months ago it flared up again. The worst symptoms for me at the minute are migraines and fatigue, the pain is just something I've become accustomed to. It bothers me more when I'm immobile for long periods.'

'I'll be telling the nurse tomorrow – you need medication. The company medical insurance covers clients – you can't keep putting yourself at risk by not taking medication. You'll end up seriously ill. What will happen then? And not eating or being adequately hydrated will add to your symptoms too, no doubt. Come on – it's time for food. You need to eat.'

Paige nodded and let herself be pulled up by Gabe. He didn't let go of her hand as he led her through to the kitchen and seated her at the table.

'Just a small portion, my appetite isn't huge.'

'You'll get a decent portion. If you can't eat it all then fine, but if you can then all the better. Sorry, I know I'm nagging, but I know how important keeping healthy is when you have an autoimmune disease. Not to mention keeping your body fueled when you're stressed out. It's important. Your body can start shutting down if it doesn't have fuel.'

'The someone-you-know who has it is a friend or relative? You seem to know a lot about it.'

'My sister, Anna. She contracted it after a car accident when she was twenty. I've seen her suffer through many years of it. The meds are helping now, though – she hasn't had a flare in a good while.'

Gabe dished up a large bowl of pasta and put it in the microwave to warm through, then dished up a smaller bowl for himself. He'd eaten a couple of hours ago but was ready for some more food. He'd purposely kept plenty for the both of them.

Chapter Nine

Bland P.I.R office

Paige was nervous. She'd woken to the smell of fresh coffee and bacon and eaten with Gabe at his table. Then she'd cleaned herself up and traveled with Gabe back to his office where she was asked to sit and provide him and his team with all the information relevant to her case.

Telling Gabe was one thing; it had actually felt good letting him know what she was running from and asking for the help she knew she needed. But now, sitting in the back office of Bland P.I.R, seated around a large round table, with what felt like a dozen expectant faces staring back at her, she was nervous. She didn't know these people – to them she was the person who'd got their friend shot in the woods.

She flashed a shaky smile at the three faces seated beside her and Gabe. The other female present was the one she'd seen at the hospital. *Becca I think her name was.*

Becca didn't smile back, though; if anything her return expression was cold. *She definitely blames me for the shooting. Which I would too in her shoes.*

Paige sighed deeply then forced her strength forward. She had no reason to be nervous or afraid. She needed help, and that was what Bland P.I.R provided. Setting her shoulders slightly, she took a deep breath then explained, in brief, the reason she was there.

After what felt like an eternity, the other team members filtered from the room and the round table, leaving Paige and Gabe alone.

She exhaled shakily. 'Well, that had to be one of the most terrifying things I've ever had to do. It's not easy for me to ask for help. I know your team are the best, but it would have been easier for me if you'd explained.'

'If I'd done that then you would have regretted it. Saying the words out loud gives you strength. It also made Becca, Deacon, Grayson, and Jacko understand exactly how terrified you are of Al Graham. You did the right thing telling them the way you did. I was here – wasn't going anywhere – and if I'd thought for one minute you were out of your depth, I'd have stepped in.'

'So, what now? Can I go back to the shelter? I need to see Mags. Tell her what's happening. She'll be worried sick.'

'That's the idea. I'll take you back shortly. I want to chat with Mags too and check the security at the shelter.'

'Why? Do you think he knows about the shelter?' Paige barely managed to keep the panic from bursting forth. If The Fox knew where she was staying, he'd relay that information back to Al. And Al wouldn't let anything like a secure refuge stop him from getting at her.

'No, but I'd like to make sure the shelter is as secure as it can be in the event that anything does happen, whether it's linked to you or not. Mags' place houses vulnerable women and kids. The Fox likely doesn't know you're there or he'd have made a move, but that's not to say someone connected to one of the other residents there won't cause issues. Mags is good, but security is a big part of what we do.'

'Well, you seem to know Mags pretty well. I know she'd never leave any of us at risk. But I see what you mean. You might think of something she hasn't. I'm sure Mags is amenable to anything that protects the people who stay with her.'

'I've helped Mags out a few times, and equally, she's helped me – she's an amazing woman. Remind me one day to tell you how we first met.' Gabe grinned, perhaps remembering, then continued. 'Come on then, let's head off.'

Brannigan's Shelter

Gabe parked his truck down the road from the shelter. Parking directly outside might draw unwanted attention to the place. From the outside, it looked like all the other houses on the block – he knew differently, though. He'd had cause to attend the shelter a few times. Mags knew her stuff and was good at referring her rescues to him when they needed his kind of help. He'd had more than a few cases off her now, and they'd built a relationship of trust and friendship. Mags was easy to like – the things she cared most about were the people under her roof.

He walked alongside Paige to the heavy metal gates that led onto the driveway. Paige paused at the key code entry pad, clearly torn between entering the code with him present and telling him to turn away.

'I already know the code. Mags sends me it when she renews it every week. You don't need to worry.'

'Sorry, I know that was stupid. There's no reason you wouldn't know the code.' Paige blushed, obviously embarrassed at her confusion.

'It's fine, don't worry.' Gabe let his fingers touch her arm, something that he instantly knew he shouldn't have done. A bolt of electricity shot between them, and her skin warmed under his touch. Her eyes met his, and he was pulled deep into the blue depths. He dipped his head toward hers – she didn't move. The soft whisper of her breath ghosted his lips.

A door opening and closing behind the gates outside the car wrenched him back from the imminent kiss, and he moved his head back sharply. 'Sorry. I shouldn't have … erm … let's go inside.'

He pushed the gate, motioning Paige to go through ahead of him, and followed, closing the gate behind them with a click. *Just a few more seconds and you'd have kissed her. You're an idiot, Bland. That was a total dick move.*

He forced the errant thoughts out of his mind and dragged his attention back to the shelter. *Key code entry is good on the gates. CCTV camera in the top corner of the house – is it active or a decoy, though?*

Mags was waiting at the front door, and when he was close enough, she pulled him into a massive hug.

'Good to see you, Gabe. Thanks for bringing Paige home and keeping her safe.'

'Anytime. You know that, Mags. Is the camera at the top real?'

'Straight down to business as always. The camera is real, yes – it doesn't have night vision, though. I leave it on a twenty-four-hour loop and stop the loop in the event something happens. There's another one overlooking the back door of the house. The house alarm is activated when I go to bed. All external doors and downstairs windows have sensors.'

Gabe nodded his approval. 'Key code entry to the house now too?' He'd noticed the keypad beside the door when he'd entered.

'Yes. There was an incident a few months ago – a man managed to hop the gates and force his way inside to get at Abigail, one of the girls who used to live here. I installed the key code at the doors then and updated the alarm system.'

'Was she okay?' Gabe's voice sounded a little harsh – but he knew Mags would get that it wasn't aimed at her.

'A little bruised and battered, but I managed to tangle with him and restrain until Kyle arrived with his flashing blues and twos. She moved out a couple of weeks before Paige here arrived – Abigail's settled into an apartment a couple of towns over now.'

Mags motioned him and Paige through to the kitchen. A boy looked up from the table as Gabe entered.

'Paige!' he exclaimed, jumping up and grabbing Paige into a hug. 'I missed you. Will you read to me, please?'

Paige wrapped her arms around the boy's thin body. 'Hi, Jason. How're you doing? I will read to you and the other kids, but it'll have to be a bit later, okay? Right now, I need to speak to Mags and Gabe.'

Jason's eyes filled with tears, and Gabe's heart cracked a little. The boy obviously had issues – his gait was jerky as he'd thrown himself at Paige, and the easy tears falling down his cheeks were further evidence. Jason glanced around Paige's waist at Gabe and paled. Gabe hated to see the fear in the kid's expression.

Moving slowly, he sat at the table, instinctively lowering his height so he was more at eye level with the boy. 'Hi, Jason. I'm Gabe – what's the best story Paige reads to you?'

The boy peeled himself away from Paige and took a tentative step toward Gabe.

'*The Shmoogly Boo*,' he said shyly, his manner more like a toddler than a kid of his size.

'I've not read that one. Maybe I could read it to you?'

Jason's eyes lit up, and he raced out of the kitchen.

'That was really nice, Gabe. Jason has cystic fibrosis. You can probably tell from his speech that mentally he's younger than he appears. His mom is upstairs sorting one of the rooms out. Read to him first, then I'll get him a snack, and he can go and watch cartoons,' Mags said, putting the kettle on.

The reading only took a few minutes, but Gabe really had fun. The joy on Jason's face as the Shmoogly Boo shouted 'Boo!' was priceless. Mags had cut some cake while he read, and Jason had left seconds after Gabe had finished the book, leaving the adults in the kitchen ready to discuss security.

Joey Mendino had positioned his car just around a junction that allowed him to look at the gates to the large house he'd seen the woman he thought was Beth, and the mountain who'd thumped him in the alley behind the diner. His anger simmered beneath the surface – he didn't forgive or forget. He had every intention of getting his own back on the man who'd connected that forceful punch to his face. Even now – a day later – his jaw still smarted from the first impact, and a sizable purple bruise had spread across his nose and underneath both eyes from the second.

You will not get away with it. Asshole.

The beginnings of a plan unfolded in his mind. The first thing he needed to do was stick a tracker on the man's truck – once that was done, he'd be able to locate him no matter where his truck ended up.

The day would come very soon when the large man would get what was coming to him. Mendino grabbed a tracking device, no bigger than a quarter, from the box in his trunk. Sauntering as though just out for a walk, he feigned tripping over next to the black pickup truck and applied the device to the top of the wheel arch at the rear. Then he made his way back to his car and drove a small distance away. *No need to raise additional suspicion after all.*

Chapter Ten

Brannigan's Shelter

Gabe had left an hour ago, but Paige could tell he hadn't wanted to. The shelter was secure, and he'd had no real reason to stay. But she'd wanted him to as much as she suspected he did. He'd pressed a cell phone into her hand as he'd left with strict instructions to use it if she needed him. He'd even had the forethought to store his number on speed dial and install the emergency icon on the front screen.

Paige had helped Mags lock up the shelter and said goodnight to her friend. The house was silent apart from the heavy rain pounding against the windows. As tired as she was, though, she wasn't ready for sleep. Instead, she snuggled under a blanket on the sofa and had the TV on low, watching a documentary about snakes.

All of the happenings over the last few days were playing over and over in her mind. It was hard not to blame herself for everything that was going on. Maybe if she'd just stayed with Al and been the kind of woman he needed, then none of it would have happened at all. *If I had been, though, he'd have ended up killing me ...* But she wouldn't have stolen his black book, she wouldn't have got Dave shot, and she wouldn't have lost – *No, stop right there. Lock those thoughts back down right now.* Paige shivered under the blanket and hugged it in tighter around her.

It wouldn't do to let all those feelings out. She'd end up a gibbering wreck. It took all of her strength not to let them out. With everything that had happened of late, all she wanted to do was shout and scream and possibly cry. But she knew once those walls tumbled down, she'd be no use to anyone. Paige had been at that point before – once. And it was almost her undoing. Her mistakes had allowed Al to find her. Getting away from him the first time had been hard, the last time had been nigh on impossible. *No way can I put myself in that position again. I need to trust that Gabe knows what he's doing.*

She flushed and instantly berated herself. It was neither the time nor the place for some silly infatuation. Now her mind focused on Gabe, that was even harder to shut down.

Pulling the cell phone from her pocket, she debated sending Gabe a text. He had said to contact him if she needed anything. The phone buzzed, and the screen lit up in her hand.

Hi, Paige. Just checking in and making sure all is well before I hit the hay. Gabe.

Her flush deepened, heating her cheeks. *He probably doesn't mean anything by it, though. He's just being nice.*

Typing quickly, she shot a text back: *All locked down. Everyone's in bed except me. I'm on the couch watching TV. Thank you for your help today. Paige.*

She'd ummed and ahhed for a while over whether to put her signature 'x' at the end of the text, then opted against it in the end. Their relationship was professional. She needed a service, and he was providing it. End of. *Liar, liar, pants on fire.*

Still wide awake, Paige decided to make herself some hot cocoa. She stood, putting the phone in the pocket of her dressing gown, and turned toward the door. A loud crash suddenly sounded from the front living room window – glass shattered all over the floor, and the chill from the night air swept into the room.

Paige froze for half a second then ran from the room, grabbed the phone out, and hit Gabe's number on the speed dial just as the house alarm screeched.

'Someone's just put the window out in the living room – there's glass everywhere.'

'Wake Mags. I'm on my way.'

He ended the call so abruptly Paige didn't even register he was gone at first.

'Paige? What happened?' Mags sped down the stairs in her flannel pajamas and bare feet.

'Don't go in the lounge, the front window's been put through. There's glass everywhere.'

'Did you see anything?'

'No, the curtains were closed. I didn't want to stay in there in case …'

'You did the right thing,' said Mags, dragging on her boots from the rack at the front door. 'Go upstairs and settle everyone down. I'm going out to have a look and see who's out there.'

'No.'

'What do you mean no? Listen to me, child, this is my shelter. No one breaks a window here and expects to get away with it. I haven't got time to argue. Go upstairs and settle everyone down.'

'No. You're not going out there alone, Mags. I'm coming with you.' Paige set her expression so Mags knew she meant it.

Mags sighed in exasperation. 'Sarah, get the kids and the other women into one room upstairs, please. And call the police.'

Sarah was at the top of the stairs and nodded, taking Wendy's hand and pulling her back along the corridor.

'Stay behind me, Paige.' Mags took hold of the heavy wooden walking stick from by the door.

Paige registered that she'd never even noticed it hiding in the corner.

It was dark outside – the external light wasn't on for some reason, and the driveway wasn't illuminated. The only streetlight outside of the gates was and lit up the entrance with a dull glow. It seemed like the gates were still secure.

The only noise was the breeze rustling in the trees and the rain hitting the paved driveway. At least that's what Paige thought until a rustle sounded in the far corner of the grounds. Typically, it was the darkest corner, she couldn't see a thing over there. Mags had heard it too and had paused, staring at the corner with the walking stick raised in the air.

'Whoever's over there, come out now. The police have been called and are on their way.'

Nothing moved.

Until the sound of a footfall on the wet driveway. Spinning around, Mags went to swing the stick, but a man in black clothing snatched it and swung so hard that Mags dropped to her knees, releasing her grip.

He turned to Paige. His face was covered in a balaclava, and the only thing visible was his eyes. In the dull light they looked black, like the demon eyes from Paige's favorite show, *Supernatural*, and for a second, she froze, struggling with reality and what the program had taught her. *Don't be stupid – that's a man. There's no such thing as ghosts and demons. Get Mags and RUN!*

Listening to the voice in her head, she took a step to the side, trying to see Mags and whether she'd got up. She needn't have worried, though – Mags was on her feet and only a meter or so away from the man.

Knowing she needed to distract him, Paige spoke. 'Al sent you to get me, did he? Bet he didn't tell you I'm more than you bargained for.'

The tentative steps she'd taken backward resulted in her foot hitting a garden pot – the pot she knew was right next to the steps leading up to the front door. She couldn't go any farther. Mags was still waiting for an opportunity.

The man never spoke. He stepped forward again, now only a meter from Paige. Lifting the wooden stick, he swung backward to get momentum – his intent was obvious. He wanted to clock Paige with the stick.

He didn't see Mags behind him – and she grasped the stick and pulled, the force enough to bring his arm farther back than it should go. He yelled in pain, his grip loosening, but he didn't let go. Instead, he moved with the stick when he realized what was happening, turning with it so he was facing Mags.

She directed a well-aimed kick to his groin area which connected with a thump. He groaned loudly and stumbled. Mags stepped to the side, and Paige took the opportunity to kick the man's backside – he was already bent over slightly, and the strike sent him to his knees. Mags stepped closer and brought her knee up under the man's chin with force.

His head snapped back, and he sprawled, finally releasing his grip on the walking stick. Mags kicked it out of the way, but he anticipated that reaction. He leaped to his feet and ran past her, pegging it to the eight-foot wall surrounding the property – it had been heightened after the incident with Abigail's ex.

With one jump, the man took hold of the top and hoisted himself over.

Mags ran to the gates, pressing the interior open button on the wall. The gates clanked and shuddered then slid apart.

Stepping out into the street, Mags quickly scanned up and down both ways.

There was nothing to be seen. The man had vanished.

She secured the gates and strode back to Paige's side, cursing under her breath. 'Son of a bitch got away. I should have kicked him harder. Who the hell does he think he is?'

Paige wrapped her arms around herself – she was shaking hard. When her teeth chattered, Mags gently took her arm and led her back up the steps to the front door. Blue lights flashed on the door in front of them, and Mags hit the remote kept inside the hall and opened the gates, allowing the police cars to enter.

Gabe had the pedal to the floor – his speedometer said he was doing 90 kmph, and for a minute he wished he'd gone for speed over practicality with his truck. *I should never have left her at the shelter. I should've brought her to mine.*

He punched his fist off the steering wheel in frustration and tried to floor the pedal even more.

She'd better have called the police. What if there was more than one person? What if they've taken her? That's all on me. I should have insisted she come with me for her own safety.

He drove through the town at a far higher speed than the local limits dictated and eventually arrived outside the shelter.

Gabe swore loudly when he realized the gates were open, but as he entered the drive and saw the police cars present, he allowed himself to exhale. He needed to calm down – going in all cock-a-hoop would just cause problems. He took a deep breath, held it for a count of seven, then exhaled for ten. Repeating the process a couple of times, he felt his blood pressure drop and his heart rate slow. *I don't even know why I'm reacting like this. Paige is a case. Pure and simple.*

Liar, his mind argued back. Just the one word. Nothing else was needed.

He hopped out of the truck and headed into the house.

'So, tell me what exactly happened.' Kyle's voice was strong but sounded tired – the call had dragged him from his bed.

Gabe pushed the ajar door open and strode inside, his eyes finding Paige immediately. She leaped up from her seat, crossed the room in seconds, and flung herself into his arms.

He tried to deny how good it felt but failed miserably. Everyone in the room could likely see the attraction between them. Gently, he pulled himself from her arms – it was absolutely the last thing he wanted to do, but they had an audience, and he needed to know what had happened.

'Paige, darlin', it's okay. You're safe. Let's sit down and talk to Kyle.'

He kept hold of her hand and sat next to her on the couch.

Mags started talking. She was to the point with her explanation.

Gabe knew that was a mix of shock, and the fact Mags had seen it all. It took a lot to faze her, and she knew how reporting things worked.

'… and then the little coward hopped the wall and ran off. I tried to follow through the gate, but he'd vanished. I didn't hear a vehicle drive off so I'm guessing he'd parked a bit away.'

'Were you or Paige hurt?' asked Gabe, his voice soft, but even he could hear the undertone. *If he hurt either of them …*

'No. I scuffed my knees when he swung me to the ground. The only pain I have now, though, is the knowledge I should've kicked his balls all the way back inside. If I'd kicked harder, he wouldn't have got up.'

Gabe shuffled in his seat – he'd been kicked there enough to know that hurt like a bitch.

'What do you think his intention was? Scare tactics or something else? Do we even know who he was here about?'

Paige spoke up. 'He smashed the window first – he couldn't have known who was in the lounge. I went out with Mags. He seemed to zero in on me instantly, so I'd say he was after me, wouldn't you, Mags?'

'Yes. He was after Paige. He didn't seem bothered by me at all. He didn't speak, so I can't even attest to accent. All I can tell you is he was about five feet ten inches, average build but strong, and he was white. His balaclava covered his face almost completely.'

'He had a scar too, a small one. Near his right eye. It shined differently in the light to the rest of his skin.'

Gabe paused. He was all for helping law enforcement, but this had rapidly become personal. He remembered that scar – the lowlife who'd come to the shelter looking for Paige was The Fox. *We'll see how wily you are now. You'd best watch your back, Mendino. I'm coming for you.*

'You recognize that description, Gabe?' Kyle's voice cut through his thoughts.

Knowing he had to answer and that he wouldn't lie, he replied, 'Yes, it's Joey Mendino, aka The Fox. He's the one who tried to kidnap Paige from the hospital.'

'Okay, I'll need whatever details you have sending over for an APB. Mags, I'm positioning a cop outside the shelter. There's a chance he might wait for us to leave and try again. I'll board the window before I go and arrange for my brother, William, to come and fix it tomorrow. Gabe, I presume you're taking Paige with you? Or are you staying here?'

Gabe half wanted to stay, but Mags wouldn't allow it – the women in her care would already be petrified, and the last thing they needed was a man of his size in the house disrupting them even more. 'I'll take Paige to my place. Don't worry about paying your cops overtime to house-sit Kyle – I can sort a couple of my guys to watch over the shelter. It's all linked to the case anyhow, no need for you to be eating into your budget.'

Kyle flashed him a brief smile. 'Thanks, I appreciate that. Budget cuts are a bitch. You will keep me updated, though, that's the requirement. I want to know what's happening every stage of the investigation. And when you collar Mendino, the arrest is mine.'

Gabe nodded.

'If you're done questioning, Kyle, I'll help you board the window. Mags, you still have some wood out back in the shed, I'm guessing?' Gabe said, knowing Mags never got rid of anything that could be useful.

'Yes, the same piece you used last time is still there. Thanks for getting Will to repair it tomorrow, Kyle, that's much appreciated. You brother is sweet, and Lord knows we can all use the work. See how I'm trying to spin a positive on this bitch of a night? I'm going to make a batch of hot chocolate for the women and children. They'll all be petrified upstairs, and I doubt very much any of us will get any more sleep tonight. I'll make enough for you all too. And some toast.'

Gabe and Kyle stood to leave the room and work on the window.

Joey Mendino loitered in the shadows a block away from the shelter, observing. His initial instinct had been to run like hell after hopping the wall, but then he figured it would be more useful to observe and see what kind of response came from the encounter. *A lot.* His thoughts were filled with dark and ruthless intentions. He rubbed a hand over his sore balls for the hundredth time. *Those bitches are going to get what's coming to them real soon. No one kicks me in the balls and gets away with it.*

He froze when the headlights on the police car parked in the drive turned on and the car pulled out, followed by the mountain man's big black truck. The streetlights glinted off the windscreen, highlighting a tired and worried-looking Paige Matthews – or Beth Robson as she was better known to him. He was certain now she was Beth – seeing her up close outside the shelter had confirmed it to him.

He smiled in the gloom. He'd let Al know where his precious Beth was soon – first, he intended to have some fun with both her and the beast of a man she was now leaving with.

Melding back into the shadows then out onto the night-black street, Mendino made his way back to the car. He had a long drive and an important meeting tomorrow – more money was due to be paid. And Al always wanted him in the office to hand over the cash.

Gabe's cabin

Paige had been silent all the way from the shelter to the cabin. Gabe was worried about her. If she didn't tell him, he couldn't have any idea what could be going on in her mind.

'You okay?' he asked and put the truck in park on his drive.

'Not really,' said Paige, her voice quiet, contemplative.

'You're safe here. Everything's going to be okay. Once we get inside, I'll update the team, assign a couple of them to start searching for Mendino. You're our number one case, Paige, it will be okay. We'll get Mendino before he can do anything else, and we will go after your ex.'

Paige didn't answer. A single tear dropped from her cheek onto her lap, and Gabe gently pulled her round to face him. 'Paige, listen to me. None of this is your fault. You're the victim here, we will take care of it. I give you my word.'

'I hate that word *victim*,' said Paige softly. 'And you can't promise no one else will get hurt, Gabe. All of this hurt, it's on me. What if he goes back to the shelter? What if he hurts someone else searching for me? I should go back and face the music. My life isn't important, not like yours and Mags' lives. You both help people. What do I do? I go around not eating, passing out, and getting people who want to help me hurt.' Another tear streaked down her cheek.

She believes that tripe she's spewing.

Not tripe when you believe the same for yourself, is it?

Shotgun was my fault – it was my op. I was in charge.

Doesn't mean it's your fault. It was an accident. Beat yourself up all you like, but Paige feels the same as you do. You can't begin to help her deal when you haven't dealt yourself.

'You're right, I can't promise that no one else will get hurt. But I can promise that I will do my damnedest to make sure that doesn't happen. You can't deal with this alone, you need help. And that's something I can do – it's my job. Let me protect you, Paige.'

She didn't reply; she nodded once, which Gabe had to take as a yes. He hopped out of the truck and opened the passenger door, taking hold of Paige's arm to help her out, and led her into the cabin.

'Come on, darlin', let's get you settled inside.'

Chapter Eleven

Graham Industries, the docks, Carlstown, near Astoria

Al Graham was seated behind the intricately carved desk in the office of one of the warehouses he owned. His broad shoulders filled the back of the expensive office chair, and his gray pinstripe suit gave him an air of professionalism. The Rolex glinted on his wrist – his wealth obvious and in the face of anyone who entered the room.

The desk was one of the few things he truly treasured. It had cost him far more than he'd wanted to spend on such a frivolous thing, but he had to have it. It had been there since the day he'd started the company ten years before. He ran his hand over the woodwork thoughtfully.

A glimmer of satisfaction fluttered over him. He loved his job. It was powerful; he got hard just thinking about all that it gave him, ordering the people who ran around after him about was just one of those things. He was a passionate man, in all fields. Nothing was too much for him.

He signed his name on the bottom of some paperwork in front of him with a flourish, the shiny, gold Montblanc pen another testament to his wealth. Narrowing his eyes, he stared at the man seated in front of him.

'You do what you need to do. Find me that bitch of an ex. I want her alive. Follow the leads you said you had the other day and report back to me every twenty-four hours.'

The cash to pay Mendino was gripped between two fingers, and Al raised his hand. He paused midair, staring at the hand that snaked over to grab it.

'Do not disappoint me. I'm paying well over the odds for your services. I will not be made to look a fool.' Al stared at the man intently.

Mendino was reportedly the best in the business. Al had his doubts, however. The Fox had been on the case for a good couple of months now and seemed no further forward in tracing Beth. Al wasn't even sure the alleged leads were true. He was giving Mendino more cash to sweeten the pot, but he knew in his heart that if there weren't results within a couple of days, he'd be doing a little foxhunting himself before going after that bitch of an ex on his own.

Al's anger rose whenever he thought about her. *When I finally get my hands back on her …*

Inhaling a deep breath, he continued. 'You do know I've paid other investigators. All have come up empty. If you do the same, I'll make sure you're never employed again as anything other than a toilet attendant. Understand?'

Joey's eyes narrowed as he stared at Al. He was obviously a man who didn't take kindly to threats. *Well, tough shit. Deal with it, asshole.*

'Yes, *boss*.' Joey's response was sarcastic. He took the cash and left Al's office, passing a blonde entering the room.

'Hi, sweetie, could I have the credit card, please? I need to go and get something from the store.' Her voice was guarded.

Al knew she was lying. He stood, walked around the table, and not-so-gently pushed her down into the seat Joey had vacated.

'Kim, what have I told you about lying? I don't like it. I won't put up with it. So, tell me what you really want the card for, and I'll see if I can accommodate it.'

Tears filled her eyes – she cried far too easily. If she hadn't been pregnant, Al would have got rid of her months ago. He hated weepy women. Weepy was pretty much the only thing Beth hadn't been. They were weak. And Kim was definitely one of the weakest. The only thing that had attracted him to her when they met had been her massive rack. She had the personality of a plank and zero intelligence. He'd given her the chance to walk away even before he'd known about the baby. Now he couldn't let her go. She was pregnant with his son. The one who would carry on his empire.

'I wanted to get some more baby things,' she spurted out, then sobbed, already anticipating what was coming next.

'You've got enough. I ordered the crib, the pram, and all the clothes. It's still four months until my boy arrives. You don't need anything else.'

'It's my first baby, Al, I just wanted to choose some things myself. It's okay, though. You're right. It's a waste of money.'

Al raised his hand, and Kim flinched, awaiting the blow. He smiled in satisfaction, then pushed his fingers through his hair as though that was all he was going to do. When she relaxed, though, he brought his palm down and slapped her face hard. It was the only place he would touch – he didn't care if she sported bruises. No one came to visit her anyway. But he'd never endangered his boy. Not once.

'Now piss off and let me work. If you want a ride, George will take you home.'

He motioned toward the heavyset man in the doorway. George was shorter than Al, but his neck melded into his shoulders in a pure mass of muscle. He'd been there for Al through everything. He took care of the business Al didn't want to do, not that there was much he wouldn't do personally, but it paid to have a right-hand man. And he paid George very well for his loyalty.

George guided Kim out of the room with a hand to the small of her back, and Al sat back down in his leather chair. He stroked the dusting of light-brown stubble on his chin – he liked it. It matched his well-groomed hair. He knew he'd look good with a beard too. *Hell, I look good with anything.*

His thoughts turned to Kim and the baby. Her pregnancy had been an accident – one that was her fault entirely. It was assumed these days that the woman took care of not getting pregnant. Besides, he hated condoms. Why should he cover himself? It was the woman's job. He was glad he'd have an heir, though – the boy he'd so desperately wanted with his ex. She'd failed on the not-getting-pregnant front too.

His face darkened as he thought of Beth. That sickening auburn hair – he'd always hated it. Detested the fact it turned heads even when he was standing next to her. She'd stood fast when he'd asked her to go blonde, said it wouldn't suit her skin color. It was the one thing he'd never managed to get her to acquiesce to. *Where is she? She's not bright enough to hide forever.* She was the one who got away. His kryptonite. If she spoke … *The Fox better do his bloody job. I want her back. So I can kill her myself.*

He should have done it all those years ago, but he'd faltered, wanting to believe that the mother of his child would do as he said. His composure slipped at the thought of his daughter, and for a moment a wave of vulnerability washed over him. He recovered in an instant and turned to the computer and hit the keys relentlessly.

Gabe's cabin

Gabe had spent a restless night. He'd updated the team on what was happening and had assigned Becca and Grayson to search for Mendino. Then he'd rung Dave, knowing he'd wake him but also knowing Dave would kick his ass if he wasn't kept in the loop. The hospital were going to release him today, and Gabe wanted to be at the hospital for him but didn't know if he could be, not with Paige to take care of.

She'd slept in the loosest sense of the term, snuggled up on the sofa underneath his throw. Every hour or so she'd stirred, crying out in her sleep, and her arms had flailed around. Each time Gabe had knelt in front of her, putting her arms back down and talking in low tones to soothe her back to sleep. He doubted she would even remember him being there, but just his presence had stilled her thrashing and settled her back into peace. Until the next time, however.

Even now he glanced over at her – her dark curls were spread around her head like a halo. Every now and then she gave a small snore. He was loathe to wake her, but they needed to get moving. He needed to know everything there was to know about Al Graham and Joey Mendino if he had any hope of protecting her. And that information was mostly at the office, being looked into by the team. Gabe had scheduled a briefing for 9.30 a.m., later than he normally scheduled them for, but he hadn't wanted to wake Paige too early after the incident the night before. It was pushing 8.30 a.m. now, and if the women he knew were anything to go by, Paige would need at least half an hour to get ready. *She's not like the other women you've known.*

She moaned a little, then her eyes sprang open, and she shot into a sitting position, looking confused.

'Easy, Paige. You're at my place remember, we came here after the incident last night at the shelter.'

Paige nodded and yawned widely. 'Please tell me you have coffee.'

'Already brewed in the pot in the kitchen. You want milk and sugar?'

'Just black and hot, please.' She stretched then got to her feet. A flush stained her cheeks. 'I need the bathroom. I'll join you in a few.'

'There's clean towels on the rack if you want a shower.'

'If you don't mind, that would be great. Presume we'll need to get going soon? How's Dave? He's still in hospital, right?'

'Yeah, but hopefully he'll be released today. Have your shower – take your time. We have a briefing to attend, but it's not for a bit yet.'

Paige walked toward him then surprised him utterly by leaning forward and kissing his cheek.

'In case I forgot to say it, thank you. Everything would be a lot worse without you in my corner.'

And then she was gone. Gabe's hand strayed to his cheek, touching the area her lips had brushed just seconds before. *You've got it bad.*

He sighed once before standing and heading to the kitchen to get the coffee poured.

Bland P.I.R office

Paige followed Gabe into the office, trying not to let anxiety get the better of her. Two of his team were at computers in the main office and barely even glanced up when she and Gabe entered. The others were seated in the room at the back. They all looked up as Gabe opened the door, glanced at her, and then all moved off and sat down.

'A round table? Like the knights of old?' Paige's voice came out more of a squeak than her actual voice, but at least she'd managed to get the words out.

Gabe smiled and put his hand to her back, guiding her into the chair beside his. He poured coffee and put a steaming mug in front of her. Needing something to stop her fiddling, she gripped it tightly, enjoying the warmth spreading through her hands from the heat.

'Okay, down to business. Grayson, what have you found out about Mendino?'

'He's got a record a mile long, but you already knew that. Confirmed the most recent reports that he's into a bit of torture. None of his victims have survived but were recovered with multiple wounds – things like water in the lungs, lacerations, fingernails pulled out, et cetera. Obviously, there's no forensic evidence on the bodies otherwise the cops would have caught up with him by now. All this is rumor based on previous jobs he's been assigned to. I'm linking them to him via modus operandi only – and the fact all victims had issues with a more exclusive clientele. Basically, people who paid well for the privilege of ensuring the thorn in their side was erased. He's all over the Dark Web as being reliable and someone who gets the job done. Contact is made via that function too – payment in bitcoin, or cash on attendance. I have managed to source a potential address for him, but I'm not sure until I visit it today whether it's viable or not. He switches cars out regularly. The one Mitch got the intel for was found burned out in a field a few towns over yesterday evening, according to police reports. No leads, but I'm guessing he wouldn't torch it if he didn't already have another ride. He uses burner phones only – can't find any contracts in his name and no local amenities. Only reason I got a lead on the property was an old photo I managed to source from a few years ago – I triangulated the location using the background plants and trees. That new software you invested in, Gabe, it's the bomb.'

'Glad to know it's being used effectively. Since you like it so much, you can train the team members who haven't had the training yet if you like?'

Grayson nodded, and Gabe continued.

'Thanks, Grayson, good work. Becca? How about Al Graham? Any skeletons in his closet?'

'I've sent you a full file – he's got his fingers in a lot of pies. Some kosher, some not so kosher. He's been mentioned in the cases of a couple of disappearances as a suspect, but nothing's ever come of it. He's prime suspect in the disappearance of his ex, Beth Robson. He maintained throughout all interviews that Beth was unhinged and has run off with another man. But there were several hospital admissions in recent years – all eventually put down to her being clumsy and accident-prone, but not until after the police had spoken to both parties numerous times. Don't know why anyone would stay with someone beating them up like that. I mean, she had virtually every injury known to be related to domestic violence.'

Paige felt the blood drain from her face at Becca's words. Without speaking, she got to her feet and ran from the room. She barely heard Gabe curse behind her and kept running until she was across the road in the park. Panic overwhelmed her. Black dots spread across her vision, and she struggled to draw breath.

'Paige, easy, darlin'. It's okay. Just try and breathe. I'm here, I'm not going anywhere. You are safe.' Gabe's voice interrupted her panicked state slowly.

Her vision was still swimming, and she couldn't focus but she drew in a shaky breath.

He led her to a park bench and pushed her gently until she was sitting.

'Sorry, Becca's investigation hits close to home. I should've thought of how you would react to what she was saying and taken you out of the room.'

Paige's head shook. All the memories she tried so hard to keep back were threatening to burst through her walls and into the forefront. She drew in another trembling breath, focusing her attention on a large stone on the path in front of her.

'It's not ... I can't ...'

'Shh, just breathe, Paige. Get your head back from wherever you go when you don't want to remember. Focus on what's here now – me, the park. The birds singing. Keep breathing – nice and deep. Nothing can hurt you here.'

She registered Gabe's thumb drawing circles on the back of her hand; the contact was soothing. The spots in front of her eyes ebbed back. Breathing became less of a struggle.

Shifting in her seat, she brought her gaze up to Gabe's. His concern emanated off him in waves. She leaned her head farther toward him. Desire sparked instantly in his eyes, drawing her closer still. Her lips were almost touching his when the reason she was sitting in the park next to this man burst back into her mind. Paige backed away, angling her body away from him.

'Sorry, I shouldn't have …' She took a deep breath, knowing she needed to tell him. Turning back to face him, she said, 'Beth Robson was the name I had when I was with Al – I'm the ex that Becca was talking about. I'm sorry I lied to you.'

'I suspected your name was false. After our run-in at the cemetery, I tried to trace you. There's a lot of Paige Matthews in the USA, did you know that? I had an inkling you might be Beth but I didn't want to put you on the spot, figured you'd tell me when you were ready. Do you think you can go back inside now? Your input will be helpful building the case against Al.'

Paige nodded slowly. 'I think so.'

Gabe kept hold of her hand as he stood.

'So shall I call you Beth or …'

'No. I left her behind. I never want to be Beth again. I have everything I need as Paige. Social Security number, ID et cetera. It's all verifiable.' Paige sighed, knowing she'd just admitted to fraud. 'I'll get in trouble, won't I? It's fraud, pretending to be someone you're not. Damn it.'

'Is the real Paige Matthews still alive and kicking?'

'No, she died a few years ago. I got her details off a gravestone. She was the same age as me – same date of birth. I did some more digging and found she'd died in a car crash down in Arkansas. I figured it was far enough away that no one would link me as being the same person. I got some info online and went to someone Al hated for the ID. Someone who'd never tell Al in a million years. I'd known him since school. I'd rather not give his name. He does a lot for women who've been abused and need a sharp exit.'

'Okay. Let me speak to someone I know, make sure everything you have is top level. I don't condone it but I get that on occasion, people need to make a new life for themselves. You were running from Al – he's got enough money to find you under your given name anywhere you turn up. You did what you had to do to survive. We'll see what else there is we can help with in legalizing the identity for you once this is all resolved. I want Al behind bars for what he's done. Not just to you, but to an awful lot of people if Becca's research is anything to go by.'

'Wait.' Paige pulled his hand back, stopping him where the path through the park met the sidewalk. 'Why are you doing this? I get that you're honorable and that this is kinda what you do, but to this extent? When your staff are getting shot for me and your team are turning dirt up against someone like Al? Surely you pick and choose your jobs based on the ones you think you'll win? That's just good business sense.'

'I don't work like that. Winning doesn't mean anything. We take the cases that need our help. That's it. The fact that we tend to win is down to my team, how they work together, and the tools they have at their disposal. I've never met a problem that isn't solvable yet. You know the old adage, people do things for one of three reasons: sex, money, or revenge. That's totally true. You have to work out what motivates the main players and then you can work a resolve.'

'I never thought of it like that. So based on that thinking, Al's issue with me is revenge based. What he does to others will be to do with one of those three too. That actually makes sense.'

'Is there anything else I should know before we go back inside and speak to my team?'

Paige paused – she should tell him everything, but she wasn't ready. What was left was the stuff she kept buried deep inside. She didn't need the pity he'd display for a start. Gabe would probably find out himself anyway. She didn't need to open that box – not yet. *Not ever if I have my way.*

'No. We can go back inside.'

Joey Mendino watched Beth and the mountain man talk in the park. The drive back from Al's office hadn't taken long at all, and he'd figured there was a reason she'd been at the park the day before. The security firm had piqued his interest – he knew what she was running from. It made sense she'd seek help. He kept his face hidden behind a newspaper and was sitting on a bench a good way from them – too far to overhear what they were talking about. *Wonder what lover boy was whispering in her ear – the body language between the two of them screams relationship, albeit not a long-standing one. Wonder how the lovely Beth will fare when he's no longer in the picture …*

Chapter Twelve

Perkinsville General Hospital

Gabe parked his truck in the pickup zone outside the front entrance of the hospital. The doctor had called him to say Dave was ready to go home. He knew from speaking to Paul that he was stuck at home seeing a client. Paul had said Dave knew about the client and would be happy to wait at the hospital until he could make it, but Gabe offered to take Dave home instead.

Dave hated hospitals – they both did. A by-product of being a SEAL had been occasional hospital stays or at the very least visits to fallen colleagues. It was a tough job; injuries were easy to come by. Some days he missed the action – being dropped in a hot zone and expected to pull off an impossible mission made a person run on adrenaline alone for extended periods. The team camaraderie had always been his favorite thing about being a SEAL – knowing that no matter what happened, his teammates would always have his back. Until one day they hadn't. Gabe tempered those thoughts back down – he never let them surface. It hurt his chest to think those thoughts. Almost as if the memories themselves inserted a sharp knife into his heart and twisted. *Besides,* he reasoned with himself, *it wasn't the whole team. It was one man. Just one.*

Whatever had happened back then, it had inadvertently helped him become the man he was today. He was a huge believer in karma and he'd never have believed for one second when he was a SEAL that he'd have left and set up his own private security business. Those days were the reason his checks were so rigorous on his team members. He never wanted anyone on his team who would betray them. His team needed to know they were safe in whatever situation they ended up in. *Not Shotgun, though – he wasn't safe, was he? You got him killed.*

Sighing, Gabe pushed the door open and stepped inside. The instant antiseptic smell of *hospital* hung in the air like a wet rag. He took one calming breath, then strode toward the elevators situated at the end of the long corridor.

Bland P.I.R office

Paige felt like the walls were closing in on her – she'd paced the back office about twenty times on a loop. The rest of Gabe's team popped in and out briefly, but none had engaged her in conversation, and while she understood Gabe needed to pick Dave up from the hospital, she didn't like being away from him.

Her gut was twisting, and she had an awful feeling of dread. If she didn't get some fresh air, she was going to end up having a total meltdown. Pulling open the door, she made her way through the large kitchen and seating area to the left of the corridor – she'd walked past the main reception, and no one had moved from their computers, all absorbed in whatever it was they were doing. The kitchen was well kitted out – a person could live in these offices with no issues at all. She was relieved to see a rear door that opened out into a large yard that doubled as a car park for the staff.

Stepping outside, she inhaled a deep breath, trying to calm herself. It was quiet out the back of Main Street. Birds chirped, but they sounded far away, and the traffic from the road outside was a quiet hum. It was peaceful, which was exactly what she was looking for.

Paige took a few more steps out, wondering where the entrance to the drive was. A couple more paces, and she realized it was L-shaped, the entrance and exit running down the left-hand side to the building.

Despite her drawing in deep breaths, the feeling of foreboding grew in intensity. She shivered, fear clawing at her insides for no reason she could see. Deciding she'd had enough fresh air, she turned to head back to the kitchen door.

A strong arm snaked around her neck from behind, and the sharp prick of an object at her lower back jabbed into her.

Paige froze. *It's Al! He's found me!*

'Don't scream. Don't even utter one word or this knife will pierce your liver. Interesting fact about a bleed to a person's liver – it doesn't clot properly, so they slowly bleed out. Just one word, and we'll test that theory. Understand?'

Paige didn't respond – it was like her voice had disappeared. Her heart was throbbing so fast she thought for a moment it would beat out of her chest. *Why did you have to come outside? Why couldn't you just have stayed in the office?*

The Fox marched her to around the bend in the driveway and kept the point digging into her skin as he shifted position slightly so it appeared to anyone else like he was just holding her as couples do.

Do something! Don't just walk with him like the idiot you are.

She opened her mouth to scream, but his words resonated through her brain. She knew with certainty if she did yell out or scream that he would carry out his threat – she wasn't convinced that whatever he had to her back hadn't already pierced her skin.

They reached a gray panel van in record time. Keeping the blade at her back, he unlocked the van with the hand that had been on her arm. *If you're going to do something, now would be the time.* Deciding to chance it, Paige ran forward at speed – the blade moved from her back, and her feet kicked into motion. His shoes slapped against the sidewalk behind her, but she kept running, knowing if she stopped he would have her in seconds.

Paige didn't even dare to look back. When the shops and houses faded into hedgerows, she still kept running. A car door slammed somewhere nearby – it registered, but she still couldn't stop running. Her breath kept catching – she wasn't used to such extreme exercise. Her legs burned, her lungs even more so.

When a shadow appeared in front of her, she veered to the left, panic forcing her to run into the road. Brakes shrieked loudly, and suddenly she was flying through the air.

She closed her eyes – this was it. The moment she would die. There wasn't any of that life flashing before her stuff, nothing except air and then a hard impact with tarmac. Pain shot through her arm and up into her shoulder, and her head bounced off the road. Dizziness invaded – the whisper of voices carried on the wind, but at the same time, they sounded like they were a million miles away. *Surely it wouldn't hurt if I was dead – there's no pain when you die, is there?*

'Paige? Can you hear me?' Gabe's voice sounded like it was drifting on the wind.

She closed her eyes and let it take her.

Gabe had been driving toward the office with Dave in the passenger seat when Paige had come into view – running fast. It almost felt like every time he saw her she was running. He'd slammed the brakes on, much to the consternation of the driver in the car behind him, who honked and swerved around Gabe's truck. Jumping out, he ran across and stood in front of Paige, waiting for her to see him.

The terror on her face punched him in the gut, and he opened his mouth to speak. She registered something in front of her, however, and spun to the left, running straight into traffic. Gabe felt himself scream her name, turning and following her without thinking of his own safety.

Brakes screeched, and there was a sickening crunch as a white car hit Paige mid-stride. The force took her off her feet and threw her a few yards away. Luckily, the speed of the car had slowed drastically prior to hitting her. The female driver of the car was still inside, her mouth and eyes wide with shock.

Knowing Dave would already be out of his truck and following, Gabe ran to Paige's aid, scuffing his knees when he slid on the tarmac beside her.

'Paige? Can you hear me?' He avoided shaking her shoulders like he wanted to in order to get a response. There'd been a loud crack when her arm had hit the road – it had echoed in the street, and he knew she had a break. The left side of her forehead was grazed and bleeding slowly – more of a seep and nothing he needed to stop instantly. He was worried about the bump her head had taken, though. 'Someone call nine-one-one,' he shouted out, before gently feeling along her body for further injuries. Her left elbow was already visibly swollen, and he felt the area with his fingertips. Bone ground on bone, and he knew instantly it was broken. It happened all too often when a person's arm was straight-on impact with the ground – Newton's law of gravity applied, what goes up must come down. And Paige had definitely come down with a thump.

He couldn't see inside her jeans but he'd seen the car hit her on the right side – even if she had no further breaks, she'd be bruised and sore.

She groaned softly as Gabe probed down to her feet and ankles. Scooting back up her body so he was near her head, he ran his fingers lightly down her face.

'Take it easy, Paige, don't move too fast.'

She groaned again, her eyes fluttering. When they snapped open, they were filled with fear until she registered it was him sitting next to her. She was still scared, and her eyes darted past him to the small crowd of people now gathering. It appeared she didn't see anyone familiar, and her breath whooshed out from her lungs.

'Help me sit,' she said, her voice sounding strange and not like her own.

'Nope, you need to stay where you are, Paige. You hit your head – you might have concussion. Not to mention you've broken your elbow. Trust me, if you move now, you'll regret it – your body is in shock, lying still is masking the pain. Please, just lie still and wait for the EMTs.'

'It was The Fox,' Paige whispered, fear still sweeping across her face.

'How did he get to you? What happened?' Gabe's temper flared. Mendino had found her even despite his team being on the job? How the hell had she ended up outside? And where was the rest of the team? *Heads are going to roll! How did he get to her, though – I left strict instructions with the team that she was to remain inside. No wonder she was running if my team couldn't protect her!*

'Dammit,' he cursed softly. *I'll damn well find out where we fell down – again! This is getting to be a bad habit!* He needed to reassess the working protocols. This *couldn't* happen again.

'My fault … I'm sorry … I …' Paige's eyes flickered closed, and she lost consciousness again.

Sirens wailed in the distance, and Gabe breathed a sigh of relief at knowing the medics were close. He was really worried about the knock to her head.

'Gabe,' Dave's voice was quiet beside him, 'the driver is shaken up but not injured – she'll need checking out too, but I doubt they'll transport her. I've written our details down for her – the insurance will cover the damage and whatever medical assistance she needs. I've called the office – Grayson was pulling his hair out looking for Paige. He's on checking the external cameras now to see what happened. I'm presuming we suspect Mendino with everything else that's gone on?'

Gabe nodded curtly. 'When I get my hands on that sly bastard …'

'I hear you – I'll hold the fucker down. Becca's coming to grab your truck and me – you'll be going to the hospital with Paige, yes?'

'Absolutely, I'll call the office as soon as I know anything.'

Chapter Thirteen

Perkinsville General Hospital

Gabe wasn't used to feeling helpless. He'd all but worn a hole in the tiled floor in the ER waiting area. It felt like he'd been there forever, and he was on the verge of losing his temper. Reining it in, he made his way to the reception desk.

'Excuse me, I've been waiting here for over an hour. I need an update on Paige Matthews, please.'

'As I told you twenty minutes ago, you'll need to be patient and wait for the doctor to come down and speak to you.'

Gabe sighed loudly and spun on his heels, returning to pacing the waiting area. He was onto his fourth lap when the doctor who'd whisked Paige away came into view, and Gabe stopped, a ball of worry lying heavy in his stomach.

'She's stable – Paige has two breaks to her elbow and arm. She might need surgery on one of the breaks, but we can't do anything until the swelling goes down. We've put her in a splint so the swelling won't restrict blood vessels – a cast would be too tight in these circumstances. She has a mild concussion, a small fracture to the collarbone on the same side as the arm we've splinted, some nasty bruising to her hip, and some abrasions. She will be okay. The injuries she has will heal, though the elbow will be a slow process. I can release her later today as long as she has someone to stay with her for the next twenty-four hours and monitor her concussion. If she starts vomiting or won't wake from sleep, she'll need to come straight back in.'

'I'll be staying with her. You're sure she doesn't need to stay in?'

'I'm sure. Usually, I'd keep her in overnight for observations, but we've got a flu epidemic circulating the hospital currently. If she stays, she'll likely end up with that to contend with as well as her other injuries. She's been treated, but I'm just waiting on a couple of test results coming back. As long as they're clear, which I suspect they will be, she can go. I'll make sure she's got some pain relief to take with her also. She'll be in pain once the morphine wears off.'

'Great, thanks, Doc. Can I see her?'

'Yes. Come with me, she's awake and asking after you.'

Gabe followed the doctor up the stairs and along to a side room on the surgical ward. He motioned Gabe inside and left him to it.

Paige glanced up when he entered. She looked awful. Her skin was pale, a huge bruise spread across her forehead, and she had black bags under her eyes – eyes that filled with tears as he took another step toward her.

'I'm sorry, it was my fault. Don't blame Grayson or the rest of your team. They didn't even see me go outside. I went through the kitchen. I just needed a bit of fresh air.' She shuddered visibly. 'He was waiting for me – held a knife to my back and told me he'd cut my liver if I yelled out. He meant it, Gabe. I couldn't yell. So, I took the first opportunity and ran. Then there was this shadow, and I thought he'd overtaken me. Is that what happened? Did you get him?' Paige winced, sitting a little straighter, her attention focused.

'No, the shadow you saw was me. I saw you running and slammed the brakes on. You ran into the road and were hit by a car. Not driven by Mendino. I didn't see him anywhere.'

'He had a gray van with him. I didn't get the license plates, though. I'm going to be in here for days, aren't I? God, I hate hospitals.'

Gabe sat in the chair beside the bed and took hold of her uninjured hand. 'Everyone hates hospitals, it's like a requirement or something. And you won't be in for days – the doc is letting you go today, all being well. You'll be coming to my place to stay. You seem to have a habit of getting yourself into hot water, so I won't be leaving your side until this is all over, okay?'

Paige flashed him a grin, surprising him. 'I do seem to, don't I? Thanks, Gabe. Oh crap, I'll need to call Mags.'

'Use my phone. Here …' Gabe unlocked his cell and scrolled through the contacts for Mags' number. Hitting 'call', he handed the phone to Paige.

'Mags? … Jacko told you … I'm okay, honest. I'm at hospital. Busted up elbow and some bruises, but I've had worse. I'll be okay. Yeah, sure, I'll put Gabe on, two secs …' She held the phone out to Gabe who knew instantly he was going to get the brunt of Mags' wrath.

'Gabe? What the hell were you doing leaving her alone? And now she's injured? Boy, you better have a good explanation for this …' Mags' voice was loud down the phone.

Gabe moved it an inch from his ear in response.

'She wasn't alone, Mags, she was in the office with some of the team. I had to pick Dave up – she went for a breath of air. This was … a mistake. She won't be left alone again.'

'Well, you damn well better have her attached to your hip, Gabriel Bland. Get your team on catching her ex so she can get on with her life. Poor thing is terrified – she's so scared she hasn't even told me what happened back then. I just hear her crying in her room every night. It's heartbreaking. You will get this resolved, won't you? I can't bear any more tears from that child.' Mags' voice broke at the end of her tirade – Gabe's heart wrenched at the use of his Sunday name. She was talking to him that way out of fear and worry. First the window was put through, and now Paige was injured – he totally got where she was coming from.

'You have my word, Mags, she will not leave my side until it's sorted. Jacko is fine to stay at the refuge if you're happy to keep him there a while. Put him to work – you must have some jobs you need doing. He's more than capable. And if there are any issues, any at all, you ring me, okay?'

'Will do. You make sure she rings me tomorrow, Gabe. Regular check-ins.' Mags replaced the receiver, and it clicked softly in his ear.

'She sounded pissed – is she okay?'

'Yeah, she's okay, Paige, just worried about you. I feel like we've maybe fallen down on protecting you. What happened today should never have happened. I've got some of the team on tracing Mendino – it's their highest priority, they will locate him. We're building a case file against Al Graham too – is there anything else that we should know? The evidence you stole, for example? What exactly is it?'

'A black leather-bound book. It has details of all his business dealings. But it's in some kind of code, I didn't understand it. I took it because it was important to him.'

'Okay, encryption we can work with. Where is it?'

Seeing hesitation flutter across her face, he said, 'I know it's difficult, you have been hurt and burned, and you're still not sure who to trust. I get all that, and we've let you down, you're injured and in hospital, not to mention afraid. That book has been your insurance policy, but from the sounds of it, it contains information that we can use to take Al Graham down for good. He can't hurt you anymore, Paige.'

'I put it in a tin box and buried it along with some other things from my old life. It's at the base of the trunk of the largest oak tree on the west side of the park along Main Street in Rhododendron. It's been there for months. I figured if he ever caught me at least he wouldn't get the ledger.'

'Okay, I'm going to go and call the office. I'll be standing right outside the door. If you need anything, just yell, okay?'

Paige nodded. Now she'd disclosed the info, it looked like a weight had lifted. Either that or the energy expelled doing so, when mixed with the pain relief, had brought on tiredness. Her eyes blinked slowly, and before Gabe had even shut the door, her head lolled to the side and she fell asleep.

Graham Industries

'What the hell do you mean, you had her and she got away?' Al Graham's spoke the words through gritted teeth down the phone to The Fox. '… no, you listen to me. I'm done listening to you. I want the location and all the information you have on Beth brought here and handed over personally. And I mean everything. I will handle the matter myself. You, my friend, will not be working this case anymore. It's too important for mess-ups like that. You'd better be in my office at eight p.m. this evening, otherwise Beth won't be the only one I'm after.'

Al slammed the phone receiver down with force and swore loudly.

'Problem, boss?' George's no-nonsense tone drifted over from the doorway.

'Probably. Organize a couple of guys and get the trace in on Mendino's cell phone. I want to know where he is, where he's been over the last couple of months, and who he's been talking to. He had Beth today – and lost her. She's not bright enough to get away from him under her own steam – she must have someone she's working with. I need all the information, we'll deal with this ourselves. She is not slipping away again, understand?'

'I hear you, boss. Give me an hour. I'll be back.'

Al nodded at George who silently left the room. *Man's built like a shithouse and moves like a panther. If he didn't work for me, I'd be worried.* Al was grateful to have George on his team – he was the one person Al knew would never be bought off or betray him. He'd worked for Al's father before him – in the same line of business Al had been raised in. He knew all the ins and outs.

Al suddenly had the need to get out of the office. Grabbing his jacket from the back of his chair, he strode into the reception area. Marcia glanced up expectantly – she hadn't been there long enough to understand anything about the business, and that was just how he liked it.

'I'm going to pick Kim up and take her out for an early lunch – have George ring me when he gets back.'

'No problem, Mr. Graham.' Marcia turned her attention back to the computer screen and tapped on the keyboard.

Al didn't know what she was doing – he hadn't set her any tasks yet and knew she'd been up-to-date the day before when she'd left.

'What're you working on?' He kept his suspicion in check as he spoke.

Marcia's face reddened, and he waited for whatever lie would drip from her lips. She surprised him with her response, though.

'I'm playing solitaire, see?' She turned the screen a little so he could see the cards spread out. 'Sorry, if you want me to stop, I will, it's just you haven't set me anything to do, and I finished yesterday's stuff last night. I'm still answering the phones, and there's a stack of filing coming in from the warehouse shortly. I was just passing time.'

Fear flashed across her face – she mightn't have been there long, but it was long enough to understand he took no shit from anyone. He should slap her for playing games on company time, but she wasn't a risk to him. Hitting her wouldn't have any benefits. Not right now anyway, and if there was one thing Al could do, it was control himself.

'It's fine, just make sure George rings me when he comes back in the office.'

He got to his car in record time and slid into the bucket seat of his one-month-old Mustang. It had been a somewhat frivolous purchase, but the accountant had assured him it was a decent tax write-off. His intention wasn't really to take Kim out for lunch either – he was suspicious. She'd hidden her phone from him that morning after receiving a text – she'd tried to be subtle, just tucking it back in her bag as though she hadn't even heard the vibration. He didn't think she was stupid enough to be having an affair, not when she was nearly six months pregnant with his son, but whatever it was, he didn't do well with people hiding things from him. He intended to catch her out by turning up at home during work hours.

The electronic gates to the house sprang open at his approach – the camera recognizing his license plate. It was pretty state-of-the-art stuff – he'd learned from Beth leaving to keep the grounds more secure. He drove past the large oblong rockery, purposely not even glancing at it. To look brought back unwanted memories – the past was the past. He couldn't change it.

But he could find out what the hell was going on with Kim.

Pulling the car up to the side of the house, he went inside via the back door – something he never did.

Kim was sitting at the kitchen table with paperwork spread out in front of her. She was so engrossed she didn't hear the door click or his approach.

'What the hell is all this?' Al spoke in low tones, the threat immediately evident to Kim who jumped up from her seat and backed away, fear in her eyes.

'I just wanted … well, it was so I could put some money aside for the baby and …'

Her speech filtered off to silence when he picked up some of the paperwork.

The logo for Citigroup banking was spread across the top of the paper – it wasn't a bank Al used for any of his transactions, not business or personal. *She was opening her own bank account? Without my say-so?* He paused, thinking for a second, then everything clicked into place. *She was going to get money together and leave – with my son!*

Anger in overdrive, he moved quickly until he was standing in front of her.

She was shaking – tears ran down her face. 'I'm sorry, Al. I didn't mean anything by it – I just wanted to be more independent. I should have asked first, I should have …'

'What you should have done is not planned to leave with my son – you intended to try and sneak away money so you could escape. After knowing that Beth did a similar thing, I'd have thought you knew better. I expected more from you, Kim.' He raised his fist and slammed it into the side of Kim's face, and she fell sideways onto the tiled floor. Lifting his foot, he kicked her hard – making sure to avoid her stomach and focusing his rage on her face. She blacked out after the second kick. His rage kept him going, and he kicked her face again but eventually slowed his temper. *Wouldn't do to kill her, not until after my son is born.*

He picked her up, took her to one of the guest rooms, and dumped her on the bed. Not bothering to wipe the blood from her face, he laid her head on the pillow. Al stretched her left arm out and secured it to the metal bedpost using the handcuffs from the top drawer of the bedside cabinet.

She would have her needs catered to, but he wasn't risking her taking off with his son. Nothing and no one would ever take his child away – not again.

He secured her in the guest room. Al made his way back down to the kitchen. He left the blood on the floor – he had people to clean up for him. He scribbled a quick note to the housekeeper telling her to tidy Kim up and to ensure she wasn't freed from the restraints unless supervised. He gathered the paperwork up from the table and strode into his office, putting the papers through his industrial shredder. No way would he leave it lying around for the staff to see – no one need know Kim had been intending to leave him. *Who does she think she is anyway – she gets everything she could want or need here.*

His cell phone rang in his pocket and, pulling it out, he saw George was calling.

'We've got a location, boss. A small town called Rhododendron – we can be there in a few hours. Wayne and Jonner are prepping the car – figure you'll want tools bringing along too. If we set off in thirty, we'll get there for about three-thirty p.m. That would be before Mendino sets off, if he was intending to, I'd guess?'

'Yeah, be ready. I'll be back shortly. That bitch has taken too much. This ends today. Once and for all.'

Gabe's cabin

The trip back to Gabe's cabin took far less time than Paige had thought it would. She'd fought sleep for some of the journey, but the painkillers they'd given her at the hospital were wearing off, and it was now the equivalent of pinning her eyelids open with matchsticks. Every bump, every turn in the road, even every movement of her head sent pain shooting up through her injured elbow and into her shoulder. When the doctor had said she'd be sore, he hadn't been lying.

Gabe unlocked the front door and moved to one side to allow Paige to enter in front of him.

She couldn't help but wince as she lowered herself onto the sofa.

'I'll put the kettle on and be back in a sec with your meds. You okay for a few minutes?'

Paige nodded, not trusting herself to speak. The pain was sharp and constant, reverberating through her arm and up into her shoulder. Even breathing seemed to cause her pain.

True to his word, Gabe was back in minutes carrying a tray. He placed it on the coffee table and sat next to Paige. Handing her a glass of water, he then gathered the painkillers from the tray and gave them to her.

Paige took a large sip of water, leaned her head back, and popped the pills inside her mouth with the water. At his questioning look, she responded, 'I know I'm weird. I hate the pills on my tongue – the taste makes me gag. So, I put the liquid in first then the pills – no taste, and it goes straight down with no problems.'

'I've never seen anyone take pills that way before. Makes sense, though, I guess.' He poured them both a mug of hot coffee then leaned back on the sofa with a soft sigh. 'It has been a long-ass day. How you feeling now?'

'Better now I'm out of hospital – did I mention I hate hospitals?' she asked wryly, giving him a small smile.

'You might've. I think everyone hates hospitals, I know I do. The smell, the brightness, the fact everyone in there is either hurting or in pain of some kind. What's not to hate?' Gabe paused, thinking about whether to expand further. 'I spent a lot of time in hospital when I was a kid. My sister, Anna, was diagnosed with leukemia when she was six. I kinda got used to being in hospital as we had to visit her every day. Then she needed a bone marrow transplant, and I was a match. She's younger than me by a few years – I couldn't have said no even if I'd wanted to. She's my little sis. But it meant I had a good while in those godawful hospital beds myself.'

'And then after all that she got lupus? I'm sorry about your sister. That sucks. Is she past the leukemia now?' Paige shifted position so she was looking directly at him.

Gabe grinned – and Paige felt like she'd been hit by a truck. It was the first true smile she'd seen from him. His whole face lit up, and she couldn't help but smile back in response. 'I guess that means she's okay – that's great, Gabe. What's she like?' Paige wanted the smile to continue – she'd asked hoping it would remain and leaned back in her seat a little as he opened his mouth to speak. Her painkillers started to kick in, and she suddenly felt mellow and relaxed.

'She's great, runs a holistic shop a few towns over, nothing ever fazes her now. Anna is amazing. I'd love for you to meet her. You two will get along like a house on fire, I reckon.'

'Sounds good. How about your parents?'

'They live next door to Anna – same house I grew up in. I visit every weekend when I'm not working. It's just on the outskirts of Granton, two towns over from Perkinsville. I guess some would call it a ranch of sorts. I'd say more of a small farm – they've got a bit of land but not enough to warrant it being a ranch, I guess.'

'They all sound very happy.' Paige's eyes filled with the easy tears that seemed to appear out of nowhere now.

Swiping at her cheeks somewhat angrily, she glanced up. Gabe rushed to her side. He knelt in front of her and removed her hand from her face. Using his thumb, he wiped at the tears for her.

'What's wrong?' His voice was quiet, almost a whisper.

Paige stilled, mesmerized, and not wanting to break the moment.

'Nothing's wrong, it's lovely to see a family so happy. It reminded me of my dad – I miss him. Every day. If he knew what was happening right now, well he'd move heaven and earth to get back here and help me. He would have hated all this stuff with Al, all the people getting hurt because of me. My dad was a Navy SEAL a million years ago, before he had to give it all up to look after me. He never complained, not once. But he wouldn't have taken any crap from the likes of Al Graham either. He raised me stronger than this – I'm pathetic, all I do is cry and get people hurt. That's why I'm angry – I put myself in the position I did with Al – I should've left sooner. I shouldn't have taken all that crap. And I shouldn't be asking you for help and getting your people hurt. I shouldn't have let Diana …' Paige paused, horrified. She'd been about to tell him about her precious Diana – she couldn't open that door. Not now, not ever. Not to anyone – it was too much.

'Diana is your daughter. I can help you get her back, Paige; in fact, ever since you first mentioned her, that's been one of the top priorities – I will help you get her back.'

The tears fell freely now – no amount of swiping would get rid of them. Her heart snapped in two, and the floodgates were open. *I have to tell him – he can't believe she's …*

'Oh, Gabe, no one has ever said and meant something so meaningful to me. Ever. But you can't help me get her back, as much as I wish it was possible. No one can. Diana is …' Paige paused again, her voice hitching in her throat, trying to prevent her saying the words that made it all so real, so impossible. 'Diana's dead.' Now she couldn't control the sobs. Every wall she'd ever built up smashed into a million pieces, and the utter feeling of loss and despair echoed around her.

Gabe pulled her into his arms, her tears soaking his shirt in seconds.

Paige shook and sobbed until there were no more tears. And even then, she left her head where it was on his shoulder. His hand was rubbing her back in soothing circles, and she realized it actually felt good to let some of the pent-up grief out. She missed Diana – it had been killing her not talking about her. Diana was her whole reason for living, for staying with Al – in not talking, it almost made Paige feel now like she'd been underplaying the importance of her child. She hadn't had any support after Diana had died – no one to talk to. She'd quickly learned to lock up all the grief – it was one way to avoid further beatings from Al before she'd finally plucked the courage up to leave. That itself had taken her a while – for so long she'd thought she deserved what Al was dishing out, especially with the blame she felt for Diana's death swallowing her whole. She shuddered against Gabe, guilt now replacing the hollow feeling of loss deep inside her.

'You can tell me about her if you want to. Equally, if you want to lock it all back up, I totally get it. I won't push you, Paige.'

Gabe rocked back on his heels and gazed into Paige's eyes – his were full of hurt and concern for her. Not pity, though, which was something she always thought she'd see if she stopped to explain about Diana.

Taking a deep, shuddering breath, Paige began. 'She was just three when it happened. It was the nanny's day off. Diana was playing in the garden, and George, Al's second-in-command, was looking after her – Al made me stay inside with him and was in the process of screaming at me for something. Is it weird that I don't even remember what about?' Giving her head a soft shake, she returned to the story, ignoring the tears welling up in her eyes. 'Diana loved being outside – she loved the flowers and the trees and wildlife, her favorite was butterflies. She'd spend ages chasing them around from one flower to the next. Anyway, George was busy listening to Al beat the crap out of me again – he must have moved closer to the house. He was always just there, didn't care what Al did to me. If Al asked him to hit me, he did, if Al told him to remove Diana from my arms, he did. He's a bastard.' Paige knew her voice had turned scathing, but she no longer cared.

Paige's breath hitched in her throat, and she shuddered. 'All he heard was Al punching me a couple of times, and me refusing to cry because that made him hit harder. I remember being on the floor for what felt like an eternity – it would only have been about five, maybe ten minutes max. Al just walked round me and put the kettle on, pretended he hadn't even done anything. I dragged myself to my feet and found George glaring in the kitchen window. And I couldn't see her – I couldn't see Diana anywhere. I swear I felt my heart stop – I ran out of the kitchen, stumbling at the kitchen step and falling on my face. Al ran past me, shouting for Diana. But she didn't come … she didn't … I got to the pond at the same time as Al. But while he took the time to take his fucking shoes off, I jumped in to get our daughter. George had been so busy listening to Al beating on me that he didn't see her fall in the pond, he didn't hear her cough or splutter as she went under.'

Tears fell freely, but Paige continued.

'She was blue, and so cold. I tried to give her mouth-to-mouth; I remember screaming at her to wake up. I even … I even shook her little body so hard. Oh my god, Gabe, I tried to save her. But it was too late. My baby was gone. She was gone …'

The tears turned to more heart-wrenching sobs, and Gabe grabbed Paige, hugging her close to him tightly. There weren't any words of comfort he could offer. What could he possibly say?

So, he just held her, let her cry until her racks turned to shudders, then shakes, and finally her tears slowed. Moving back a little, he wiped her tears.

'I am so sorry, darlin'. So very sorry. I can't even imagine how hard it's been for you. Let me make you a cup of tea and you can talk about Diana all you want – I can tell you hold it all in. I want you to know, that with me, you don't have to, okay? Whenever you want to talk, I will listen.'

Paige sat back and let him stand and head into the kitchen, recognizing he needed a moment to process. Hell, she felt like she'd been processing for a lifetime and still couldn't really understand how it had happened. How she'd lost her precious Diana. What she wouldn't give to have her little girl back in her arms, laughing as she pulled away to chase the butterflies she so loved.

For the first time in a long time, the sharp pain in her chest didn't split it in two at the thought of her daughter. It still hurt, so, so much. But maybe, the sharpness of the loss was going to ease. Maybe it was just time for her to talk about Diana and not keep everything inside.

When Gabe came back into the room and placed the tea on the coffee table, Paige stood, suddenly realizing that pain wasn't the only thing she had to feel. When she looked at Gabe, she knew instinctively that he could help heal the split in her heart.

Paige slowly leaned forward. Gabe didn't move.

What the hell am I doing? She paused a hair away from his lips. *I can't do this. I shouldn't do this. But I don't want to stop.* His eyes were smoldering. She hadn't thought they could change color until they did – glittering gray initially, they were now dark gray, like thunderclouds rolling across mountains. Desire sparked lightning bolts of gold inside the gray, and Paige was drawn in deeper.

She shivered as her lips connected with his – he tasted a little of coffee and a lot of pure man. He moaned into her mouth, still not moving. She understood immediately that he didn't want to push her into anything she might regret. She couldn't possibly regret this, though – and she couldn't stop if she wanted to.

The kiss deepened, her tongue darting into his mouth, connecting with his.

Gabe tightened his grip, pushing forward slightly and kissing her back, hard.

She snaked the arm that wasn't in a sling around his neck, moving her fingers through his hair and tightening around strands of it.

He moaned into her mouth in response and, not breaking the kiss for a moment, lowered her back onto the sofa and lay next to her. Her left arm was tucked beside the back of the sofa, not in the way and not getting touched.

One of her last coherent thoughts was that he'd done that on purpose to protect her arm from being hurt.

He didn't break the kiss even as one hand fluttered over her collarbone and down the side of her ribs with a featherlight touch. She shuddered visibly, her back arching upward. When Gabe's fingers brushed over the swell of her breast, she gasped, her lips parting from his. And suddenly he was gone, off the couch and back to the kneeling position beside her. She felt empty, bereft. *How can all that come from one little kiss? I've never felt anything like it in my life. What the hell was that?*

Drawing in a few deep breaths, Gabe spoke softly, his voice gravelly and shaky. 'Wow, I don't know what just happened there, but you're in no position to cope with what would happen if this continues.'

'What position should I be in?' Her retort surprised her as much as him, her voice playful and gentle. She didn't even think she was capable of responding like that.

'Damn it, woman, you're injured. I'd be the world's biggest jerk if I took advantage of you like that, as much as I want to. You're drugged up for a start. You probably don't even know what you're doing. And I don't want to do anything that would cause you pain or regret.'

Ignoring his words, she pushed herself back into a seated position and looked at Gabe. She could see he was torn between wanting to continue and obeying whatever honor code he was trying to follow.

'It's not taking advantage if both parties want it – my painkillers have done their job, I'm in less pain. But I'm not high, and I am in full control of my faculties. I've never had such a strong reaction to a kiss before, and we are both talking way too much.' Resorting to torture, Paige kissed the side of his mouth and moved along slowly – featherlight kisses on his lower lip whispering at each step as she went. 'I … want … this …'

Gabe tried to move away, he really did. *We can't do this, I shouldn't be doing this ...* But she drew him in until he could barely string a thought together, let alone protest. He wanted to be a gentleman and protect Paige, but her kiss was making it hard. *It's not the only thing that's hard.* He shifted position slightly to relieve the pressure at the front of his jeans.

When she pulled his bottom lip into her mouth and sucked gently, he was lost. All thoughts of him taking advantage drifted away, and he was overcome with utter desire.

He heard himself growl – that was a new thing. He'd never been so swept up before. His hands found their way to her face, and he deepened the kiss, again. Tasting her, feeling her shiver under his touch.

He was harder than he'd ever been, but even knowing how much he wanted her, Gabe's underlying need not to hurt her was strong. Gently, he lowered her back onto the sofa, not wanting to ever stop kissing her.

When his hand found her breast again, he moaned into her mouth, feeling her shudder when she arched against his touch. He knew his way around a woman – he'd had his fair share, but none had ever made him feel like this. At this moment, there was nothing in the world that could touch him.

He unbuttoned her shirt, but all he wanted to do was rip the buttons; it was like agonizing torture, but he did it. He slipped his hand under the vest and cupped her breast again, his fingers stilled at the touch of simple cotton and lace. He broke the kiss to push her vest up, his lips seeking out her nipple, his teeth grazing the lace even as she cried out. Her hand was wrapped in his hair again and, instinctively knowing what she wanted, he bit down, not too hard but enough to make her buck into him.

I need to slow down – this is going too fast. She can't take me – not as she is. The decision that this would be all about her was an easy one, even though his cock groaned its denial almost audibly on the denim he wore.

He unbuttoned her jeans and didn't take his eyes off her. She lifted her hips, allowing him to draw the denim and her matching cotton panties down her legs.

Gabe's erection pushed farther against his own jeans. He registered the black bruises to her hips and leg, the scuffs to her knees, and a frown marred his face. Once her jeans were discarded, he moved his position and lowered his head, slowly kissing every single one of the bruises.

Paige could barely contain herself. His lips gently touched all the discolored skin on her hips and legs – she'd half expected it to sting but all she felt was warmth spreading across her whole body. She exhaled in short gasps, desire overwhelming her. Gabe's lips drew closer and closer to the juncture of her thighs, and she shivered uncontrollably. She didn't know what to expect – she'd never had anyone pay her attention like this before. His tongue swiped through her sex, and she almost jumped off the sofa in shock. *Holy shit!*

He licked again, and her orgasm built instantly – whatever this was, she didn't ever want it to stop. She wound her fingers tighter in his hair. He pushed her close to the edge then pulled back slightly. His finger dipped inside at the same time as his tongue hit her clit. Her orgasm exploded, and she cried out loudly, throwing her head back. He continued, drawing the explosion out of her for what felt like an eternity.

Floating back down, Paige groaned when he removed the welcomed intrusion and sat back on his heels.

'Seems like a good position to me?' His voice held a hint of humor.

'Mmm-hmm.' Paige couldn't say anything else – she was suddenly overcome with exhaustion. It was deep in her bones, and she tried to fight it, knowing Gabe hadn't finished, but even though she wanted more, it needed more energy than she had.

She barely noticed Gabe carefully putting her panties in place and covering her with the throw from the back of the sofa.

Well, that's a new one on me. Gabe grinned at her – she was already asleep. He tucked the throw around her and stood, wincing at the erection straining against his jeans.

He couldn't have had sex with her – not like this. But he was pleased to have at least satisfied her. Gabe acknowledged he'd never seen any woman he'd ever been with fall apart like that. He'd barely even touched her – it had taken a mere minute or two.

Imagine her exploding around your cock like that. He groaned loudly, running his hand through his hair in frustration. Needing a cold shower, he made his way to the bathroom.

Once he'd finished in the shower, he checked on Paige briefly before heading into the kitchen. He was starving, which meant she would be when she woke. He opted to keep it simple and whipped up a batch of bacon and eggs – not exactly dinnertime food, but it was quick and filling, which was what he wanted.

He wolfed his down in minutes and poured himself a large mug of hot coffee and sat in the recliner beside the couch with his laptop open.

An email from Jacko assured him all was well at the shelter, and another from Becca confirmed that she and Grayson were heading to the potential location they'd advised him of during the debrief for The Fox. She verified she and Grayson would call him when they'd got there. The email was timed ten minutes before he'd checked. They'd just be leaving the office now. *No point trying to contact them.*

Grabbing his phone, he dialed Dave's number.

'Hiya, Dave, how you doing, brother?'

'I'm good, glad to be home. I hate hospitals.'

Gabe grinned down the phone. 'You and the rest of the world. Paul okay?'

'Yeah, he's good. Listen, I've been digging into Graham Industries – they've got their fingers primarily in import and export, but there's a few subsidiary companies that provide other services – likely to be Graham's way of cleaning the excess money he makes from the illegal stuff. There's actually quite a few I've not identified as yet too, just inklings of something else below the obvious. I've tried hacking into his system already, but he has some serious firewalls and blocks in place. I'm going to keep at it, but it'll take a while. How's Paige?'

'She's okay, she's sleeping right now.'

Gabe kept his tone neutral, but Dave picked up on the undertone without even pausing for breath.

'You didn't? Gabe, she's a client. Please don't tell me you've taken advantage of her when she's laid up and injured.'

Dave sounded appalled, and Gabe winced at his tone, knowing he was right. 'What? No. Why would you even think that? I …' Knowing Dave knew him like the back of his favorite book, he paused. 'I didn't take advantage, I helped her relax is all. Which was wrong, I know, but I didn't do anything for myself.'

'Well, that's something, I guess. We know how this turns out, though, Gabe. You keep going through life saying you're not the relationship kind. I don't believe it for one minute as you know, but don't go pissing on this girl's cornflakes after making her fall for you – she deserves better than to be hurt like that after everything she's been through.'

'I'm not going to hurt her. What happened tonight happened, but I've no intention of a repeat performance. Like you said, she's a client. And I'm *not* the relationship kind.'

As Gabe hung up the phone, though, he frowned. Dave was right – he never had been the relationship kind, not really. Not many women were built to put up with last-minute missions with no explanations, so he'd always kept himself distant, never allowing himself to fall fully for anyone. Never really allowing them to fall for him either – he'd always laid his cards on the table, or thought he had. The incident with Helena, well, that was one he could've avoided if he'd been thinking with his head and not his cock – she still haunted his nightmares on occasion. But he thought he'd been plain with her at the time.

Maybe the others just weren't the right one, though. Maybe Paige is …

Pushing the thoughts of possibilities back, he focused his attention on the laptop, shaking his head.

Chapter Fourteen

Rhododendron Inn

Al's driver pulled up the SUV outside the inn.

'Are you sure this is the only hotel in town?' Al's voice was grating as he took in the floral arch where the path met the porch steps, the gnomes in the garden, and the overall nicey-nicey feel to the whole place. Normally he much preferred to stay in a five-star hotel – this was way below par.

'Yes, boss. The nearest decent hotel other than this inn is thirty miles away in Fallow. You've stayed there before when we've been visiting one of the sub-companies. We can go there if you'd prefer. I know this place is … quaint.'

'Quaint? It's like something from *The Waltons*. I almost expect to hear shouts of *'Goodnight, John-boy'* – it couldn't be more hick if it tried.'

The front door opened, and a woman stepped onto the porch, assessing the vehicle with her hand to her forehead to block the sun. She was pretty – girl-next-door kind of pretty but appealing nonetheless. *Maybe it won't be so bad staying here after all.*

Stepping out of the vehicle, Al approached the woman.

'Hello there, miss, I'm in need of four rooms tonight – for me and my employees. We're just passing through and saw the sign for your lovely establishment. I do believe in keeping economy up for local entrepreneurs.' He smiled widely – the toothy grin he used to disarm and charm people. It always worked.

Until today.

'I'm sorry, sir, but we're full. I was just heading out to put the no vacancies sign up.'

'Full?' Al glanced around the empty car park and back at the woman, his eyes narrowing in disbelief.

'Yes, I've got a party arriving shortly – they've booked up for a week. Tourists looking at the area's attractions. There's a motel twenty miles or so toward Perkinsville, or if you travel through there, you'll end up at Fallow which has a few larger hotels.'

'How about I pay you full room bookings for two weeks – every room you have, of course. It should cover any shortfall you might've made and mean that me and my friends don't need to travel farther afield. It's been a long day already.'

'I couldn't do that – I'm sorry. My guests would be devastated – I've promised to show them around and whatnot.'

Al frowned. He wasn't used to people saying no to him. If he pushed further, however, he could encounter problems.

'Okay, well, thank you anyway, Mrs. ...'

'Ms. actually. But Alice is fine. Do you need directions?'

'No, my driver will find the hotels you've suggested. You have a good day now.'

'You too.' Alice turned and went back inside, and Al got back into the SUV.

'Hotel it is. Watson Hinkle is the hotel, I believe?' George said.

When Al nodded his acknowledgement sullenly, George reciprocated briefly and tapped the driver on the shoulder, making him aware of the direction to take.

Bruce put the car in gear and reversed out of the driveway.

Probably wouldn't have been the best bet booking in a little place like this with Mendino in the boot anyway – he's no doubt going to be a vocal one.

Al set his jaw determinedly. There were many more pleasant ways to get information from someone, but he was right in the mood to do some serious damage, and Mendino might just turn out to be the perfect release.

Gabe's cabin

The sudden invasive ringtone of Gabe's phone cut through the silence in the cabin. Paige groaned, not wanting to open her eyes. Every part of her hurt, and she thought if she opened her eyes, they would too, so she was trying to put off the inevitable.

The song registered, and she frowned. *'Moves like Jagger?' Who the hell has that as their ringtone?* Memories suddenly flooded her mind, and her eyes flew open. Gabe was in the armchair opposite – his head lolled back on the cushion, and his eyes were tightly closed. His laptop lay open at his feet.

How can anyone sleep through that? That's not even music!

Grimacing, she pushed herself up to a sitting position and leaned forward to place her weight over her knees and stand. When pain shot through her hips and down her legs, she couldn't stop the gasp that escaped.

It was the gasp, not the hideous ringtone, that woke Gabe.

'Where the hell do you think you're going?' His tone could have been offensive but for the concern in his eyes softening the harshness.

He registered then that his phone was ringing and grabbed it, swiping at the screen before standing and gently placing his free hand on her arm and guiding her back down to the sofa.

Paige could've cried at the soft fabric touching her sore hip – but she ground her teeth together and tried not to wince. *I was hit by a car, it's bound to hurt. It's also time you stopped crying like a baby and started accepting responsibility for yourself.* Steeling herself, she shifted position and glanced up at Gabe who was listening intently to what the other person on the line was saying. Her keen ears picked up the tone as being female. *Becca maybe?* She ignored the sudden flare of jealously *– you have no right or claim to this man.* Drawing in a deep breath, she continued to try and convince herself that she was right.

'Slow down,' said Gabe quietly. 'Alice, what do you mean men came to the inn? Are you okay? Did they do something to you?'

Relief washed over his face, and Paige read the meaning that Alice was okay.

'Four men, black SUV. Smarmy? Anything else? … Did you get the plates? … Crap. Okay, stay inside, lock up. I'll have one of the team come and check on you.' Gabe frowned as he ended the call.

'What was that about?' Paige asked, but she wondered momentarily if she really wanted to know.

'Four men tipped up at the inn. Alice was nervous, they wanted to stay, but she told them she was fully booked. Alice doesn't get nervous easily – might be something, might be nothing. Don't have any plates to run, but I'm going to try and access the CCTV at the inn, see if we can't turn something up.'

'The inn has CCTV?' Paige didn't know why that shocked her. Alice often let Gabe and his men stay there from what she'd gathered from the short conversation Gabe and Alice had had in her presence. She'd already seen how much extra security Gabe had provided at the shelter. It made perfect sense he'd protect the inn the same way to reduce risk to his staff.

'Damn it,' Gabe cursed softly, his fingers tapping on the keyboard – two fingers only, the index fingers of both hands. It appeared to work for him, though – he was pretty speedy at typing with just those two.

With more patience than she thought she had, Paige waited for him to expand on his cursing.

'CCTV is offline. I totally forgot we'd scheduled automatic system updates to upload today. Same with Mags' system at the shelter. It'll be down for a couple of hours yet. I'll search farther afield shortly. You must be hungry?'

Paige nodded, her stomach growling loudly in response to Gabe's offer of food.

'I've already prepped bacon and eggs, I'll just go put some toast on and be back in a minute.' Glancing at the clock on the mantel, he nodded almost to himself. 'You can eat then take your strong painkillers – some sleep will do you the world of good. Okay?'

Paige didn't like being ordered around – and she scowled at his back. He continued speaking and walked toward the doorway. Then she shook her head a little. *Stop being a bitch. He's right, I'm exhausted. And Gabe isn't the type to boss.* She should know, she'd put up with it for years of Al. And Gabe was nothing like Al.

Not that she really trusted her judgement at the minute. She'd been awake for about ten minutes now, and not once had he mentioned their time on the sofa or even looked at her as though he remembered. Self-doubt trickled inside her – *maybe he wishes it hadn't happened. It's not like he got any pleasure from it. I wouldn't want to go there with a selfish lover like me either. Though you didn't really give him chance to say anything, did you? He got the call and went to make food for you. Stop being a child.*

Sighing, she used her good arm to push herself off the sofa and saw that her jeans were folded over the other sofa arm. Gingerly, she pulled them up, gasping when the denim scraped her thigh and hip. It felt like it took forever, but she gritted her teeth and managed to secure the button. The zip would have to stay open – no way could she manage that as well.

Every step toward the kitchen felt like she was dragging the car that hit her. She'd never have guessed a person could hurt and ache so much in one go. She paused at what she thought was the door to the kitchen. It was spring-loaded and opened into the kitchen itself. *Spring-loaded means heavy.* Sighing again, she used her good arm to turn the handle and positioned her hip to push the door with her weight.

She didn't anticipate the door suddenly swinging inwards, taking her forward with the momentum. Her hip protested, and she yelped when her weight distributed none too gently on her front leg.

A plate smashed loudly in front of her, and Gabe was by her side, steadying her with his chest. Her hand had instinctively gone out to break her fall but had connected with pure muscle. Her eyes moved slowly up to Gabe's. He had tensed, like a tiger, alert and aware. Paige's pain ebbed– Gabe was the only thing she felt. Her fingers spread farther apart, and her gaze shifted to his chest – hard as rock and shirtless. *When did he get rid of his shirt?* The thought left as she stared, almost dizzy with a rush of desire. *Holy shit. Tattoos.* She knew the dark shadow under his shirt would be tattoos.

She touched them – somewhat religious, they displayed angels fighting demons, fire and brimstone, Heaven and Hell. Paige exhaled in a loud 'whoosh.'

'You need to stop touching me like that, darlin'.' Gabe's voice was hoarse and raspy – his skin rippled under her touch, and she knew with certainty that he hadn't forgotten what they'd shared on the couch. *He's trying to be professional – and trying not to take advantage.* But that was something she wanted him to do more than anything she'd felt in a long time. She could cope with ten times the pain she was in if it meant having Gabe in all his glorious entirety.

'Paige, no.' Gabe's hand removed hers from his chest and gently pushed it back toward herself. 'You're in too much pain, and I'm in no condition to take it easy. Please.'

He dropped his head and kissed the ends of her fingers. 'This is not me saying it won't happen, Paige. But it can't happen until you're feeling better. I won't put you in the position where I increase your recovery time because I acted like a horny teenager.'

Gabe stepped back and muttered just loud enough for Paige to hear, though she was pretty sure her hearing wasn't his intent.

'Horny teenager. What the hell? I doubt I ever felt like this as a teen.'

He turned and grabbed a dustpan and brush from the utility room at the back of the kitchen and made quick work of sweeping the broken plate and food remains. Paige didn't move. She couldn't – his jeans were taut over his ass as he bent over. *Oh my …*

'Stop staring at my ass.'

Paige snickered in response to the humor in his tone. 'Shouldn't have such a peachy one. Kinda makes me want to spank it.'

Who the hell is this flirt, and what have I done with the normal me?

Gabe stood, grinned at her widely, and gently turned her around, pulled the kitchen door, and tapped her on her butt.

'Sofa, madam. You're incorrigible. I'll whip up some more dinner – sit in there and do not move. Okay?'

'Yes, *boss*,' she replied sarcastically.

Cracking more eggs and frying off bacon, Gabe couldn't help but smile. *She's going to be the death of me, that one.*

He'd just plated up when his phone rang again. *That bloody ringtone – I'm going to hogtie Dave and beat him till he changes it back!* Gabe didn't have a clue about phones really – Dave did all the technology updates and maintenance. And trained his Neanderthal friend how to use the features he needed. Which had never included learning to change ringtones. Every time Dave handed him the phone back it had a different one – all equally horrific. *At least 'Moves Like Jagger' constitutes pop in some form – it's better than the 'Fraggle Rock' theme he put on last time!*

Swiping the screen to answer, he greeted Becca.

'Hey, boss, we've found Mendino. He's at the crappy motel near Perkinsville. Not too many places for him to hole up when it all comes down to it. We've been observing – he's just packed up his car to leave – emptied the room, in fact. Figured he was heading back to Al Graham, or the rock he crawled out from under, whichever was nearest. But there's been a snag.'

'What snag?'

'Well, we were going to follow him, see where he was heading. But four guys in a black SUV just jumped him and threw him in the trunk. No plates on the vehicle, the men are all armed. They're about to leave now. Shall we follow covertly?'

'Hell yes, maintain contact. Check-ins every ten minutes, Becca. I'll settle Paige and head to the office. You and Grayson stick to each other like glue, you understand me?'

'Yeah, of course. If we get the opportunity, we'll plant a tracker to avoid detection. If not, we'll maintain distance and standard protocol.'

'Good. Thanks, Becca.'

Grabbing the plates, he made his way back through to where Paige was sitting on the sofa. She'd found the remote for the TV and put a foodie program on. He put the plate in front of her and motioned at her to eat.

She obeyed without speaking. Gabe assessed her as she put bacon in her mouth and chewed slowly. It was obvious she was trying not to show her pain, but she might as well have been sobbing and wincing for all the good it did. He'd masked pain enough times himself to be able to see the signs.

Paige started to tire after eating only a third of her dinner; her pace eased up, and chewing was more of an effort.

'Okay, Paige. It's time for meds and bed – no arguments. I'm going to get you settled and head to the office. I'll set the alarm but will write the code beside the bed. You'll need to disarm it if you come out of the bedroom before I'm back. I don't anticipate being too long, and this house is the safest place you can possibly be at this time.'

Gabe knew how much she was hurting when her only response was to nod wearily.

He guided her out of the living room and up the few steps to the master suite. It had an en suite, and he figured having the bathroom nearby would be a blessing if she needed it. It was also the room he slept in and wasn't filled with art stuff like the spare room.

The artist Alice had hinted at back at the inn was Gabe. He'd always had a knack for transferring what he could see to canvas. Alice had seen his collection years before and insisted the second she had her own place, his pictures would adorn the walls. And she'd stood firm with that when she'd inherited the inn, insisting on paying him even though he'd been adamant he didn't want payment.

Paige was exhausted – he watched her swallow her pain relief without even registering she'd done it. Her eyes drooped, and he lay her head on the pillow and covered her with the duvet, tucking it around her shoulders, knowing nighttime could get chilly at the base of the mountain.

She was asleep before he'd even turned to write the alarm code on the pad on the bedside table.

Chapter Fifteen

Bland P.I.R office

Gabe pushed open the office door, not surprised in the slightest to see the office lit up. Dave was seated behind his desk, staring intently at the screens in front of him. Paul was sitting next to him, also staring at the screens, his hand nestled on Dave's knee. *Silent support – that's what marriage is. You could have it too …* He pushed the stray, niggling thought back – he had other things to think about. *Any other thing will do – I will not think of Paige as anything but a client.* But he remembered the touch of her fingers on his chest which burned a trail where they'd been. *Good luck with that …*

Deacon Marshall and Mitch Lockley were sitting at their own computers to the left of the office. Gabe didn't even need to ask what they were doing – Mitch had been working undercover for months now and was close to his case finalizing. Deacon would be monitoring Becca and Grayson as they followed the SUV.

Gabe crossed the office and stood behind him.

Deacon was the newest member of the team. He'd only worked there for six months, but his record was impeccable so far. He'd arrived with good recommendations, and Gabe was pleased with his progress.

'Boss,' Deacon acknowledged as Gabe knew he would. 'Becca has been in contact just a couple of minutes ago – the SUV has noticed the tail and is currently trying to lose them. Grayson is driving. She says they know what they're doing.'

'Okay, on the next check-in tell her I said not to put themselves in danger. They don't have full armory in the car, and backup would be too far away to assist quickly given their location.' Gabe had clocked the company car entering the industrial estate on the outskirts of Fallow on Deacon's computer screen.

Fallow was a large town; heavy on the industrial side, it provided jobs for a lot of the people living within a decent radius. It was also an easy town to get lost in.

'Okay, they've uploaded the dashcam footage to the server – it shows all four men exiting the vehicle. One stands to one side while the others manhandle Mendino into the trunk. He was punched a few times but was definitely alive when he was shoved inside.'

'Thanks.' Gabe nodded and made his way through the main office to the back room. Using the larger display in there made more sense to him. He could look at the footage while building an electronic case file. He needed to send the details over to Kyle at the police station – it was a potential kidnapping at the end of the day. Within minutes, he'd attached the dashcam footage and documents containing pertinent information on Mendino to an email and sent it. Pulling his cell from his pocket, he dialed Kyle's number.

'Kyle. I've forwarded you some video footage as well as information on a potential kidnapping victim. We think the vic is the same guy who's been trying to grab Paige. No idea why he's been snatched – could be linked to our case, but equally might not be. I've got two of my team following the SUV – Mendino was shoved in the trunk by the occupants. They know they're being followed, however, so are trying to lose my men. Last sighted entering Ridgedale Road off the highway at Fallow just five minutes ago …' Gabe grunted in acknowledgement when Kyle said he would dispatch officers – it was all Kyle could do, but the reality of the situation was that it would be likely the SUV would be in the wind by the time the cops got there.

'Yeah … I'll keep you updated on the location as best as I can. Not sure how much longer we'll be able to continue the tail. Can one of my guys access Mendino's vehicle? It was left behind – we need to know what information he has on Paige and what exactly he's passed on. We'll do it forensically – though your guys can monitor if that'll make you feel better.'

Gabe nodded to himself, realizing belatedly that Kyle couldn't see – the movement was reactive. He had no doubt that Kyle had likely done the same throughout the call.

'I'll have Deacon meet your tech guy at the vehicle in fifteen minutes – it's parked outside the Cheapside motel near Perkinsville. Blue Honda Civic.'

Before he could say goodbye, Kyle had ended the call himself.

Gabe pulled up the footage on the screen in front of him and squinted as the men from the SUV came into view. He sighed loudly. It wasn't clear enough for any facial recognition software, and he doubted even the best enhancement software would be able to improve the clarity enough to make an identification. The issues were caused by the distance between the dashcam and the SUV.

It could be Al Graham. I wonder if Paige would be able to recognize him. He's a similar build to what we have on file. Right hair color too.

Clicking the mouse to zoom, he hovered over the face of the man who'd stood to one side while his goons grabbed Mendino. The image was grainy and too pixelated to be able to make out much detail. Even the best software couldn't clear up images from a crappy dashcam. He quickly penned an email to Dave asking him to look into better upgrades for the team vehicles' dashcams.

With the image as poor as it was, there was no guarantee that Paige would be able to associate the man as being her ex.

Gabe sighed, and not for the first time in the last few days, felt totally helpless.

It's like everything's just a little off since Shotgun died. Everything is hazy and running below par. Or maybe it's just me who's running low – all the issues we've had so far involving Paige have been largely things that I should've been able to resolve before they happened. He frowned to himself; it was natural to miss Shotgun. With his easy manner and likeable character, he'd been a massive asset to the team. But it seemed wrong to blame the sudden issues on his demise. Gabe shook his head, effectively shaking off the negativity he was feeling. He had a job to do. *Focus on that and not all the stuff on the peripheral.*

Even as he made the decision, tension mounted in his shoulders. This was no time for working weights until he dropped in the gym – there'd be time enough for that later. He squared his shoulders, picked up the phone, and rang his dad. If the gym wasn't viable, speaking to the one man who'd seen him through everything would be.

'Gabriel? How you doing, son? Your ma's asking if you're coming for dinner tomorrow? She's making your favorite, apple pie.'

His mom was in the background chiding his dad.

'So, what you mean is you want apple pie tomorrow, and if I come, Ma will feel obligated to make it, yes?'

His dad chuckled softly down the line, confirming his suspicions.

'Tell Ma I'll do my best – working on a case, though, so not sure I'll be able to make it.'

'You need a sounding board, son?'

'If you have a minute?'

'Always time to speak to you, son. I'm sat in my armchair so shoot whenever you're ready.'

Gabe drew in a deep breath and told his dad everything – holding back from his parents was something he'd not done since he was a teenager, and with every word the load felt lighter.

When he'd finished, Gabe felt less like the weight of the world was on his shoulders.

'She sounds like a special gal, Paige does. Don't be pushing her away – you've got this idea in your head that you're not entitled to happiness. Gabriel, it breaks your mother's heart. You are fully entitled to happiness, boy. If there's one thing forty years of marriage has taught me it's that everyone, no matter who they are, should grab on to everything that makes them happy and cling on for dear life. You only get one shot at this life – might as well make the most of it. Bring her for dinner tomorrow, your ma says. Anna's coming too.'

'I'll see, Pops, like I say I'm working a case. And I know Dave's out of hospital, but Paige still has injuries that are going to take a while to heal. I'm not sure she'll be able to handle the drive to the farm.' He didn't know for sure she wouldn't be okay with the drive, but there was everyone on the farm to consider too. The last thing he wanted was to put everyone there in potential danger. He frowned to himself. *Maybe it would be doable - it would require careful planning, but it's an idea – Lord knows Paige could use a break.*

'Love you, boy,' said his father softly before replacing the receiver.

Gabe didn't know why he'd felt the need to talk to his dad – but in equal parts, he was glad he had. He and his dad had been close forever. His dad had raised him to become the man he was. He'd retired from the Army after thirty years of service, opting to spend his retirement on the farm he'd bought as a base to love his wife and raise his children when he was younger. *It suits him, farm life. I never would have thought it would have when he'd first bought the farm. Pops always seemed to be living it up around the world on tours. Never thought he'd be one for becoming a homebody.* Yet somewhere inside, Gabe knew his dad had bought the farm for that very reason. It gave him a home to come back to – especially when he had kids to raise. Gabe had been just eight when his dad had retired from 'the life' as he called it. *'Pays to prioritize, son, and you and Anna will always be the top of my list.'* – his dad's words appeared from nowhere, springing Gabe back to being eight years old and worried about his dad suddenly being at home.

'But who'll protect the country when you're here, Pops?'

'Plenty of other men and women, Gabriel – there wasn't just me on those front lines. A lot of people go to fight for what they believe in, and some don't come home. I needed to make sure I was coming home, to you, Anna, and your mother.'

'When I grow up, Pops, I want to be just like you.'

'You'll grow into your own man, boy. But you're making damn good headway from where I'm sitting. Not too big to give your pops a hug yet, are you?'

Gabe smiled at the memory – he remembered flinging himself into his dad's arms and telling him he'd never be too big to hug. *Always kept that promise.* His heart cracked a little, and a tear trickled down his face. *I'm sorry I didn't keep you safe, Shotgun. I promise I will keep Paige safe – no matter what happens.*

Turning his attention back to the computer screens, he worked in a comfortable silence for a while.

Empty warehouse, Fallow Industrial Estate, Fallow

Joey Mendino couldn't stop shaking – both with fear and a large amount of anger. *Who the hell does Al Graham think he is?*

Shoving me in a trunk like I'm nothing. His thoughts were all bluster, however, and he knew it. His wrists were secured behind his back with handcuffs – the kind the police use that tighten when a person struggles. No way to pick those locks even if he had access to his lock kit, which he definitely did not since it was tucked away in the glove box of his car.

Think, asshole, think! How the hell are you gonna get out of this?

That said, it was harder said than done to think of a resolve when he was lying trussed up like a Thanksgiving turkey in the trunk of an SUV.

Joey had seen Graham's goons grab his laptop bag from his car before they'd closed the trunk, plunging him into darkness. *They don't have the password – they can't access jack shit.* He groaned loudly, remembering Al Graham's vicious nature – he'd heard the stories before he'd taken the job. Even done some research on Graham Industries – that Graham was a man with his fingers in a lot of pies was evident. *Should've done more, should've at least had a viable escape plan. Every idiot knows to have a failsafe. Way to fail, asshole.*

The SUV pulled to a slow stop, and the sound of metal grinding reached Joey's ears. He cocked his head to listen. Then the car moved forward at a snail's pace, and a clanking recurred. A feeling of foreboding overtook Joey, and he knew that wherever they'd ended up, wasn't a good place.

He acknowledged too, that he was in shit up to his neck. There would be no last-minute rescue, no one to rush to his aid. Instead of finding a hot beach somewhere, with an even hotter babe in a bikini to hang on his arm, he'd never get the chance to spend the money Al Graham had already paid him.

Whatever this was, it would result in his death. He was sure of it.

He steeled himself as the trunk was lifted open, and glared daggers at the over-muscled sidekick of Al's who dragged him from the car.

I'm not giving them anything. Not one little thing that will help them.

His determination was commendable, but even through his inner strength and cockiness, he knew that the more likely scenario was that the information would be pulled from him, strand by tiny strand.

George pushed him down into a chair in the middle of what looked like a large warehouse – it was empty, and the thick layer of dust on the floor told him it had been that way for a long time.

'Are you going to make it easy on yourself and just tell me what I want to know?' Al's voice was low.

If Joey hadn't known better, he'd have thought Al was being nice. *As if that prick knows how to be nice.*

In defiance, he remained stoically silent but made sure his eyes relayed the message he was thinking very clearly. *Fuck you.*

Al stepped closer, unbuttoning his shirt cuffs and rolling them up his arms slowly. Then he unclipped his Rolex from his wrist and handed it backward to George who pocketed it without word.

Taking it off so he doesn't get blood on it. Prick!

Waiting until Al's shiny Oxfords were within reach, Joey pooled his saliva and spat at them, taking some satisfaction as the bubbly globules covered the toes of both feet.

Tension simmered in the oversized room – Joey was watching Al intently, waiting for a reaction. He didn't hear the footfall behind him until hands came around the side of his face and snapped duct tape in place roughly. *To stop me screaming as they cut me up. BASTARDS!*

Now that Joey couldn't speak even if he wanted to, Al raised his fist and slammed it into the side of Joey's head. His neck cracked loudly with the movement, and he did his best not to groan or react, knowing there'd be plenty more where that was coming from.

Two more rapid punches from Al to either side of Joey's face had his ears ringing, and stars sparkled in his vision. He shook his head, trying to force them away.

'No?' sneered Al, bending close to his face. 'No more, please? No more punches? What exactly are you saying no at Mendino? Oh, wait, I forgot. You only get to speak on my terms now. And Al says, be quiet.'

He stepped back and punched again, so hard Joey was certain his cheekbone had cracked. Blood poured down his face, and one of his eyes swelled instantly, impairing what little vision he had. *Maybe you should just talk – tell him all the stuff on Beth and let him get on with it?* But it wouldn't make a difference. He wouldn't make it out of here alive. But he'd be damned if he gave all his work up – for exactly nothing in return. Because he knew from the look in Al's eyes, that now he'd started, there would be no quick death. Even if he told, Al would draw it out and make him pay for not finding Beth sooner, or passing over the information quicker, or *fucking whatever – whatever I do ends in death. I'm not making it any easier for him.*

Bland P.I.R office

Deacon burst through the door into the back office, swearing loudly.

'Becca and Grayson have lost the SUV. The industrial estate is massive, and the driver clocked them tailing on entry – losing them was intentional.'

'Shit, thanks, Deacon. Tell them to wait near the entrance to relay last location to the cops attending. I've already sent everything we have over to Kyle. To be fair, Mendino isn't our case, Paige is. Kyle will keep us updated regardless.'

Deacon nodded and left the office again.

'Dave?' Gabe said, hitting the dial for Dave's desk. 'Becca and Grayson have lost the SUV they were following – any way to get an update as to Al Graham's current whereabouts?'

'I can't ping his cell. We don't have enough to do it legally, and he's got several listed under his business, so I'm not sure which is his. It's not listed on the website. I can't even connect with the SUV GPS without the license plates or VIN number. I'll try calling the headquarters address and see if I can get in contact with him that way – I'll say I'm from a company wanting a quote for exportation of goods.'

'Okay, keep me updated. Also look into whether he's got any buildings in the Farrow area. It's a tenuous link, but he might have something in the vicinity that he's using as a base location. Hack his credit cards too. I want to know if any recent transactions pop up in our area.'

Dave acknowledged his requests, and the receiver clicked in Gabe's ear.

He sat for a moment wondering if there was anything he'd missed. The only other thing was Paige. Maybe she could identify the grainy images from the dashcam. *Maybe not, though – they're not exactly clear.* He knew there was only one way to find out – he sent the stills he'd taken off the footage to his email and made his way through to the main office.

'I'm heading back to the cabin to show Paige the images from the dashcam. When you're finished whatever tasks you're on, get yourselves off home. It's late – you all need food and rest. Back here at zero-six-hundred. Everyone kept in the loop, please – don't need anyone going off half-cocked. Deacon, tell Becca and Grayson to get their report done ASAP and emailed over when they get back.'

Nods all round was the go-ahead he needed to leave the office. He knew his team well enough to know they'd all do what he said. Glancing at his watch, he shook his head – time passed far too quickly when he was busy.

He put his foot down a little, suddenly feeling the need to get back to Paige. He'd left her asleep after she'd taken her meds– likelihood was she'd sleep all night. People did that when they were healing – not him so much, but most people. Gabe hoped she wasn't in the minority like he was and would still be dead to the world when he landed.

Frowning at his mind's choice of words, he floored the pedal and grinned in satisfaction as his engine responded and his speedometer went up rapidly.

Chapter Sixteen

Empty warehouse, Fallow Industrial Estate

Al Graham rubbed his bruised and bleeding knuckles thoughtfully. He hadn't thought for one minute that Mendino would hold out as long as he had, not without giving up what he knew about Beth anyway. It had taken nearly an hour of intermittent beating to finally claw out of him that he'd placed a tracker on a truck that he knew Beth was seen in. *Knew she wasn't the type to be able to evade me without help. Fucking bitch.*

Mendino had also eventually given up the password to the laptop – George was sitting hammering at it with his fat sausage fingers even as Al stood to one side nursing his sore hands.

'He's right, boss. The app for tracking the truck has picked up a location as a remote setting – possibly a cabin or some such thing. There's no guarantee whoever owns the truck has Beth with him – or even if he's anything more than a lift somewhere. We can track him through the night and catch up with him tomorrow if you'd prefer. It's been a long day, and I'm guessing you could use some rest? If you want to go tonight that's fine too, though, boss.'

'No – tomorrow will be soon enough. I've waited six months to catch up with that bitch again, another few hours won't matter. Finish it with Mendino – I don't want his body left here, our guys move in next week to start renovations.'

'No problem, boss. There's a river out back, we'll dump him in there.'

Al waved his hand in their general direction before heading back to the garage section of the warehouse where they'd left the car. Hopping in the back, he put some ice from the compact freezer between the two front seats inside a towel and wrapped it around his sore knuckles. The less swelling the better. *I'll be needing this fist the second I find Beth – she won't be getting away this time. I was so fucking close to getting my ledger back six months ago – she'd almost broken. She will not escape me again.*

A few minutes later, his men clambered into the car beside him.

'All done, boss. He won't even be talking to the fishes – gave him a Colombian necktie to avoid any suspicion falling on us.'

This was why George was the best right-hand man he could ever have wanted. Al would have just slit Mendino's throat or shot him and ditched the gun. He'd never have thought to place blame elsewhere. Being able to research the ins and outs of local drug cartel kill methods was just another reason George was invaluable.

'Remind me when we get back that you're due for a raise, George.'

George flashed him a single grin, his mouth tight with the motion. Smiling was not something George did very often, and for good reason. Al spared a glance at the scar that went from one side of George's mouth to his earlobe. *Maybe one day I'll ask him how he got it.*

Al rested his head against the back of the chair and closed his eyes, seeing Beth's awful curly hair, the bitter-cold blue of her eyes, and overly rotund figure. *I'll kill you myself – make you understand once and for all, you don't get to leave me. Ever.*

Gabe's cabin

Paige stirred and slowly opened her eyes. She still felt groggy but better for the sleep, except for the throbbing in her arm anyway. Using the other arm, she pushed herself into a sitting position and flicked the switch for the lamp beside her.

She saw the note illuminated; she frowned, trying to recall what, if anything, Gabe had said before she'd ended up in bed. *How did I end up in bed anyway? I was in the lounge, wasn't I?* Figuring she must've been so close to sleep she wasn't registering anything, she picked the note up.

You probably won't remember but you were dropping after you'd eaten dinner. If you leave the bedroom, you'll need to disable the alarm – the code is 24368211. There's more food in the fridge, and I left the coffee pot on warm for you. I won't be too long – just heading to the office to sort some stuff out. See you soon, Gabe x

Paige couldn't stop the small Cheshire cat grin glancing over her lips. *He signed it with a kiss.*

For a second, she allowed herself to hope it meant something then played it down, telling herself that he was probably just being nice. *He probably signs every note he writes someone that way. I do – heck, half the population is obsessed with Xs and emojis.*

Getting to her feet, she read the code again, committing it to memory, then opened the door and headed down the few steps to the hall. The alarm system bleeped at her, getting louder in tempo after a count of five. Not knowing how much of a lag it had before activation, she quickly pressed the numbers to disarm, and the glowing red light clicked to green.

She stilled as she heard wheels spin on the gravel outside, wondering whether to unlock the door. The question answered itself, however – there were no keys she could see anywhere near her. She stepped back toward the coat rack; she opted to let him enter at his own pace. Her cheeks flushed what must be a deep red, and she registered her legs were bare – she was standing in her panties and T-shirt. He must've taken her jeans off to make her more comfortable. *Oh crap.* She turned to run back to the bedroom, but the door swung open behind her, and after a millisecond pause, she felt arms around her waist and stopped running.

It was then that panic set in – she hadn't even checked if it was Gabe! She'd just disarmed the alarm and wanted to hide her embarrassment. *Idiot!*

The arms round her waist loosened before she reacted.

'You okay, darlin'?' Gabe's voice was soft – he'd obviously noticed her tense up under his touch.

Paige turned, and her breath caught. She paused, taking in the view. He was standing in the doorway, the porch light setting a glow round his head that was almost akin to an angel's halo. His eyes were searching, worried. *He thought he'd hurt me – no, no, no.*

She stepped forward before any doubt could crawl into her mind. Paige stopped a hair's breadth from him. Her eyes were level with his chin, and she glanced up, her gaze captured by his eyes which darkened instinctively with desire, and *what else* ... no other words formulated in her brain. She was caught.

Gabe's head lowered millimeter by millimeter until his lips were almost touching hers. Then he stopped. Confused, Paige gazed into eyes, searching for answers as to why he'd stop.

Vulnerability – that's what the look was. He's not sure about this – not sure because he's a good man and this isn't what he does.

Wanting to put him at ease, to make him understand that kissing her was what she wanted and wasn't wrong, she leaned forward, keeping her eyes open and focused on him. Her lips connected with his and, not allowing him to pull back, she deepened the kiss, her tongue darting between his teeth and connecting with his. Her joints turned to liquid, and she leaned into the kiss even more. She moved her hand around his waist and settled at the small of his back, but she needed more. Lowering it, she grabbed his butt cheek, grinding his groin into her core, groaning when his erection pressed against her

With a growl, Gabe shoved the door closed with his foot and dropped the bag he was carrying, plunging his hands deep into the loose curls of dark hair on her head. He plunged his tongue into her mouth, tasting her, letting her taste him. She'd never had anyone kiss her like Gabe was, and her body responded instantly. What had started as a pool of desire was now a blazing inferno. She moaned into his mouth, the rough denim of his jeans causing friction – it wasn't enough. She needed more. She winced a little as his movement grazed her bruises, but it was fleeting. Shivers of excitement and anticipation skittered over her skin.

He untangled his fingers from her hair and gripped her backside, lifting her gently, even in the middle of something so passionate, taking care that he wasn't hurting her. He settled her core right at the top of his erection. Moving slowly, he positioned her back against the wall and thrust his hips toward her. She moaned her disappointment when his lips left hers, but then they were on her neck, nipping lightly, his tongue swiping her flesh. Paige didn't register him stopping until his hand slipped up her T-shirt, his rough palm covered her breast, then his fingers tweaked her nipple, just hard enough to make her gasp.

She bucked against him; his finger slipped beneath her pantie line and was thrust inside her. She was on the verge of orgasm already, and he'd barely done anything. Determined not to come so quickly this time, she used her chin to maneuver his face back up to hers, capturing his mouth in a long deep kiss. His finger was joined by another, his hand pushing farther into her than she would have thought possible. All thoughts of keeping her orgasm at bay flew from her mind, and she cried out, her inner muscles gripping his fingers tightly. His lips were on hers again, and the only coherent thought Paige had was that she needed him fully inside her.

Her fingers clawed at the buttons on his jeans, and she groaned her frustration. 'Who the fuck has buttons on jeans – give me an easy zip any day!'

He withdrew his hand from her, and it joined hers, batting her hand out of the way and yanking hard –buttons all came loose together. His cock sprang free, and her hand encased it, and she moved up and down urgently.

Gabe covered her hand with his and stopped her. 'Whoa – darlin', wait. We need a condom, but if you keep touching me like that there won't be time to move, let alone roll one on.'

Ever the gentleman …

'I'm on the pill – and I'm clean.'

'I am too – get checked every three months the same as the rest of the team. You sure?' His last words were ground out because her hand had begun the motion once more. Up and down his length, like the purest form of torture known to man.

Paige kissed him, giving him the go-ahead without needing words. He pulled edge of her panties aside, and he positioned himself beneath her. The head nudged inside her folds. She cried out again, and he sank inside her fully. He paused like that for a minute, plainly giving her time to adjust, but it was time she didn't need or want. She tried to move her hips, exasperated when she couldn't.

Gabe took control, angling himself so he didn't put pressure on her arm and pumping his hips slowly, in and out. Paige had never felt anything like this before – ever. It was raw and natural, and within seconds another orgasm started to build. 'Oh god, Gabe, I can't …'

He withdrew and thrust in again, and she came apart, crying out loudly, her head glancing off the wall as she threw it back. Gabe tensed in front of her, and knowing he was about to join her, she clenched her muscles around his length, and he cried out when he came, pumping in and out a few more times and groaning his release before dropping his head to hers and kissing her again.

'I've never had a "welcome home" like that before,' he said breathlessly against her lips, cracking her a rueful grin.

His eyes grew serious, and he pulled out of her, adjusting her panties to capture any leakage. She was surprised at the gesture and smiled at him, suddenly embarrassed.

'I'm … '

'Please don't say you're sorry – I shouldn't have let that progress – you're injured for one, but damn, you caught me by surprise, and I'm absolutely not sorry it happened. You are something else, Paige. I've had women, probably more than I should mention, but I've never felt like this.'

'Me neither,' she said.

'I shouldn't have done it, though – you're injured – I've hurt you, haven't I?'

'No, my arm is throbbing, but it's been doing that since I woke up. I can't believe we just had sex against the wall. I didn't even think that was possible – I thought it was the stuff romance writers made up! Thank you, for letting me manipulate you into something I know you weren't convinced about. Just so you know I'm not … expecting anything. I know I'm just a client. But thank you – you gave me something I didn't even know I needed.'

Paige untangled herself from his arms and made her way back up the stairs to the bedroom and then into the adjoining bathroom. She closed the door and sat on the toilet, suddenly mortified at what she'd done. *Crap – I practically forced him into it. He said earlier he didn't want to, and I went ahead and plowed on regardless. What if it wasn't as good for him as it was for me? Oh god, I'm an idiot.*

Gabe felt like an absolute dick – he'd let her thank him for sex and then walk to the sanctuary of the bedroom without even saying a word. It had been the best sex of his life, and *she'd* thanked *him*.

What the actual fuck – are you on another planet or what!

He needed to let her know that she didn't have to thank him for anything – what had happened had brought every wall of restraint he'd ever felt crashing down around him – knowing he couldn't leave her thinking she'd forced him into anything, he headed up to the bedroom and opened the door without knocking.

He could see the light on under the door of the en suite, so he hovered outside.

How do I do this? How do I make her understand I wanted to respect boundaries but that those boundaries came crashing down the second I met her in the cemetery?

It felt like a lifetime ago – he had always said he wasn't the relationship type, still wasn't sure he was to be honest, he didn't know the first thing about making a woman happy. But for the first time in his life, he felt like he wanted to learn.

He raised his fist and knocked at the bathroom door gently.

'Paige, can I come in?'

He heard something that sounded like a sob behind the door and pushed it open.

She was sitting on the toilet with her head in her hand, hiding her face from his view. Her shoulders shook almost imperceptibly.

Kneeling, he tipped her chin up so her eyes met his. Tears glistened in her eyes, and he knew without doubt, that tears were something he never wanted her to experience again, especially not tears over something that had been so magical.

'Talk to me, Paige. Tell me why you're trying to hide away from me.'

'Because I'm a slut – I all but forced you to have sex with me out there. I've never acted that way – not even once. You must think I'm …'

'Hold it right there – you think you forced me to have sex with you?' Gabe couldn't stop the incredulousness in his voice. 'Darlin', I shouldn't have to tell you this – my actions should have said it for me, but there is no way in hell that you forced me into anything I didn't want to do, and you are absolutely, definitely *not* a slut. I wanted that as much as you did – you're all I've thought about since you ran into me in the cemetery. Now I know I'm not very good at showing that, I've always thought women deserved better than what I could offer. I still do in some ways. But, darlin', I have never brought any woman back to this cabin, not even in relation to a case, I've never made love to a woman against a wall, and I've never, ever, experienced an orgasm that rocked me to my heels like that. And all of that is because of you. Whatever this thing between us is, it's been building since day one, and I get the feeling we're both a little in awe of that. But don't feel embarrassed or ashamed over what happened – I promise I wanted it as much as you, and I don't make promises easily.'

Paige stared at him, obviously a little shocked at his openness.

Hell, I'm as shocked as you are – I've never needed anyone like I needed you.

Gabe leaned forward and caught her mouth in a tender kiss.

'I think we could both use a shower and some sleep, don't you?'

He laughed aloud at the suggestive look she gave him.

'Hope you mean together? I might need your help.' Her voice was still a little shy, and he instantly grew hard again.

'I doubt that very much, you're a force to be reckoned with. But yes, my intention was together.' He pulled the hand she offered gently until she was standing, gazing up at him, and his breath whooshed out. He bent and put his lips on hers once more whilst turning the shower on with the hand that wasn't cupping her butt.

Chapter Seventeen

Gabe's cabin

Paige stirred and stretched slightly, feeling the body next to her stir in response. Her eyes flew open and connected with Gabe's – *I swear I could drown just in the look of those eyes. I've never seen anyone have such cloudy gray coloring.*

'Morning,' she said softly, leaning forward and placing a kiss beside each of his eyes.

'Morning, darlin'.'

She shivered. Before Gabe, she'd hated any endearments, all those people who said love, sweetie, and petal at the end of a sentence had always grated on her – probably something to do with Al always calling her by one: peaches. She still shuddered at the word. But with Gabe, 'darlin'' rolled naturally off his tongue, and she soaked it in as if the word was designed solely for her. It was confusing – she wanted not to like any endearment, but he made it special.

Gabe raised his head, putting his lips to hers in a brief but soft kiss, before removing himself from underneath her. He pulled on a pair of lounge pants he had draped over a chair in the corner and held his T-shirt out to her.

Paige took it, blushing lightly. After all they'd done, her being naked shouldn't embarrass her, but it had.

'Here – put this on. It's not like anyone can see anyway, but my T-shirts are long length and will cover your … lady bits.'

A burst of laughter escaped from Paige's mouth, and she accepted the T-shirt and shrugged it over her head, her splinted arm secure inside. 'Lady bits?'

Gabe shrugged and grinned. 'Everyone calls it something different. I didn't want to be offensive.'

'So you went with lady bits?' Paige chuckled, following him out of the bedroom door. 'For the record, I don't care what you call it. Anything but lady bits is fine – that just sounds like something my granddaddy would have said.'

'What do you call it then?' His voice turned rough, and he glanced back over his shoulder at her, desire sparking instantly.

'Horny much! Down boy.' She giggled and slapped his behind gently.

This feels so weird – I've never been comfortable enough to have this flirtation thing work – if that's even what this is. If I'd said anything like this with Al …

She felt her expression darken and knew Gabe had seen the change too as he stopped and turned to face her.

'Don't.' He took her hand in his and continued. 'Don't visit that place your mind just went – your ex is a dick – a dangerous dick who we will be taking care of one way or another. I'm not, nor would I ever be, offended or annoyed at what you just said. Not ever. I know I never meant for us to … for *this* to happen, but that was never for one second because I wasn't attracted to you. I will never hurt you, Paige, not intentionally anyway, and if ever I do it unintentionally, we will talk it through and it wouldn't happen that way again. Understand me?'

'Sorry.' Paige paused. 'I was actually thinking if I'd said anything or done anything like that with Al it would have ended in a beating. I didn't mean to imply you were like that – I absolutely know you're nothing like that. I was thinking how it was great that I'm so natural with you after such a short time. It was a comparison in your favor, trust me – I haven't seen or heard anything that places you anywhere near Al. He's an obnoxious, violent, arrogant prick – you are … everything that isn't those things. I wish I'd never met him – life would have been so different.'

Her voice turned wistful, yet more tears filled her eyes.

Gabe swiped a thumb underneath them both, catching the tears before they fell.

'I know you haven't dealt with all the shit you've been through yet, all the injuries, seeing that dick kill a man, losing your daughter, and god knows what else. And I know the day will come when you will be ready to deal with it all.' Gabe stalled whatever she was going to say by pressing his lips to hers for a second, then continued. 'I'm here for you when you need me to be. But please, until then, don't shed tears for *him*. He doesn't deserve anything but a six-by-four cell, and that's being kinder than I want to be. I will be doing everything in my power to make sure he gets nowhere near you, and I will make sure he gets that cell he deserves.'

'I know you will. In case I forget to say it later, thank you, Gabe. For everything you have done and are doing.'

'Okay, we're done with the heart-to-heart for now, unless you want to continue which is also fine. Toast or cereal for breakfast, then we need to head into the office for a briefing at six. You good to go? I'm not rushing you – you're welcome to stay here if you'd prefer, but I thought you might want to hear all the updates?'

'Getting there for six is good with me.'

They ate in comfortable silence and were in the truck and ready to go within twenty minutes.

Bland P.I.R office

'Gabe?' Kyle's voice was curt and straight to the point as Gabe picked up his phone.

'Yeah, it's me, what's up?

'We've found a body, a floater in the river to the back of Fallow Industrial Estate. From the file you sent over, it looks like Mendino.'

Gabe sighed. He'd suspected a body would turn up but half hoped the police would catch up to the perps before it had happened.

'He'd been given a Colombian necktie as a parting gift. This job you're working have anything to do with the Mervana Cartel?'

'No – no links to drugs at all that I'm aware of. Anything else suggest he ran with a rival drug cartel?'

'Nothing I've turned up – if there was, you'd have picked it up on your analysis, I'm sure. We've hit a wall with leads to the black SUV. I've got CCTV incoming from the industrial estate, but you know how those units work – if something breaks, it's not fixable until another ten things break.'

'Yeah, I remember. It wouldn't kill these people to invest in protecting their livelihood a little better.'

'You're not wrong. I need to go, but keep me updated, Gabe, I don't like the fact these assholes are pissing in my yard. The sooner this is all resolved the better. For everyone.'

'Agreed. Watch your six, Kyle, your guys too. If you get any leads on the SUV, hit me up – you'd have to get SWAT in from North Hampton, and that would take far longer than it will take me to mobilize a team. I'm betting they had more weapons stored than was evident on the dashcam. So please, don't go in half-cocked. Use us – it's what we're here for.'

'I know when I'm outmanned, Gabe. But I will speak to you soon. Watch your backs too.'

Gabe jumped to his feet and instantly commanded the attention of everyone in the room, including Paige who was sitting not far from him. She'd looked at the stills but couldn't confirm that it was Al Graham and his men. Two of the men matched Graham and his sidekick, George's general build and appearance, but without certainty it wasn't prudent to presume. Before he started speaking to his team, he asked Paige to head into the kitchen – it wouldn't do her any good to hear all the blood and gore his team would be talking about

'Mendino's body has been found floating the Fallow River – he was given a Colombian necktie – probably not linked to the Mervana Cartel despite this being their MO. Ring any bells for anyone else? Thinking about the info we've got on file relating to this case, obviously.'

Mitch was the one who answered – he was currently undercover with one of the rival cartels. What Mitch didn't know about gangs wasn't worth knowing. Gabe had no doubt Mitch's information would be accurate.

'I've not had any dealings with the Mervana crew for a few weeks – word on the street is their leader, Carlito, is ill, to the point of almost off this realm. There's fighting in the ranks for who'll be taking his place. Their concentration is focused in-house currently. I'd say it could be the Bangers – their style is bloody, but they're not into making murder look like someone else's work – they like all the credit, no way they'd pass the buck for a kill like Mendino. He's pretty well known when it all comes down to it, so it would have been a relatively high-value hit, more so reputation wise.

'There is a new crew moving in on the territories – don't know too much about them – they're into using snake venom to disable people, but again, I can't see them averting blame. They're all for the glory at the minute cos they're still building a rep. The Denesiders, who I'm UC with at the minute, are more into hooking up bad ecstasy and coke in the local clubs – they have little interaction with any of the others, and I'm pretty sure Freddie would have let drop if they'd hit Mendino. I shouldn't be under with them much longer – I've uploaded pretty much all the intel I can to the DEA. I'm just waiting on finding out the contact Freddie's getting the coke from – I'm at a meet tonight with him and the seller. Once that's done, I'll be handing it all off to Supervisory Agent in Charge, Henderson, and getting the hell out of dodge. Please say we're done with the DEA for now?'

Gabe nodded slowly. 'Yeah, nothing else in the wings with them at the minute – the fact you're under was a favor to Henderson. He owes me one now, and we all know those kind of tickets come in handy to cash in at times. Thank you for doing the deed, Mitch, it's appreciated.'

Mitch nodded and then headed back out of the rear entrance as silently as he'd entered.

'Anyone else?'

They all shook their heads.

'Anything else on the SUV or any potential identities for the males who were packing?'

Again, everyone shook their heads. It was common knowledge Al Graham had numerous black SUVs, but then so did half of America. Gabe tried not to let his frustration show, but he was pissed – all the knowledge and technology they had and they still weren't able to narrow the suspect pool from 'could be anyone' to 'could be one of a few.'

He made his way into the kitchen and found Paige sitting at the table there, silently wringing her hands, her expression troubled.

'What's up, darlin'. Talk to me.'

'What's a Colombian necktie?'

Gabe paused, startled. *She can't have heard me talking to the team from in here, can she?*

'I eavesdropped – sorry. I know I shouldn't have. It doesn't sound like a very nice thing, a Colombian necktie. Bet it's not silk and cotton.'

'It's not a very nice thing – you'll not like the answer, so I'd prefer not to tell you unless you really want to know.' Gabe kept his answer short and to the point but frowned at her and spoke again. 'How much did you overhear, Paige? I'm a little pissed you thought it was okay to eavesdrop to be honest – you know what we do here. Confidentiality is key – you didn't overhear anything not pertinent to your own case as it happens, but what if you'd overhead sensitive information that if people knew you were aware of, would result in danger? They could come after you and torture you until you gave it up? What if it was information you knew that could put someone else in danger?'

She looked devastated, and Gabe gentled his tone.

'Sorry for sounding pissed, but this is for your own protection as well as that of my team. You could be in danger if you know things you shouldn't about the cases we're working on.'

Paige knew listening in was wrong – she'd known it the second she'd started doing it and had pulled back after the first few sentences. *He doesn't know that, though, does he? Doesn't make it right, but tell him what you heard.*

'You're right – I didn't think initially. The only thing I overheard was you asking about this Colombian necktie thingy – I moved into the kitchen after that because I realized what you were saying could contain confidential information. I'm sorry, Gabe. It won't happen again.'

'Okay. I know you're out of your depth here – you need someone with you which I've totally got covered, but it's not practical for you to be in the office with me all the time. It'll be driving you insane for one. How about we head over to the shelter – you could do with some time with Mags, and I know she'll be worried about you. I need to speak to Jacko anyway. Afterwards, if you want to, I mean, and there's no pressure because I'm totally happy leaving you at the shelter if that's what you want, but my parents have invited me and Anna over for dinner – and asked me to ask if you wanted to come too. The team are running what leads there are on the Mendino killing as well as your case. There's no harm in taking a few hours to visit if it's something you'd like.'

He didn't look certain about extending the invitation for whatever reason, but she figured it was probably because he didn't ask clients to meet his parents.

Oh god! He wants me to meet his parents? Get a grip – you're not thirteen heading home with Tommy whathisface this time. Gabe's just being nice because he was going anyway.

'That actually sounds good. I do want to see Mags – and the rest ... um, can I see how I feel after speaking to Mags?'

Paige couldn't believe what he'd said – never in a month of Sundays would she have thought it was a good idea to meet parents just a few days after meeting Gabe. *I mean sure, we had sex – fantastic, amazing sex.* She shivered, recalling the rough feel of the wall against her shoulders while Gabe held her steady and pumped his cock so deep into her, she'd never wanted to release him. A blush spread across her cheeks. Nerves fluttered throughout her body – it was a big step, for her especially. She never seemed to react well publicly. *So talk to Mags before you go – see what she says. He's not forcing you.*

Gabe smiled and nodded. 'Come on then, darlin', let's go see Mags.'

Brannigan's Women's Shelter

Gabe pulled the truck up to the gates and entered the code, surprised when the gates didn't open immediately. A dull buzz sounded from the code entry system, indicating he'd made an error. He frowned, trying again, and got the same result.

Hitting dial on Jacko's number, he waited while it rang several times without answer.

Alert now, he tried the landline for Mags.

No answer again.

Dread settled in his gut. *What the hell is going on?* He was just on the verge of reversing and ramming the gate fast enough to crack the hinges, when the front door opened and Jacko stepped outside, followed quickly by Jason, the young lad Gabe had read to what felt like an eternity ago.

Jacko froze when he recognized Gabe in his truck, and made his way down the drive and hit the button on the interior wall to open the gates.

'Why didn't you answer your phone? Why didn't the code work?' Gabe ground out, his adrenaline still in overdrive.

'My phone? It didn't ring?' Jacko took his phone out of his pocket and examined it, then groaned. 'Jason, were you playing with my phone when I left it on the table at breakfast?'

Jason grinned then giggled and ran inside the house.

'Sorry, boss. I didn't realize the little monkey had put it on silent. As to the code, Mags changed it this morning. She mustn't have had chance to send you the new one. I'll text it when we're inside.'

'Okay – where's Mags?'

'Dealing with a new intake – came in an hour ago. Didn't know it was so busy here. It's a good job she has such a big house.'

Gabe's adrenaline ebbed, and he nodded his acknowledgement before moving the vehicle through the gates so it was secure.

Rain started to fall as he parked up and helped Paige out of the truck. Puddles were rapidly forming with the deluge. They all rushed to the house to avoid getting soaked.

Chapter Eighteen

Watson Hinkle Hotel, Glebe Road, Fallow

'Where are we at with tracking Beth's location?' Al yawned and stretched his arms above his head, before shooting one of his best tell-me-or-die looks at Bruce.

Despite that, though, it was George who answered. 'The vehicle tracker just pinged at a house on the outskirts of Rhododendron – seems to be staying in that area pretty much. It moved from the rural location early this morning then onto Rhododendron Main Street then over to this house. I Google Mapped it, and it's a residential area. I'd bet my incoming pay rise that's where Beth will be.'

'We'll head out in an hour. I need a shit and a shower before I do anything else. Ring down to reception and order some croissants and fresh coffee. I need the hit today. That bed was crap.'

'I'll advise the management regarding the bed. Coffee will be here and waiting after your shower.'

Used to getting things done and everything he wanted, nodding, Al made his way through the penthouse suite to the luxurious bathroom to the rear.

Never fear, Beth, or Paige, or whatever the hell you're going by now. I'll catch up with you soon – and prove to you that leaving me and stealing my ledger was the last thing you'll ever do. Al had spent hours the night before scouring all the information they'd recovered from Mendino's laptop and from the man himself. *Before he'd been disposed of. People will learn one day that I'm the boss – there are consequences to being a dick to me.*

Brannigan's Women's Shelter

Paige had spent a good couple of hours catching up with Mags and assisting her with the new intake – all the rooms at the shelter were full now. A sudden stab of guilt poked at her that other women wouldn't be able to get Mags' special brand of help because she was taking up a room there. *Maybe I could speak to Gabe about staying in a hotel or something – it would make it easier on Mags.* But then she remembered, yet again, that she didn't have any money. *I need to sort this shit out – I need to report it all and hand over the evidence and then maybe, just maybe I can start living again instead of just existing.*

She was a little surprised at her newfound trickle of enthusiasm for life. But when she thought about everything that had happened, her mood dipped. Thoughts of a curly-haired child with a toothy grin jumped to the forefront. It hadn't been two minutes since she'd thought she couldn't live without Diana. And all of a sudden, she saw … *What? A future – without my daughter in it?*

She exhaled a long breath, contemplating. It had been a little over two years since Diana had died – it still felt like Paige's chest was being torn in two whenever she thought about her. She still couldn't face thinking about how Diana had been cruelly ripped away from her. Those memories were still locked away tight. But it was that feeling of being torn in two that had always made Paige believe that she couldn't live without her daughter – but today, she noticed that the split in her chest, though still there and painful, didn't make her feel quite that way. *Maybe there is hope for the future – maybe it doesn't have to end in me joining my beautiful girl. Maybe I can ... survive?*

Paige made her way back down to the kitchen – she felt like she needed to hug Mags, give her some reassurance that she was doing okay. For the first time in a long time.

Jacko was already in there with Mags, standing on a chair with a screwdriver in hand, fixing the cupboard door that had been loose for as long as Paige had been staying there.

'Mags, can I speak to you for a minute?'

'Of course you can, child. Come on, let's go and sit in the garden for a bit. The rain's gone, and it looks glorious out there now.'

Paige followed Mags out to the side of the house where a swing seat had been set up, somewhat secluded but still with a view of the gates. *Mags is always so security conscious. I wonder what happened to make her that way. I can't believe I've never asked.*

'I wanted to say thank you. Without your help and support I'd never have got to anywhere near the stage I am right now.'

'You're ready to fight?' Mags couldn't hide the undertone of pride in her voice.

'Yes. You've let me stay here for months – you've given me money when I had none, and fed me, even clothed me. Yet you've never asked why I'm here. You instinctively knew I wasn't ready to talk and that if I did, I'd end up running, didn't you?'

'Didn't take a rocket scientist to work that out, Paige – I've been doing this a long time.'

'How come? What made you wake up one day and decide to run a shelter for vulnerable and at-risk women?'

Mags glanced at Paige, possibly assessing whether to tell her anything, but she figured it was more likely Mags was thrown by the question. *Has no one ever asked her before?*

For a minute, Paige thought Mags wouldn't answer, but the older woman took her hands, pressed a peck of a kiss on her cheek, then said, 'Well, it started with my dad – horrible man, he was. My mother was an ill woman – psychiatric problems that weren't assessed back then like they are now. She didn't see anything but my dad, well, let's just say that when I blossomed into a teenager, he *saw* me.'

Paige sat horrified, her mouth dropping into a soft 'O.'

'I finally stole enough money to make a run for the hills and that's exactly what I did. I ran – even when the police took me back three times, I still upped and ran. Eventually people stopped looking. I found a little job in a diner washing dishes in exchange for food. Life happened – most of it not good – and I ended up with a man just like my daddy, had four miscarriages due to his beatings, and eventually broke free. After a lot more soul-searching and finding myself, I realized that no woman should ever have to put up with that kind of behavior and feel like they can't escape. Then I got word that my mom had passed away – cancer – and left me all of her estate. I hadn't even known she came from a wealthy family – we never had any money spare as I grew up. Of course, I know now that my mom was savvy enough when she first got involved with my dad not to let him see her real monetary worth – whatever problems she had, she'd kept the money from him so I would have a future. And I just knew that the money had to be used so other women could see they had a future too. That's the short version of how I set the shelter up anyway.'

'Wow – Mags, I had no idea. I've known you are amazingly brave and all for taking care after us, but the amount of pain you suffered to get to this point? You're truly an inspiration. Thank you. Seriously – even without that history you're awesome.'

'You want to talk to me about how you ended up here now?'

Mags had shared her story, as painful as Paige knew it must've been. It was time for Paige to open up.

King Street, outside Brannigan's Women's Shelter

The black SUV pulled up on the street near the gates to the shelter.

'You sure this is the right place? Beth has no money – no way could she afford to rent this place. Even if she's found a job, she's qualified to do jack shit. Definitely nothing that would pay the amount needed to rent this joint. Maybe she's whoring herself out?' Al had no qualms about his words – as far as he was concerned, every single one was true.

'It shows the exact longitude and latitude for this location from when the car stopped earlier this morning. I did say there's nothing to prove she's here. Maybe this is just a relative or something for the owner of the car. It's been at that remote place too many times for that not to be home. We should scope out all of the stops the tracker shows – build a better idea of how it's even connected. We should have questioned Mendino for longer – I'm certain his laptop doesn't hold all of the information, and it's highly likely he didn't tell us everything before we ended him.'

'Shit!' cursed Al, clenching his fists at his sides. He'd already known what George had said, but sitting here, outside a large house that rivalled his own for security, Al didn't need to hear it explained or like what was said.

'Drive – we'll scope out the other locations. We might just hit pay dirt.'

Bruce, the driver, coasted past the gates as Al stared out of the window. He caught sight of a dark-haired woman just off the side of the house chatting with someone with blonde spikey hair. *And pink – she has pink at the ends?*

He honed his gaze and froze – something about that dark-haired one was familiar. *It couldn't be … could it?*

'Stop!'

Bruce slammed the brakes on, and the SUV stopped right outside the gates. Al drew the electric window down and focused on the women just as Beth – the very person he was searching for – glanced up and caught him staring. Her mouth dropped open, and she quickly covered it with one hand – the other was in a sling.

Al knew she'd seen him – so he smiled a wide smile and tipped his head forward an inch.

Let the games begin …

He tapped Bruce on the shoulder, indicating to him to put his foot down, and the SUV jerked forward.

Brannigan's Women's Shelter

Paige froze mid-sentence, staring at the man grinning at her from inside a black SUV. *That's like the one on the dashcam footage …* It took a moment longer for her brain to register she was staring at Al Graham, and that he was staring right back at her, obviously knowing who she was.

Her hand flew to her mouth, and Mags peered past her, searching for whatever had caused the reaction.

'Inside – now!' Mags shouted at her, jumping up and grabbing Paige's hand and pulling her forcefully into the house. Once inside, Mags set about securing the doors and windows, barking orders at Jacko to call Gabe.

Paige couldn't move – she was immobilized by the knowledge he'd found her. The one person she never wanted to see again had found her!

Her breath was coming out in short, sharp pants – panic was taking over.

Mags returned to the kitchen and maneuvered her back until she was sitting on the soft cushion of one of the kitchen chairs.

'Breathe, Paige. Come on, nice deep breaths.'

The voice floated on the wind, but Paige couldn't begin to comprehend – her breaths grew shorter and faster, black swirls flew in front of her eyes, and her weightless body sank toward the floor, her eyes fluttering closed.

When Gabe roared through the front door what seemed like only minutes later, Paige was still unconscious. Jacko had carried her into the living room and laid her on the sofa while Mags herded all the women and children together in one room on the upper floor.

He knelt beside her, his heart all but in his mouth.

'Tell me what the hell happened.'

Jacko slipped out of the room silently, and the front door closed behind him with a click. *Good – he can patrol with Deacon.*

Mags was the one who answered him. 'Me and Paige were nattering outside – she told me what she was running from. Then she went white, and there was a black SUV outside the gates – a man was inside, smiling at her. Hell, Gabe, his expression was enough to make me shudder. I grabbed her and ran inside, but then she passed out – panic attack. I can only assume the man in the car is the one she's been running from.'

'How the hell did he find this place?' Gabe's question wasn't aimed at anyone in particular – there was no one there to answer him other than Mags anyway. He'd left Dave in the office to contact Kyle while he had sped to the shelter with Deacon. The rest of the team were out on assignment. He could call them back in if he had to, but right now, he needed to calm down and figure out his next move.

Getting Paige somewhere safe – somewhere no one knows about.

They were already scheduled to go to his parents for lunch – the team knew the location, but very few other people did. *Maybe I can stash Paige with Dad – he's got enough weapons in his gun room to arm a small country. But it's also a massive open area – plenty of places to hide and sneak up on the main house.* He shook his head. He wouldn't leave Paige where she could potentially be exposed – not even with his dad, who would no doubt swear like a sailor when he heard the reason they'd now be skipping lunch.

Mags put her hand on his shoulder, reminding him she was still there.

'Not to sound selfish, but I'll need to get the five families we have here to another location securely – I don't trust that this man won't have the means to get past the security. And I know you can't leave any more than Jacko here – not that he's not competent, he totally is. But him against god knows how many?'

'I'll sort it – go up and have everyone pack what they need. Know it'll be teaching your granny to suck eggs, but try and reassure them it's nothing to do with them. I will be assigning some of the team to keep you all safe until I know the threat has been eliminated, but you're right. Graham has the money and the means to breach security here with little problem.'

Mags patted his arm once, then turned and left him alone in the room with the still unconscious Paige.

She's so pale – it was like the day in the hospital all over again. Except now it wasn't from missing a few meals. *It's because I failed – she needed help, and I jumped her bones rather than getting her safe and sorted.*

Cursing, he grabbed his phone and hit the speed dial for the office.

'Dave – I need the bigger safe house setting up for guests – five families and Mags. It'll need kitting out with groceries and extra security. Call Becca and Grayson back into the office. They'll be standing guard as live-in help – they can help with the security setup too to make it faster. Bring Mitch back in too – he's pretty much finished with his case. I'll be taking Paige to the forest location. Need-to-know only on that one – me, you, and Mitch. I'll need him outside. Also, I need new wheels – I don't know how Al Graham found the shelter, but it's possible Mendino tagged my truck or something. I'll be taking Paige and going dark.'

Dave acknowledged with one word – Gabe knew he'd be springing straight into action to get everything done.

The only thing he could do now was wake Paige, prepare her to run, and wait on Kyle's arrival. The police chief would be pissed not to be involved further, but he'd have to make do with a promise to share info after it was all over with, and to put it out there on the police band that they were searching for Al Graham. He doubted it would have much impact – Paige had all but implied Graham paid for police protection, and he knew it would be the case. There was always a bent copper somewhere looking to make a quick buck.

Turning his attention to Paige, he gently shook her shoulder while saying her name.

'Paige – come on, darlin', time to wake up.' He cupped a hand to her cheek and said the same words again.

This time she stirred under his touch and suddenly shot upright, her eyes scoping the room instantly.

Her fear was palpable. He could almost taste it. And it nigh on destroyed him. *I will keep her alive if it kills me. No one should ever be this scared of another human.*

'Al,' she gasped. 'He's here. How the hell did he find me? Oh god, the shelter. I need to leave.' Paige shot to her feet and faltered, swaying slightly.

'Easy. I'm moving everyone from here to a safe place. Me and you will be heading to a secure location – no one knows about it. It's not on the books in any form. We just need to wait for Dave to sort out a new vehicle. We will be dealing with this, Paige. Al Graham will not get his hands on you or anyone else here. Understand?'

He pulled Paige into his arms, and a short burst of pain shot through his chest as she stiffened in resistance before finally relaxing against him.

'How did he find me, Gabe? I mean, I know he got the information from The Fox, but how did *he* find me? I did something wrong, I must've. I shouldn't have stayed here. I should have kept moving. Then you and Mags, and everyone else wouldn't be involved in all of this. I can't believe I was so stupid. Do you know, I'd started to think that maybe I'd get through all this and learn to live without Diana? But now … maybe I should just give him the ledger back. Maybe he'd leave me alone then?'

'From what I know about Al Graham, leaving you behind has never been his intention. You know that. You should know we recovered the box you buried at the base of the tree. It's been forwarded to an analyst at the FBI, a close friend of mine. They're already building a case. I promise you, he will not harm you or anyone else. I will keep you all safe.' Gabe meant every word that fell from his mouth. It hadn't been long, but he already knew his heart would shatter if anything happened to Paige. He froze – his mouth dropping open in shock. He'd just realized that Paige was the woman who'd stolen his heart. This moment where her fear was so deep he could taste it and his heart felt like it would shatter into a million pieces if Al Graham got his hands on her had flooded him with feelings he'd never felt before. Not even once. And it scared the hell out of him.

He stepped back, breaking his hold on Paige. *I can't protect her if I'm constantly worrying about feelings.* It was a war between his heart and his mind. And for now, his mind won. He shoved his emotion back down inside and gently pushed Paige back from him.

Gabe felt like he'd been sucker-punched when confusion clouded her face.

'Sorry, Paige. I didn't intend for any of this to happen. But right now, I need my work head on – I can't protect you fully if I let my heart rule my head. We can see where we are after everything's sorted out. But until then I need to focus on getting Al Graham. I'm not trying to hurt you, I promise. There are feelings involved, and I know you feel that too.

But I need to take a step back, just for now. I can't let him hurt you, Paige.'

'Okay.' The single word which spoke volumes. She stepped away from his hands, stared at the floor for a moment, then looked up at him. Her blue eyes sparked with renewed determination, surprising him.

'Let's get this sorted. I want him caught and behind bars – Mags needs the shelter back, and I deserve … a life, dammit, I deserve my life back. I'm sick of running and being afraid. Tell me what I need to do. Like you say, we can assess "us" when it's all over and done with.'

'We're going somewhere secure. Me and you, along with Mitch, one of my men. You met him briefly in the office the other day. You need to do what I say, when I say it. Okay?'

Paige nodded and followed Gabe out of the shelter.

Gabe drove in silence to the Bland P.I.R office, and they switched vehicles to a nondescript sedan parked in the rear yard. Dave would sweep his truck to check for bugs – he really couldn't think of any other way that they could have been tracked to the shelter. His truck was the only commonality. Which also meant that Al Graham likely had his cabin's location.

As they made their way out of town, Gabe cursed and hit the dial button on the steering wheel.

'Kyle – it's Gabe. We've got a lot going on at the minute, and I can only give you a brief overview. I'm taking Paige somewhere secure – Brannigan's shelter has been compromised. I'm taking care of Mags and the families, so if you need anything regarding that, speak to Dave directly. He's in the office.' Gabe paused, giving time for a grunt from Kyle to acknowledge where they were up to.

'I also have reason to believe my cabin has been compromised – it's alarmed, and there's no secure data there they can access. I don't want your guys anywhere near – Al Graham and his men are not afraid to use violence, and I don't want you involved in the crossfire. I'll get alerts anyway, but just making you aware in case you get any calls along the way.'

'You're sure they can't access anything confidential?' Kyle was aware of the setup at the cabin.

Gabe knew that but answered anyway. 'Certain. I'll give you a full update in due course. One thing you can help with, though, Kyle, is getting a BOLO out on Graham and any and all vehicles linked to him that may be found in the area. If you get any hits, I'd advise not to engage. Report locations back to the office and monitor from a distance. There will be an APB at some point, but the Feds are taking over that side of the case. My next call will be updating them.'

'Okay, Gabe, got it all. Consider the BOLO in force. Who's your FBI contact? Just so I know who'll be coming a-knocking. Don't want involvement in any jurisdictional crap, so thank you for keeping me in the loop.'

'Mason Henderson is the guy I've been dealing with – would think it'll be him following through.'

'Look after your lady, Gabe.'

Gabe nodded silently as the call cut off. *My lady ... I like the sound of that.*

Chapter Nineteen

Remote cabin, Crockhill Mountain Nature Reserve

Paige had been silent while Gabe drove – he was making phone calls and speaking to people she'd never heard of, and she didn't want to interrupt. It gave her time to think, though – time in her head to try and sort through everything that had happened over the last few days.

She stared out of the window. The town changed to country and the country changed to forest. The mountain stood tall above the forest, and she recognized it as the one that Gabe's cabin was at the base of. They carried on past and onto a winding backroad. So far, they'd been driving for nigh on an hour, during which time Gabe had made another four phone calls. One to the FBI contact he'd mentioned to Kyle, one to his dad foregoing the lunch invitation and giving a brief explanation of why – his dad needed to be on the alert just in case anyone linked Gabe back to him. Then a call to Dave in the office who was quick to reassure Gabe that all was in hand. The final call had been to Mitch – the man who was reportedly meeting them at wherever they were headed.

Paige sighed quietly – it was a lot to take in and handle. All this mess because she hadn't been brave enough to stand up to Al before now. She hated it. Hated that she was essentially responsible for people getting shot and hurt, for upending Gabe and his company. *I need to take responsibility and deal with all of this. Gabe and his team would be better off if they'd never met me.*

Determined not to wallow in the self-pity that was now threatening to take over, Paige turned and glanced at Gabe. His face was set in a grim expression – the silence was comfortable, but she could see Gabe was running a hundred different outcomes over in his head. She'd heard the hushed tones as he'd told Dave to check his truck for bugs, and in that instant, she knew just how far Al would go to get her back in his grasp. It was no longer a case of he might beat her or whatever, but more what he would do to others to get to her.

It was terrifying – and Paige didn't know how to cope with the responsibility of so many other people being at risk. She wouldn't blame Gabe for just handing her over to be fair – it would seem she was rapidly becoming more trouble than she was worth. *I wish I'd handed that stupid ledger over months ago – no one would be in this position now if not for me being so stupid.*

Gabe had navigated the sedan around windy roads, passing the driveway entrance for his own cabin and continuing around the base of the mountain. Eventually, he pulled onto what looked like a dirt road with weeds sprouting in the center and trees overhanging above – it made the track appear dark and creepy. The overgrown plants showed it hadn't been used for a good while. Paige had spent the journey staring out of the window and biting her lip – she couldn't get away from how quickly Al had found her. And the worry for Mags and the rest of the families in her care was weighing heavily.

'Are you sure Mags and the others are safe?' Her voice sounded small and pathetic even to her – Gabe had already promised her they were, but she needed to hear it again.

Gabe nodded then hit the call button on the steering wheel. Paige was surprised to see Grayson's name flash up on Gabe's phone which was in a mount on the dash.

A gruff male voice filled the car through the inbuilt speaker system. 'Boss, everything okay?'

'Paige wants to check in with Mags – put the loudspeaker on.'

'Paige? Are you okay?'

Tears pricked Paige's eyes at the sound of Mags' voice.

'I'm okay – worried about you and the others.'

'We're okay, child. Gabe's sorted a lovely big house out a few towns over. We're all here, the fridge is stocked, and Gabe's colleagues are here to make sure nothing goes wrong. Stop beating yourself up – you couldn't have known any of this would happen.'

'How is it you always know what I'm thinking? I don't think I've ever told you, but I love you, Mags. I should have told you about Al sooner. You've been so good to me, and now I've brought all this shit down on you.'

'Stop that right now – you are not responsible for that monster's actions. And I love you too – you're the daughter I never had. You make sure you take care of my girl, Gabriel Bland. I'm warning you.'

'Scout's honor, Mags. Try not to worry. Paige will not be leaving my side.'

He ended the call with a quick press of the red end-call key. The car jolted over a pothole on thin track, and Gabe grabbed the wheel, maneuvering around the steady stream of gaps on the track until they eventually reached what could only be called a clearing, though the trees surrounding it hung over the center, obscuring much of the view. The tiny wood cabin appeared basic but inviting. *Anything would at this point – I feel like I could sleep for a year.*

Paige sighed and popped the car door open.

'Wait.' Gabe said softly, placing a hand on her leg.

Paige tried to ignore the bolts of electricity that passed through her leg at his touch, and half turned so she could see his face.

'I need to clear the cabin first – just to make sure.'

And just like that, the electric sizzle faded and was replaced with the dull ache of fear. Paige drew the door closed. She knew she was tense – she sat upright, her muscles frozen in place. *What if there's someone inside? What if they get Gabe? What if …* Shushing her anxious mind wasn't easy, but it was necessary. She drew in some deep breaths and focused her gaze on the front door to the cabin. Gabe had got out of the car and dipped inside the cabin seconds before. Her heartbeat was pounding in her ears. *I can't lose him …* The thought shocked her. *I never really had him, did I?* She thought back to the previous day – his body hard against hers, taking her against the wall, the tenderness he'd displayed making sure he didn't hurt her arm or hip. Desire pooled deep inside her. What she wouldn't give for that feeling again – she'd never had anyone make her feel that way. Closing her eyes tightly, she tried not to think about the way he filled her so completely. She tried her best to rid her mind of the image of him naked. So hot and chiseled … *Stop – right now. There are no guarantees it'll ever happen again – don't you go falling for him just because he's the one man who's showed you attention after Al.* Thinking of Al had the same effect a cold shower would have had, and she wrenched herself from her reverie, reopening her eyes.

Her heart leaped into her throat as her gaze fixed on a man's face at the car window.

Paige scrambled to lock the door and screamed.

Gabe cleared each room in the cabin methodically – it didn't take long, the cabin only had three rooms. It was definitely rustic, but it had running water, and a generator out the back provided electricity. He was certain no one had been inside since his last visit three months before. He was just about to open the front door when a scream ricocheted around the dense clearing.

How the hell has anyone found us here when we've only been here minutes?

His gun still drawn, Gabe opened the door and peered around the doorjamb, not sure what to expect but fully prepared for any number of people to be present outside. His mind had already run through several scenarios. What he didn't expect, however, was to see Mitch looking helplessly inside the sedan as Paige moved about inside and screamed again.

He holstered his weapon, stepped outside, and strode over to the car.

'That's what you call covert protection?' he growled at Mitch who raised his shoulders in a shrug.

'Sorry, boss. I literally just got to the car when she opened her eyes and saw me. She screamed and locked the doors. I didn't think she'd panic that way. You told her I would be here, right?'

'Of course I did – but she literally only saw you for a minute, for fuck's sake. She won't remember you! You were only in the office two minutes when we found out about Mendino.'

Gabe moved to the door next to Paige and tapped on the window, not sure if she'd seen him approach – panic did that to a person.

Paige glanced at him, recognition flaring. Seeing no issues between him and Mitch, she unlocked the door. Before he could even pull it open fully, she'd launched herself out of the car and straight into his arms.

Instinctively, he wrapped his arms around her. He inhaled her scent without thinking – jasmine and strawberries. Gabe glanced up, and the questioning expression on Mitch's face changed to one of smugness. Gabe couldn't stop the flush reaching his cheeks. *Damn it – last thing I need is my staff to think I can't keep my brain on the job.*

Moving back a little from Paige, he glared at Mitch over her shoulder and mouthed 'Not one fucking word' silently.

He could see Mitch trying and failing to hold in the knowledge he'd just acquired. A hint of a smile played on his lips, and he winked at Gabe.

Gabe released Paige from his arms and found himself grinning as she spun round to face Mitch herself.

'What the hell, man? You think it's acceptable to sneak up on a woman who's been through the shit I have? You're lucky Gabe took his gun with him …' She was plainly annoyed and took one step toward Mitch who backed off with his hands held out to the front, the grin he'd had seconds before ebbing rapidly.

'Sorry, I thought Gabe had told you I would be here. My apologies, ma'am.'

'I'm not ninety – Paige will be fine.' Paige stalked toward to the cabin while Gabe grinned widely.

'Seriously, Mitch, not one fucking word. I don't need that wrath turning on me – it's much more fun watching you get a roasting.'

'I got here an hour ago. I was doing a perimeter check when I heard the car so I doubled back round. No signal out here, and I've not kicked the genny into gear yet.'

'Okay, do I want to know where your car is? Actually, scratch that, I don't need to know. We'll leave the sedan on the front in case we need a rapid exit. We weren't followed – I triple-checked and I know all the vehicles were scanned prior to any of us leaving. Dave found one more bug – on Lou's car of all places. She's barely even been in the office, so I don't know how Mendino would think she'd be involved with Paige. The Fox was fucking clever too – two different bugs, two different frequencies.'

Elouise 'Lou' Garrett had been working from home since Shotgun's death – she and Shotgun had been seeing each other for over a year. His death had understandably hit Lou hard. Gabe understood – it had hit them all hard, but her especially. She needed the time to get in the right headspace before coming back to work fully. She'd called in after Dave had been shot, though, expressed her wish to come back to work in the very near future. Gabe had said they'd sort it out in a couple of weeks. It had felt like the right decision, but now he wondered whether Lou was itching to get back to work. He was no good at sitting on the side-lines, and it was the same for all of his team, Lou included.

'That is odd. But maybe he didn't know who was involved so hedged his bets. Lou's car was parked next to your truck in the yard if I remember rightly. Probably just luck of the draw.'

'Yeah, you're probably right.' Gabe ran a hand through his hair and sighed. 'You sure you don't want to stay in the cabin? It's getting pretty chilly at night. Especially this side of the mountain.'

'I'm good, thanks. You know me, hate to be cooped up. I'll be fine. Got everything I need, will be setting up shortly. The radios are already in the cabin. I've locked the bandwidth so they can't be hacked into externally. I've got mine and a spare battery. Fridge is stocked, but you'll need to crank the genny so there's enough power to run it. I'll pop back in a couple of hours and eat with you guys – don't fancy MREs when there's proper food on offer.' Mitch shot Gabe a cheeky grin then melded backward and into the tree line.

Gabe lost sight of him almost instantly. It was no wonder Mitch'd had the call sign 'Ghost' when he'd worked for special forces. He pushed the heavy feeling he felt whenever he thought of Shotgun to one side and opened the door to the cabin.

Watson Hinkle Hotel

Al Graham sat in one of the chrome-legged chairs at the glass-topped table in the lounge area of the suite he and his men inhabited. His laptop was open, and he frowned at the map image on the screen.

'Where the hell are they? Looks like Timbuktu from this aerial view – I thought satellites were supposed to pick up intricate detail. The tracker the stupid orderly put in Paige's bag at the hospital verges on useless. Which reminds me – get rid of him, we don't need any loose ends.' Al picked up his coffee and took a long slurp, enjoying the burn on his tongue from the sweet heat.

'I wouldn't care, it's not like Senator Charles doesn't have funding to access better satellites than this crock of shit. I thought satellites were all state of the art and would show you a freckle on an ass cheek. To have that kind of money and power, and have to use crap like this … well, it's a good job I'm not senator, that's all I'm saying. I mean really, a one-square-mile area? I'm sitting here staring at fucking satellite images of a fucking forest. Can't it cut through the trees a bit? Or can we not get a drone out there? Anything's got to be better than this.'

Al pushed at the laptop, sending it careening across the glass table and onto the seat at the other side. George dutifully recovered it and reset it on the table. Sitting, he examined the images sent by the satellite.

'According to the senator's aide, the satellite last passed over the area ten minutes ago – so we can assume these images are the most recent. I'll do a grid analysis and compare to land records and mapping to see if anything pops. How did you manage to even get access to the satellite anyway, boss?'

'Let's just say this senator has some skeletons he'd prefer were kept in the closet. A well-placed reminder of something he'd rather nobody found out about had him racing to get me the info. Now, I need someone to bang – my balls are bursting. It's been four days since I saw Kim. And she wasn't overly happy or accommodating then. Something about pregnancy making her tits hurt. No way I was getting off without those bad boys, though – I paid for them. Don't know who she thinks she is telling me no. Get me booked in at Madam Rossiter's place.'

'I'll make a call – head downstairs, and I'll get the driver to take you over. There'll be someone there for you, I'm sure.' George's voice was quiet yet commanding. He pulled his cell phone from his pocket and scrolled through his contacts.

'Make it two or three someones. I want to forget this whole mess for a couple of hours. Make sure you have a better location for me when I get back, though.'

Remote cabin, Crookhill Mountain Nature Reserve

Paige stomped into the cabin and resisted the urge to slam the door. *He has the nerve to call me ma'am? After scaring me half to death?* The door opened behind her seconds later, and she turned to glare, expecting to see Mitch following her inside. Once she realized it was Gabe, her expression softened. Her heart was already trying to beat its way out of her chest, but the adrenaline eased, and her heart beat for a different reason. He didn't speak, but his gaze intensified as she stared.

Heat pooled at the apex of her thighs. *I should not be feeling like this from him just walking into a room.* She didn't know who she was trying to kid, though – how she felt about him was as obvious as the nose on her face.

She thought she heard him groan, then he strode the four steps across the room to her and his lips were on hers. Fire ignited instantly – his hands slipped around her hips and settled on her ass, tugging her to him. The outline of his cock was nestled against the top of her thigh – hard already and straining at the cargo pants he wore. Even now, he was being mindful of her arm and held her from the left side.

His grip loosened on her ass, and she moaned her frustration into his hot mouth. She didn't want him to ever stop kissing her – and wanted so much more than just kisses. He rubbed his thumb over the hardened peak of her nipple, and she gasped loudly, a jolt of electricity shooting straight to her clit, and for half a second, she believed she could orgasm just from that single touch. His lips blazed their way down her throat, his teeth nipping gently, navigating toward her breasts. When they grazed the same nipple, she felt herself go light and weightless.

Without Gabe breaking the hold on her, his mouth found hers again, and he guided her away from the kitchen counter and into the bedroom. The bed hit the back of her knees, and she would've collapsed ungracefully onto it, but he held her and lowered her down carefully. Then he pulled away from her suddenly, leaving her feeling bereft and frustrated. She managed to force her eyes open, half thinking he was leaving her there, in that state, and when he ripped his T-shirt over his head, his abs rippling with the motion, she was lost. His abs were defined, his muscles big but not massive. He undid his belt, not taking his gaze off her for a second. His gray eyes smoldered. There was no coming back from this one. Seeing his erection straining against his boxers, knowing how close he was to losing control, gave her a sense of power. Pushing herself up with the hand that wasn't in a sling, she sat on the edge of the bed and watched openly. He bent to remove his boots and kicked his pants away with his socks.

All that was left now was the thin cotton of his boxer shorts – shorts that hugged his hips tightly. A damp spot appeared where the tip of his cock met the material, and she hooked her finger into the top of his boxers, bringing him closer to her.

Gabe almost lost it as her slender finger hooked into his boxers and brought him toward her. The fingertip grazed the top of his cock with a featherlight touch, and he jerked forward, stopping mere inches from her face. Her tongue snaked out and licked her bottom lip which she then drew into her mouth and bit ever so slightly, and he was a goner.

Somewhere in the dark recess of his mind, he registered they'd said they'd wait and see what happened after the case was wrapped up, but they were safe for now. Mitch was outside, and no one would ever sneak up on him. All coherent thoughts of the case, Mitch, and anything else flew out of his mind the second her hot mouth closed around the tip of his cock, teasing, tasting. Her tongue gently scraped across the center, and Gabe damn near jumped out of his skin. All he wanted to do was ram it home and have her milk him for all he had. But he refrained – letting her take control was too damn sexy. She held him with both hands, slowly drawing him deep inside, and his balls tightened.

He was going to come in two seconds flat if he let this continue, and he stepped back, ignoring her squeak of frustrated annoyance. Kneeling, he nudged her legs apart with one shoulder while his other hand unbuttoned her shirt and trailed his fingers lightly around her ribs to the back. With one quick snap her bra was undone, and he slid the straps down her arm, releasing her tits in all their magnificent glory. Lowering her down, he found one with his mouth and sucked it inside, swiping his tongue across the tip. She moaned and bucked beneath him, and he teased the same nipple with his teeth, groaning in response. His hands replaced his mouth, his thumbs brushing over the hardened tips, and she cried out loudly. He loved the sounds she made when he did that. And it also served as a distraction – she was so busy enjoying what his hands were doing that she didn't notice where his head had lowered even farther down her body.

He dipped his tongue into her slick folds, and she screamed, her hips thrusting against his waiting mouth. His right hand joined his mouth, and he sank one finger into her, groaning loudly over her clit, loving that her muscles drew his finger in even deeper. Shudders coursed through her when he added a second finger, slowly thrusting in and out.

Suddenly feeling selfish, he withdrew and stood. Her legs spread even wider, accommodating his hips, and his cock probed at her entrance. He was taken aback by the utter beauty of his woman, her hair strewn all over the bed, her darkened nipples tight with desire, her one free hand holding the bed throw tightly, and totally lost in the moment, she gazed at him.

Sliding his cock into her, he felt every shiver and shudder as she gripped him tightly. He withdrew almost all the way out and then thrust again, going even deeper this time. He grabbed her hips, lifted her a few inches to improve the angle. *Sweet Jesus; if she moves even an inch I'll blow my load ... Not before her, though ...* Her legs wrapped round him, freeing up his hands. He leant forward ever so slightly, tweaking one nipple whilst his thumb pressed down on her clit, circling rapidly. Paige flew apart with another cry, shuddering around his cock.

'Shiiit,' he groaned, pumping into her one last time and came so hard he saw stars. 'See what you do to me, darlin'.' He helped her sit, then gently pulled her bra back over her breasts and reached behind to fasten the clasp.

'You could just leave it off ...'

Gabe leaned forward and captured her mouth with his, soft this time, not hard and demanding. So damn soft he didn't want it to end. Her teeth grazed his bottom lip, and he deepened the kiss instinctively. *Jesus, a man could lose himself forever in this sweet paradise.* The kiss slowed, and he kissed either side of her mouth gently.

'Not now, darlin'.' At her disappointed pout, he kissed her hard again, but only briefly. 'As much as I want to stay in this bed and fuck you till you've seen every star in the universe, are aching so bad you think you'll never walk again, and tell you every single thing I want to do to this amazing body of yours before proving I mean those words, we absolutely need to stop. I need to stop and get some focus. I can't protect you if I'm naked in this bed.'

Paige pouted again but then nodded, obviously knowing he was right.

'Why don't you take a shower. I'll go start knocking up some dinner. I'm not a master chef or anything but I can hold my own in the kitchen.'

He bent to grab his boxers and jumped when her left hand connected sharply with his ass. Ignoring the sparks of electricity, he turned back with a pretend glower. 'Stop it, woman, you're making me crazy. And don't think I won't spank you back …'

He jerked his cargo pants over his boxers, flashing her a grin that showed he meant those particular words, and left the room.

Chapter Twenty

Watson Hinkle Hotel

Al felt lighter when he returned to the hotel from the whorehouse; more in control and ready to face the news from George about a precise location to find Beth. He'd had a bit of time to think as he'd laid back and been serviced. He knew she'd witnessed him killing Fred Donnington – he'd made sure no one would ever find Fred's body, of course, and the warehouse had been cleansed. But with Fred's disappearance, if Beth ever talked then suspicion would fall on him, and he could do without the extra scrutiny. He paid well for loyalty, but there was always someone willing to fess up at the end of the day. He'd make sure Beth wasn't one of those people if it killed him.

He knew she hadn't said anything yet – he'd not had law enforcement sniffing around and had been ultracareful since she'd stolen his ledger. If the Feds ever got hold of it, they'd have had more than enough evidence to put him away. If they could break his code, that was, which he doubted would happen. He'd designed it himself, after all – it wasn't one they taught in code-breaking school or wherever those people went to be trained. Even George wasn't trusted with that information.

He clicked his fingers loudly, said 'coffee,' then sat beside George at the elaborate table. A steaming coffee pot, two mugs, and a tray of nibbles magically appeared, and he took the mug with more finesse than a man like him should have.

Taking a long sip, he turned his attention to George.

'So, have we found a more precise location for Beth?'

'Yes and no. There's a track which has to lead somewhere, but the vegetation is too dense to show anything else – if there is a shack or something it's fully obscured by the trees. I've checked land records, and the land is owned by a holding company – I can find no mention of any buildings in the location at all. If there is one there, they're completely off the grid.'

'Tell me you've at least got decent surveillance of the surrounding areas – do we even know what we're rushing into?'

'Not really. I've run the plates on the car Mendino hit with the tracker – it's registered to a business called Bland Inc. I can't find a whole lot on Bland Inc. – they're very good at covering what it is they actually do – there's a basic website with some office pictures on, contact information et cetera., but it just says they're specialists in their field. So, they could sell window blinds or they could be something else. The site is vague enough not to call attention but detailed enough to deter anyone doing any deep searches. They could be the CIA for all I can find out. I'll keep at it, though, unless you want to get Hansel in – you know he's the tech guy, not me.'

'No, I don't want anyone else involved at this stage. We're too close. Besides, the track you mentioned has to lead somewhere. We can always just drive up – if there is a building and it's totally off the grid, it can't exactly have a state-of-the-art security system, can it? We're so close I can almost taste Beth's fear right now. That bitch deserves all she's going to get and more.'

Al's phone rang, and he glanced down. The name Frank flashed on his screen and, frowning, he swiped to answer.

'What's Kim doing now?'

'Well, boss, the thing is, she seems really in pain. She's crying and holding her stomach. You said to keep the baby safe. Do I call an ambulance?'

'Put the phone to her ear.' He waited until he could hear sobs down the phone. 'Kim, do you remember the conversation we had just before I left the house …' He waited again until she hiccupped, knowing he had her attention. 'Well, I did what I threatened and have posted two of my worst guys outside your mother's house – twenty-two ninety-one Lake Shore Road. Now I know you're not that close to your mother, but she's still your mother at the end of the day. These men are under strict instruction not to go inside, but, well, if your mother were to come out to attend to her sick daughter because of some kind of ruse, well let's just say outside is fair game. So, if you really are in pain and need a doctor, best tell me now. I'll arrange the best physician I know to come to you at home – and I'll call your dear mother and express how worried I am about you. Of course, if you're faking to try and get Frank to feel sorry for you, then I'd reconsider. Carlos and Juan have both done time for rape – and I happen to know they prefer a little fight, especially from the older women.'

'You bastard … you leave my mom alone, Al. You're sick – I'll stop, I'll be good, I swear. Please, Al, leave her alone.' This time her sobs were real, and Al knew it.

'If I hear one more word from Frank about how you're trying to use our child as a means to escape, I will not only kill your mother, but when I come back, I'll rip that baby out of you and leave you to rot. They can survive from twenty-six weeks, you know. You're thirty weeks. Think about that next time you try and fake illness to escape. You will leave when I say you can leave.' Al didn't really know at what age a baby could survive, but he figured it would be close enough. He knew that many born premature survived – Diana had. *At least for a while …* He frowned as Frank grunted down the line and ended the call, pulling him from his thoughts.

'God, women! Honestly, how hard is it to find one who toes the line and behaves? Enough of stressing about Kim, she's not going anywhere. How soon can we have a team down here to go in and get Beth back? I've no doubt she's with her new boyfriend or whatever the hell he is. We don't know who he is or his skill set, so better to be prepared, yes?'

George nodded. 'I already requested a two-man team to follow us down. That'll be six including us, Pike, and Tony. They'll get here in about an hour. I'd say set off straightaway – the darkness comes quickly here – we can use it as a cover and go in, get Beth out, and be heading home by ten.'

'Good – I'm going for a nap, all that sex has tired me out. Wake me in forty-five minutes.'

Remote cabin, Crookhill Mountain Nature Reserve

Gabe was antsy – it was almost like he knew something was going to happen but couldn't figure out how it would happen. There was no way Al Graham could know where they were. They'd scanned the car, Paige, and even himself for more bugs before leaving. The cabin was remote – it was on the team database of safe houses, but no one had managed to hack their system since they'd first started five years before, and he knew Dave kept the security top-notch. But he still couldn't shake the feeling that something was going to happen.

He'd left Paige in bed; she was exhausted, and he didn't want to worry her with his thoughts. He could worry Mitch, though. Standing, he made his way to the door at the back of the kitchen and opened it softly.

Almost like magic, Mitch appeared.

'There's a strange feel to the air tonight, boss. Something's coming, and it ain't the good kind of something. I'm thinking we might need more backup.'

'That's exactly what I wanted to talk to you about – get on the sat phone and get Deacon and Grayson out here too – full kit with weapons. And a second team in the area as backup. I don't know how, but I think Al Graham knows where we are.'

'They'll be a good couple of hours before they get here – the pass leading to the track has had a landslide. They'll park up and head in on foot from there.'

'I've no idea how you know that already, Mitch, but thanks for letting me know. I'll wake Paige shortly and put her in the basement. I have an idea that no matter where we take her, this guy will be one step ahead. And the basement is a lot more secure than anyone who doesn't know this cabin thinks. Might as well get this over with on our own turf. We know this forest, they don't – that's an advantage. Speak to Kyle and make sure he's aware of the situation too. He'll have some arrests tonight, all being well.'

'Will do, boss. Gear up – I get the feeling this isn't going to be an easy fight to win.'

'You too – make sure you've got your armor on, which you probably already have. I just can't lose anyone else, Mitch. So, humor me and pass the message to Grayson and Deacon. No one dies tonight.'

'I know – Shotgun dying …' Mitch's voice turned a little raspy, 'that's on all of us, boss. We all feel it. The void he left behind. All we can do is stick together and get through each case one at a time. And the one thing Shotgun would be saying now would be to protect Paige and kick ass.'

'Yeah, he sure would. And that's what we're going to do.'

Gabe stepped back toward the door to the kitchen as Mitch melded back into the darkness outside the cabin.

Track leading to remote cabin, Crookhill Mountain Nature Reserve

'How the hell did you not know there'd been a landslide? Are you even sure we're on the right track, George?' Al's temples pounded with an impending stress headache. He hated change at the best of times. He had an awful feeling George was about to tell him they needed to hike the rest of the way, and as fit as he liked to keep himself, he was no match for what would likely be a treacherous trek in the dark.

And it was dark – Al couldn't even see the track for much farther than the glow from the SUV headlights gave. Clouds covered the moon, and even that had chosen this moment to retreat away into shadow. It was blacker than anything Al had ever seen before, and for a moment, he felt a sense of foreboding.

'We're on the right track, boss. And I didn't know about the landslide because it's not been on any news or local channels, probably cos this goddamn track to "nowheresville" doesn't have any residents. We're going to have to hike in. From what I found out online, the track leads to an old hunting cabin that's been abandoned for years. There's a few of them dotted about these parts. If it's even still standing, that is. You can see by the condition of the track even here at the entrance, that it's not well used, but despite the overgrowth, there are tire tracks – besides, I triple-checked the satellite footage, it's definitely the right track.'

Al sighed, rubbing his temples.

'Okay – Tony, Pike, grab the torches and gun bag from the trunk. Stevie and Ray, take a torch and scout ahead.

Keep noise to the minimum. I don't want these assholes knowing we're coming. Let's go – I've got me an ex to find.'

Remote cabin, Crookhill Mountain Nature Reserve

The air stilled, and the night wildlife fell silent, as if the forest itself knew something was about to happen.

Mitch was close to the cabin but not visible to anyone prowling about – nobody would be able to see him until he was ready for them to. He'd applied camo paint to his face, neck, and ears – his clothes were black. Even the earpiece he wore was black, blending in perfectly with the paint.

His armor pressed gently under his jacket, and he knew without a doubt he'd be glad later that he'd donned it as instructed by Gabe.

Mitch had watched his boss slip from the cabin seconds before, locking the kitchen door from the outside. The whole team had worked on getting the cabin to be the secure haven it was. With limited cell service unless you had a sat phone, and a wealth of trees and brush for remaining hidden, it was the perfect location to defend. The only official entrance was the track – only the team knew about the underground basement, and only they had the code to unlock the basement door from the outside. Working on its own generator that was situated inside the large room, it was impossible to power down from the outside even if a person knew it was there.

He cocked his head to one side, hearing the slightest rustle near to the point the track widened in front of the cabin. A whisper carried on the wind, too light for him to distinguish words but loud enough that he knew it was a man.

Knowing with one hundred percent surety that it wasn't Deacon or Grayson, he covered his pencil torch with his fingers and flashed once, fully aware that all that would be seen by Gabe was one sliver of light between his fingers for less than a second. It would be enough to warn the boss in case he hadn't heard the approach.

Moving silently, Mitch navigated the woods until he was a few feet from the track entrance.

Al split off from George and the rest of his men and, as quietly as he could, made his way through the trees. The cloud covering the moon had thinned slightly – enough that he could see the dark structure not too far in the distance. He needed to be the one to get his hands on Beth – he wouldn't trust this task to anyone now, not even George. He'd force her to tell him where his black book was, which he had no doubt she would, she was terrified of him. Then he wanted to feel the life ebb from her as he gripped her throat and squeezed.

Closer to the cabin he crept, on high alert for any small noise. By the time a loud grunt sounded a few meters away, he was nearing the front door. He turned slightly and scanned the area in front of the cabin. He could barely make it out but was almost sure three shapes were fighting to the left – when another grunt sounded, he was sure. Without knowing where anyone else was, he worked quickly.

He took the lock picking set from his pocket, inserted two thin metal pieces into the lock, and patiently but efficiently moved it around until there was an audible click. He grinned to himself in the dark. *Damn, I'm good.* He twisted the pick and applied pressure to the door firmly – surprised when it didn't move. He pushed again, harder this time, and the door still refused to budge.

'You really think I'd be stupid enough to have the door secured with one small lock?' a voice came from beside him.

Al jumped in shock, swiveling quickly, ready for an attack. He couldn't see anyone, but his senses went into overdrive, the hairs on the back of his neck standing on end.

Sensing movement to his left, he ducked fast, feeling the whoosh of a fist traveling at speed past his face and connecting with the heavy wood of the door. That punch told him a lot, the other person knew where he was, and was likely wearing night-vision goggles, and the door was solid – it had barely shuddered with the connection.

He figured entry would come later, so he kept his back to the door and scanned the porch to the left and right, fully aware that the other person was still there but that he couldn't see them. The air moved to his right this time, and he aimed another punch blindly in the approximate direction

---

Gabe felt the punch dislodge his NVGs slightly and stepped back out of range, stabilizing his stance so he was ready for the incoming body weight. As predicted, the man at the door launched his body Gabe's way.

The impact caused Gabe to grunt, but he held his stance steady, kept his head back and his shoulders squared, absorbing the brunt and putting him in the position to be able to secure around the man's arms. Firmly, he constricted his hold, anticipating the backward headbutt from the man he had pinned.

A soft shuffle behind him got his attention, but he couldn't spin away quick enough to avoid the impact from something heavy and hard. It dislodged his NVGs even more, and bright stars exploded into his vision, but still he kept taut hold of the man from the door. Blood trickled down his cheek, but he held tight. A fight was expected, and he'd been hit round the head more times than he dared to count. He spun his body weight around, ignoring the wave of nausea that bubbled up from his stomach. Using the momentum from his own body weight, he spun around quickly, feeling his opponent judder as he impacted with whoever had clocked Gabe from behind. The second man grunted in pain.

Gabe fought the wave of dizziness and forced the man he held into the balustrade surrounding the porch. He let go; the weight of the man sent him tumbling through the railing and four feet down to the ground. Landing hard, the man groaned loudly.

Gabe pulled his NVGs back down over his eyes and switched his attention to the man who'd hit him. He was big, easily as tall as Gabe and definitely wider. Whatever pain he'd been in when he'd been hit had obviously passed. He swung a thick wrench toward Gabe, who stepped backward. This guy had come prepared – his own NVGs glowed against his face, and in the opposite hand to the wrench he held a knife. *A hunting one judging by the serrated edge to the four-inch blade.*

Refusing to entertain a knife fight, Gabe pulled his gun from his holster and fired quickly into the man's left shoulder. His arm dropped to the side, the knife hitting the porch deck with a clatter.

'Drop the wrench, don't make me fire again.' Gabe's voice was no-nonsense – it didn't take the smartest tool in the box to know he meant business.

But the other man ignored him, stepping forward and swinging the wrench hard.

It caught the end of Gabe's .45, knocking his aim off, and he relaxed his finger off the trigger the instant it happened, not wanting shots to stray toward Mitch, wherever he was. The man raised the wrench again, and Gabe bent and rammed his shoulder into the other man's stomach, forcing him backward and onto his ass – over two hundred pounds of pure muscle hitting an object at force would do that.

The wrench glanced off Gabe's shoulder, and he drew his gun back and brought it round hard onto the man's temple. With a loud thud, his head hit the deck this time – his breathing slowed, and Gabe knew he was unconscious.

Stars swam in front of Gabe's vision again, and he dropped to one knee, forcibly slowing his breathing to get through the dizzy spell. His head was pounding, the blood trickling down his cheek hadn't slowed, and he knew it meant a concussion. But he also knew he had to keep Paige safe.

Gabe used cable ties from his utility pants' pocket to secure the wrists and ankles of unconscious man's hands. He left the man facedown and drew in several deep breaths, before standing and glancing through the broken railing at the ground where the other man had landed – there was no one there.

Cursing, Gabe jumped down the steps and scanned the area in front of the cabin. Mitch was still fighting with one man; two others lay at his feet. Gabe was sure there'd been six in total – meaning two were unaccounted for. 'Two foxes in the wind – heading to the back of the henhouse.' He kept his instruction short and sweet, unsure who could potentially be listening on the team frequency.

He caught a sliver of light through the trees beside the track and grabbed his own torch, flashing back twice. He exhaled, knowing that Deacon and Grayson had arrived. He waited for a second, making sure they were heading to assist Mitch, then ran round the cabin to the rear.

Gabe scanned the trees, his NVGs not picking up the heat signature of any people, and when he got round to the door to the kitchen, he wasn't shocked to find it ajar.

'Foxes have breached the henhouse,' he whispered, holding his gun tightly in front of him as he entered the kitchen. The pantry door was open, and he quickly scanned the inside then moved forward through the kitchen toward the lounge area. His breathing slowed, and he focused everything on keeping his tread silent.

Suddenly, one single vibration emitted from the phone in his pocket. The emergency alert – one of his men was calling for immediate assistance.

He was torn – the entrance to the basement was in the pantry which he knew hadn't been disturbed; the basement was virtually impregnable – Paige was as safe as she could be despite someone being in the cabin.

'Status report,' he said into his mic.

'Tracker one down – tracker two down. Tracker three intact and dealing.' Deacon's voice was reassuring through his earpiece, even though he sounded hurt himself. Tracker was the call sign assigned to his own men – Deacon had given instruction that Mitch and Grayson were injured but alive.

He breathed a sigh of relief, knowing he needed to find the remaining two men.

'Stay alert, two foxes in the wind.'

Silence was the only answer Deacon provided.

Al had done a quick search of the cabin and hadn't found anything – but he knew she was there somewhere. There wasn't a single thing indicating his theory was correct, but he could smell her on the air inside. Or what he now imagined she smelled like – it wasn't a manly smell, it was softer, more feminine. Most people wouldn't have even noticed it, or if they had wouldn't have associated it as being a woman, or even a person. But he did. He crept back out of the bedroom, and a barely audible whisper came from the doorway to the lounge from the kitchen.

Drawing his gun, he fired once into the general area, the boom loud enough to echo.

Paige froze as a loud boom thundered above her – it sounded exactly the same as when Fred had been shot in the warehouse, and she knew instinctively that it was Al who had fired the gun now, just as he had back then.

Gabe had given her strict instructions not to leave the basement – assured her she was totally safe and to stay inside under all circumstances. And she was utterly determined to do what he'd asked. Until she'd heard that loud boom – now every possible scenario was running through her head. *Is Gabe okay? Has he been shot? Has someone else been shot?* Guilt stabbed through her repeatedly.

And quite suddenly, a streak of something else she didn't immediately recognize.

Defiance.

Who the hell did Al Graham think he was? Up himself so much that he thought it was okay to beat women up, force them into sex and hold the things they loved dear to ransom? That he was and always would be above the law? *It's not fair that these people are fighting to keep me safe when I'm so scared I can't breathe! I have nothing to be scared of – he's a man. Nothing but a fucking arrogant, violent prick of a man. I will not be scared of him anymore.*

She couldn't change the past, she knew that. There was no saving her precious Diana any more than Fred – but all of that was in the past. This was the here and now, and her ex had potentially just shot Gabe – the only person other than Diana she'd given her heart to in her whole life.

I'll be damned if I'm going to let him take everything away from me a second time.

With shaking fingers, she deactivated the security to the basement, crept up the stairs, and carefully pushed the door that led into the pantry.

Chapter Twenty-One

Remote cabin, Crookhill Mountain Nature Reserve

Paige's heart was pounding loudly – so loud, that for a moment she wondered if anyone else would be able to hear it. The cabin itself had fallen strangely silent. She listened hard and crept out of the pantry and into the kitchen.

Unable to tell where the boom had come from within the cabin, she moved forward. She reached the end of the kitchen bench and paused as she saw a foot in front of her. Knowing it was Gabe, she forgot her fear and rushed forward.

Gabe groaned loudly under her probing fingers, his eyes flickering open.

'What the hell are you doing out …' his voice ground through gritted teeth.

'I came to help you – looks like you need it. Can you stand?' Paige had totally forgotten that Al was potentially in the cabin too – until his shadow blocked the light from the lounge window and he stood in front of them both, his gun pointed straight at her head.

Paige froze, her eyes wide.

'Move the fuck back, Peaches.'

'Don't call me that – you don't get to call me that anymore.'

'Grown a set of balls while you've been away, have you?' He jabbed the barrel into the side of her head. 'I said move the fuck back.'

Cautiously, Paige shuffled backward on her knees until her back impacted with the edge of the kitchen unit. She was now a meter away from Gabe and glanced at him, but he didn't make eye contact. Instead, he shifted slightly in position, his hand moving to his waistband so quickly that she would have missed it if she hadn't been staring directly at him.

Thinking he obviously needed time for whatever he was planning, she glared at Al. Her heart was still pounding, and she was terrified, but somehow the fear seemed a little less overwhelming with the knowledge Gabe was close by.

'It's me you want – or rather you want what I took from you. So, if I give it back, what then? You'll expect me to cry and beg for my life, like I used to? I'm not the same person I was back then, Al. You have no power over me. Not anymore.'

'That is precisely where you're mistaken, Peaches. I have all the power. Your new boyfriend here is injured – he's doing a good job of disguising it to give you hope, but look closely at his shirt – it's soaked in blood. Now I could call my men and request some assistance for him – but let's be honest, that ain't gonna happen. I might be tempted, though, once I've got my ledger back and you safely in my helicopter on the way back home.'

At his words, Paige stared at Gabe more intensely. There was a darker stain down his right arm – he was bleeding. Her breath caught in her throat in shock. Gabe shook his head once at her – not speaking. Just silently telling her he was fine and not to lose focus. It was the nudge she needed.

'I'll tell you where the ledger is, but you have to let him go. Please.'

'No deal – don't know what you see in this chickenshit anyway, he almost cried when my bullet hit him, you know. Besides, I don't need you to tell me where it is – you're going to fucking show me.'

Pointing his gun back toward Gabe, he held it there and roughly grabbed Paige's arm, dragging her to her feet.

'Move, pretty boy – and I'll just kill her right here and now.'

With the arm not trained on Gabe, he rammed his elbow outward, catching Paige in the nose. Pain burst across her face, and blood poured from her nose. She'd almost forgotten how painful it was to have her nose smashed – and it was definitely something she'd rather she never went through again.

Her eyes were streaming, but she ignored them and glanced at Gabe, shaking her head almost imperceptibly.

Mitch was around somewhere – he'll come find Gabe and then they'll both find me. Of this she was certain. A ball of fear settled in her throat, but she swallowed it down, along with a mouthful of blood that made her gag. She stumbled backward in the kitchen toward the rear door.

Reaching it, she steadied herself by holding the frame for a second, trying to see past the tears still filling her eyes. Her whole face throbbed in time with her heart, but despite all the pain, all she could think of was that for once, she wasn't terrified of Al Graham. A hysterical laugh bubbled its way up her throat and escaped from her mouth, and Al lost it completely.

The gun barrel connected with her cheek, sending her careening backward and out of the kitchen door. She lost her balance, landing hard on the splint on her arm. It gave way with a loud crack that echoed round the trees, rapidly followed by the snap of the already weak bone in her arm. It'd barely had time to fuse let alone heal, and intense white agony shot up her arm to her shoulder. She bit down on her lip, trying not to show her pain, knowing it would turn her ex on and make him even more aggressive.

His boot connected with her ribs, and then something barreled into him from the side, knocking him away from her. Paige couldn't help it – she curled into a ball, hot tears streaming down her cheeks, hugging her arm tightly to her chest.

Gabe had no choice but to let him go with Paige – Al's gun was pointed at his head this time; no amount of body armor would be able to stop a bullet to the brain. As soon as Al had moved off toward the door in the kitchen, Gabe pulled the knife from his belt and silently got to his feet. Blood dripped down his right arm – the bullet from Al's gun had hit his shoulder, millimeters from the edge of the body armor. It hadn't exited through his back and was pressing on a nerve – ignoring the sharp tug of pain, he held the knife firmly in his left hand. He was adept at double-handed combat – the same as they all were.

When he heard Paige's hysterical laugh, he knew it would trigger Al into hurting her even more. He was still seconds away when Al's gun connected with Paige's cheek, sending her flying outside. Anger fueled Gabe into action, but even as fast as he ran, he couldn't stop the double crack from echoing round the trees and couldn't stop the boot to the ribs. He could stop anything else, though – his body weight propelled him into Al like a rocket, and the momentum threw them both to the ground, him on top of Al. He heard the gun skitter off into the brush somewhere nearby and knew he had the upper hand. *No underestimating, though, keep it tight.*

Using the knife still held tightly in his hand, he slammed it into Al's shoulder; Al emitted a scream that was more animal-like than human. Al fought back, twisting beneath Gabe, trying to get free.

A gunshot sounded suddenly, and both he and Al paused, unsure of who had fired at who. The area lit up with a bright torch beam, and Gabe saw the dead man on the ground not a meter away, a gaping wound in his chest.

Not one of his – which meant Al was the last one standing.

Al used the distraction to his advantage, flinging his palm upward and connecting with Gabe's chin. His teeth clashed together, and he bit his tongue but still maintained his grip on Al Graham. Without saying a word, he flipped Al onto his front and secured his arms behind his back – it was a move he'd used a hundred times, and it was always effective.

'Cable ties,' he muttered in the direction of Deacon who was approaching to his right. Quickly securing Al's arms with double ties, he left him with Deacon and ran to Paige's side.

'Paige, come on, darlin', untuck those legs and let me see you.' More light flooded the clearing, and he realized Grayson had turned on the powerful lamps hidden around the perimeter.

Gabe's heart seemed to leap into his throat as he saw the blood covering Paige's face and the careful way she was holding her arm.

She tried to turn into his arms but couldn't complete the move without crying out in pain.

'Listen to my voice, Paige. You are safe – Al is not going to hurt you anymore. I need you to uncurl yourself so I can have a look at you. Can you straighten out your legs for me?'

Paige hiccupped, and he knew she'd heard him – she was present. For a second, he'd thought she'd slipped away into her fear like she had in the alley. Slowly, she uncurled her legs and allowed him to gently turn her onto her back. Supporting her, he helped her sit up so the blood from her nose didn't travel down her throat.

'Lean forward a little for me, don't want you choking. Now I know your arm and nose hurt, but are you hurt anywhere else?'

Paige shook her head. 'He kicks like a stuffed mule – I'm fine.'

Gabe saw that she said it through gritted teeth and was really hurting – but he was proud of her for not showing it to Al Graham and saying the words loud enough for him to hear.

'I'll kill you, you fucking bitch. I swear to god, you won't be able to hide from me. I will fucking find you!'

Gabe heard Deacon say 'shut up' then Al howled – whatever Deacon had done shut him up again. *Probably temporarily, but it's better than nothing.*

'Boss, if Paige is okay, I need a hand, please. It's Mitch.' Grayson's voice sounded weak and came from the track entrance.

It reminded Gabe that one of them had set the emergency alert off.

Kneeling beside Grayson, he took in his gray pallor. Even without worrying about Mitch, he could see Grayson needed to help too.

'You're hurt – sit. Now. Lean against the tree. Tell me about Mitch then tell me about you.'

'Mitch took a knife to the leg – femoral artery. I've been applying pressure, but it's still bleeding, and he's passed out. Boss, there's so much blood.'

Gabe heard the fear and desolation in Grayson's voice and, feeling Mitch's neck, he confirmed that Mitch was still alive, though his pulse was thready. He'd lost a lot of blood. Moving down his body, he checked the leg – the blade was still lodged in his thigh near the groin, and whoever had used it had twisted it. Grayson and Deacon had secured a utility belt above the wound tightly – and it had done the job, but the blood was still seeping from Mitch's leg.

As if he knew Gabe was there, he groaned softly.

'It's okay, brother, just stay still. We've got help incoming.'

He'd heard the update from Dave on his earpiece moments before that Lou and Becca were mere minutes away. Dave always handled the comms remotely when he wasn't directly involved in the mission. And Lou was never any good at staying away from the action when the team were in trouble. Gabe found the sound of Dave's voice comforting today.

'Now you, Grayson – where are you hurt?' Gabe tried not to let his guilt or worry come through in his tone – all Grayson and Mitch needed to know was that he was there and that help was coming.

'When we came into the clearing, one guy rammed me with a tree – at least I think that's what it was. Heard a few cracks – definitely some broken ribs, boss. Nothing I can't handle, though – I'm okay. Take care of Mitch.'

'You're not okay – you're bleeding internally judging by the color of your skin. Sit there and do not move. You need to tell me if you start feeling like you're going to pass out, okay?'

'Okay, boss.'

Gabe kept his fingers on Mitch's pulse, concerned when it fluttered against his fingers. The whirr of their all-terrain vehicle (ATV) sounded on the track – it would carry two people out quicker than going on foot, but he wasn't sure Grayson would be okay with that kind of movement, let alone Mitch.

Seconds later, Lou and Becca were in the clearing, jumping off the ATV almost before the engine stopped.

Ignoring his surprise at the fact Lou was with Becca, Gabe said, 'Helo status?' He knew he sounded short, but his worry for Mitch had his temper on the edge.

'On the ground waiting for us two klicks south. The Feds will be there in a few minutes – Dave held off updating them until we knew what was happening. We've given Kyle the location of the cabin, so he'll head in this direction too. Let's get them loaded and on the way back to the helo.'

'No can do – Mitch's femoral is shot, and his pulse is thready. Grayson has internal injuries and broken ribs; Paige has had her arm broken again and has a broken nose. Not sure about Deacon. I need you to do emergency surgery here, Lou, Mitch won't survive the jolts of moving him now.'

Lou's skin paled – it was too soon after Shotgun's death, but he needed her to save Mitch. Lou was the best at field surgery.

'We can't lose anyone else, Lou. Can you do this?'

Her expression hardened, and she knelt without any further acknowledgement and packed her field kit.

'Get the torch held over the wound – I need to see what I'm doing.' Lou's voice was to the point but quiet.

Without speaking, he placed one hand over hers, providing both strength and comfort, which was just enough. She glanced at him and gave him a tight smile, before pushing his hand off – a clear indication she was ready to carry on.

Lou worked methodically, taking each step slowly. Deacon had dragged Al closer, Becca brought Paige to Gabe's side, and both hovered above, wanting to help but not wanting to interfere.

'Becca, I need your thin, piano-player fingers in this wound now – pinch the artery hard above the damage to stop blood flow while I get the clips in place.'

Becca knelt immediately, unintentionally moving Gabe from Mitch's side.

When Grayson suddenly moaned softly and slumped to the side, Gabe left them to it and nodded at Deacon to help him.

Carefully, Gabe opened Grayson's jacket and undid the Velcro fastenings on his armor. Lifting his T-shirt, he could see that Grayson's chest was covered in a large purple-and-black bruise which spread across the left side of his ribs and chest. Gabe gently pressed against the bones, feeling them crunch under his fingers.

Grayson's lips slowly turned blue, and he gasped for breath without managing to breathe much air into his left lung.

'Damn it, his lung has collapsed – I need to reinflate.'

Deacon passed Gabe his field kit, and quickly, Gabe pulled gloves on and ripped open the packet with alcohol wipes in. Working swiftly, he wiped Grayson's chest down. Deacon, anticipating Gabe's needs as if he was doing the necessary himself, had a scalpel unwrapped and in his hand for Gabe to grab within seconds.

Gabe felt his way up Grayson's ribs, and when he got to the point he needed, he pressed the blade against Grayson's skin and cut through the skin and muscle and into the lung. The cut itself wasn't long – only an inch in length, but it was all that was needed.

Deacon handed him a small piece of plastic tubing which Gabe inserted into the cut, pushing firmly to ensure it ended up where it was meant to be. Grayson inhaled with a loud gasp, the cyanosis fading on his lips as he drew in another breath.

Gabe sealed the tube in place then put packing around the tube to hold it still while they moved Grayson.

'Pretty sure he's bleeding internally too, but his breathing is better, and his pulse is strong – we can get him out of here and the hospital can deal with the bleeding unless his condition worsens.' Gabe yanked the gloves off, turning his attention back to Lou and Becca.

Lou finished applying the last bit of glue to the exterior wound on Mitch's leg and added two dressings, one on top of the other.

'It's not the best job in the world, but it should hold until he gets to surgery – his pulse is still weak, but his stats are better than they were.'

Gabe pulled his phone from his pocket and hit 'call' on Kyle's number.

'Kyle, we could do with some backup to help carry the wounded. You'll also need to bring extra men – there's some fatalities, none of my men. We've got Al Graham secured and ready for hand off to the Feds. Is Mason Henderson there?'

'Fair to say he's here and spitting feathers – turns out the Feds don't like other people pissing in what they think is their pond …'

Gabe could hear the wry tone in Kyle's answer even down the phone.

'Put him on the phone, please.'

'Bland – who the hell do you think you are going forward on this without updating us on what was going down before now? Did I just overhear that you've got fatalities? You do know you'll be held accountable? I'm …'

'Mason, shut the fuck up and listen. I already spoke with Assistant Director I'Anson and updated him fully on the situation – as I do with any mission we complete that will involve the FBI. He gave his blessing to let my men deal with the situation and that you would be here as backup – because you're part of his best team, his words. Now I've got three of mine injured and in need of immediate medevac to Perkinsville where I've got a trauma surgeon on standby. You can stand there and bluster needlessly – or you can get here with Kyle and his men, arrest this asshole, and let me get my men to hospital.'

Gabe cut the call off, not willing to entertain anymore conversation with Mason.

'He sounds like a prick,' said Becca with a grin.

'Mason's actually a good guy – he's just pissed not to be updated sooner. I probably should have involved them more – you know how the Feds are about getting credit for the jobs they do.' Gabe gave a tight smile and glanced around at everyone.

'You guys came through, as always. Good job – I know we're not out of the woods yet, literally, with Mitch and Grayson, and we'll cover what we could have done differently in the debrief, but for now know that I appreciate everything you've done. I could not ask for a better team.'

Chapter Twenty-Two

Perkinsville General Hospital

Gabe had paced so much he felt like he'd worn a hole in the floor. Six hours had passed without so much as a doctor peeking their head out of the surgery doors to let him know the condition of Paige and his men, all of whom had been rushed into surgery the second they'd landed. He was almost at breaking point. *Someone has to be able to tell me something!*

He started walking back toward the reception desk, ignoring the glare from the receptionist he'd already bugged one too many times for her liking. He didn't care, though. He wouldn't leave that desk without an update this time.

His team needed the update as much as he did. Lou was sitting in the corner on her own, staring into space. Dave was sitting next to Deacon with his laptop open on the chair beside him. Becca was sitting with Jacko who'd joined them from the house where Mags and the families had been stashed.

It's too much – it's all just too damned much. With Shotgun, then Dave, and now Mitch and Grayson. He couldn't cope with anymore losses, let alone the rest of them. Gabe couldn't change the past, but as strong as his team were, and they *were* strong, the strongest people he knew, in fact, there was only so much people could take. It was Sod's Law that in the first five years, they'd had nothing major impact on them as a business or a team. Then in the last six months, they'd had nothing but trauma and heartache.

The process needs to change. I need to look at a training matrix or something, ensure everyone's skill set is up to par and frequently reassessed. They're all ace on the range and at their job, but maybe some of the stuff we've dealt with might have been able to be handled differently.

Pulling himself from his thoughts, he realized the receptionist was staring at him with an expectant glare on her face.

'Mr. Bland, I've told you four times already that I can't give you any information. Last I checked they were all still in surgery.'

'Please, could you check again? I just want to know what's taking so long. I'm worried.'

Her gaze softened, and he turned on the charm a little more.

'I know I'm being a pain, bothering you when you're obviously busy, but they're like my family. Every last one of them. Would you mind possibly having another check? They were in such bad condition when they arrived.'

'Okay, Mr. Bland, I'll have a look.' She tapped the keys on the keyboard swiftly – probably years of practice allowing her to touch-type – and after a few long seconds, she smiled at him.

'Grayson is out of surgery and in recovery – I can't give any more information on that one. Paige is the same – out of surgery and in recovery. Mitch is still in surgery – I can't say how long it will take. I wish I could.'

Leaning forward and reading her name badge for the fourth time, Gabe gently took the receptionist's hand. 'Thank you, Laura. Honestly, I can't thank you enough.'

Tears filled his eyes as he turned and glanced round at the faces staring back at his own. His team had sat up sharper in their chairs, were awaiting his update, trusting him not to break down. Because they all needed him strong. He'd seen the doctor about his gunshot wound when he'd arrived – only because they wouldn't leave him alone. No sedation, just a quick tug on the bullet and a few stitches. It was nothing. Nothing compared to what his friends were going through.

'So far, so good,' he said. 'Paige and Grayson are out of surgery and in recovery. Mitch is still in surgery, but he's alive. That's all Laura can tell us at the minute.'

It was another two hours before Gabe and the team finally left the hospital. Becca went home with Lou at Gabe's request – she'd seemed even more fragile by the end of the long hospital stretch.

He felt strange, heading back home without Paige in the truck with him – the doctor had advised she'd be staying in for a few days so they could monitor her pain levels and provide relief when needed. She'd needed pins inserting and an arm brace to hold the pins in place. The second break to the bone had caused it to shard. The doctor was confident she'd retain the majority of movement in her arm once it had healed, though had said she had a hard slog ahead of her.

Grayson's internal bleeding had been stopped, and he was also staying in for a short while, more to make sure he didn't tug his stitches. Apparently, the doctor had an inkling that the people on Gabe's team didn't always do as they were told. Gabe had grinned at that comment – plainly the doctor knew them well.

Gabe sighed, his thoughts moving to Mitch. Mitch was alive, but the damage to his leg was extensive – the surgeon had managed to repair the artery as best he could, but there was a lot of muscle and nerve damage that couldn't be addressed straightaway. Mitch needed further surgery, a skin graft, and what sounded like months of physiotherapy. He'd be like a bear with a sore head when Gabe could finally get in to see him tomorrow. Out of everyone on the team, Mitch was the one who hated to be cooped up – he hated being still. Gabe knew it was a knock-on effect from the PTSD he'd suffered since his discharge four years previously. He'd openly told Gabe on numerous occasions that he preferred the stars over his head than a ceiling. This was going to be really tough on him.

Gabe sighed deeply, pulling up the track to his cabin. He turned the truck engine off, pushed the door open, and inhaled one deep breath. He closed his eyes, letting the peace of the cabin wash over him. This, right here, was the reason he'd spent so much on this place. The smell of pine and wood warmed him, his senses taking it all in. He inhaled a long, deep breath. He could smell the water from the nearby lake, and, coming down off the mountains was the scent of snow. Exhaling slowly, he felt some of the tension leave with his breath.

It had been a long week – he was more than ready for a hot shower and a cozy bed.

Shame Paige isn't here to join me ...

He didn't even know if Paige would want to see him again – her case was technically over. He'd broken his own rule of not getting involved personally with a case, but to what end? His feelings were already way past where they should be now the case was coming to a close. What if she didn't feel the same? *That's something you'll never know the answer to unless you talk to her. Is it even fair, though? She's had it so tough – the last thing she needs is to be with me. Trouble follows me around like a bad smell. And she's had more than her fill of evil.*

His mind felt heavier than ever, and with a sigh, he disembarked his truck and made his way inside. *Shower first, worrying later.*

Chapter Twenty-Three

Perkinsville General Hospital

The dawn broke after the team had reconvened at the hospital – they all knew that the FBI would be in the debrief in the office at 9 a.m., and every one of them wanted an update before they went into that meeting. Gabe had merely smiled and shaken his head when he realized everyone was there before him, and he thought he'd been early getting there at 6 a.m.

Dark circles surrounded his eyes, his hair was mussed and uncombed, and he had a five o'clock shadow that was more like a two-day growth – a total indication of his lack of sleep, but no one said anything. They all had the same gray shading under their own eyes, their hair was equally messy, and not one of them had slept all night.

Dave handed Gabe a cup of steaming black coffee. 'The receptionist, Laura, has been very helpful this morning – she's let us invade the staff canteen for a generous donation to the tea fund from our petty cash. Better than the shitty machine coffee at any rate.'

Gabe inhaled the aroma and took a long sip, grateful for its warmth as it made its way down to his stomach. 'Thanks. So, what do we know? Any doctor shown their face yet?'

'Nope. Laura has checked on Grayson and Paige personally – both had an okay night, albeit without much sleep, but that's to be expected. The day doc is starting his rounds at seven a.m., and their ward is the first. She didn't have an update on Mitch per se, just said he's had a comfortable night. I can hack the hospital files if you want a clearer update before you speak to the doc.'

'No, it's fine – whatever their condition, we'll deal with it and be here no matter what.' Lowering his voice, Gabe added, 'How's Lou this morning?'

'Okay, I think – Becca stayed with her overnight. They must have talked because Lou seems to be in a better place today. She's interacting which is a good start.'

'Good. Do me a favor, discreetly contact the shrink that we dealt with when we got back from Iraq seven years ago. Rachael Stones I think her name was. I want everyone booking in for mandatory counselling. Myself included. We'll pay her more than her going rate to prioritize – in fact, if she'll come on board permanently then make her an offer. We could use someone on staff like her.'

'I already sent her an email this morning, figured you'd ask.'

'There's a reason you're my second-in-command, Dave, thank you. Now, it's seven-fifteen a.m. I think that's enough time for the doc to have seen our guys and gal, don't you?'

Paige shifted uncomfortably in the hospital bed. Everyone hated hospitals, but it felt like she'd seen more than her fair share. She hadn't slept well at all – the nurses coming in every two hours to check her blood pressure hadn't helped. Apparently, her pressure had tanked when she'd been brought to the ward from the recovery room. She didn't know what they expected, though. They'd had her under anesthetic while they'd operated, and she always reacted to anesthetic, something she'd told them as they'd wheeled her down, or at least she thought she had.

The fact her arm was inside a metal brace, with pins holding bone in place, the whole thing resting on a pillow left her virtually immobile until the doctors said otherwise, had made for a very uncomfortable and long night. Her body was reacting to the shock by periodically spasming in different areas – it hurt like a mother – and was just exacerbated by the pain in her arm. The nurses kept giving her pain relief, as well as medication for her lupus at Gabe's request. The meds made her space out and then sleep for a bit, but the pain was a constant around that bit of sleep.

And, when they had brought her up to her private room on the ward and managed to stabilize her blood pressure, they'd only let Gabe in for two minutes. He'd been ushered back out quickly with instruction that she needed to rest.

She probably did, but she needed to see Gabe more. She needed to know he was okay – she knew he'd been bleeding, and she'd seen him helping patch up Grayson and Mitch, but then hadn't really seen him since. She'd been too out of it to ask how he was during that brief visit. And the nurses wouldn't give her the cell phone from her bag, just telling her over and over to sleep.

She'd felt herself getting more and more frustrated and was definitely nearing the end of her tether now.

The door opened, and she readied herself to make demands, not something she was accustomed to. Her mouth dropped open when Gabe entered, and any words she was going to say quickly flew from her mind. Her mouth went dry; her heart pounded.

'Hey,' he said softly, crossing the room in three long strides to get to her bedside.

'Hey yourself. You okay?'

'That was going to be my line – how's your arm? Is the pain really bad?'

'Not as bad as some pain but worse than others – I'm okay.' Suddenly remembering he'd been shot, she pushed her back up off the bed and sat up, hissing as pain radiated up her arm into her shoulder. 'You were shot,' she added, her tone almost accusatory.

'I'm fine, lie back on the pillows – it was a scratch. Promise. Only needed a few stitches.'

'I was worried. They only let you in for a minute last night. I didn't know if they were rushing you to surgery or something. Are Mitch and Grayson okay?'

'They'll be fine. Grayson has to stay in a little while yet, Mitch is being moved to a rehab facility in a few days – his recovery will take a bit longer, but he'll get there. The others are in with them now. I popped my head in but I needed to see you. Doc said you'd had a rough night.'

'Well, if they hadn't woken me every two minutes to prod and poke at me, I might have had a less rough one.' Paige pouted, only half joking.

'I'm sorry you got hurt. Rest assured, though, Al Graham will never get his hands on you again. The Feds shipped him out of local law enforcement custody last night. You'll be needed to stand as a witness at court, but from what my FBI contact said, it's a pretty cut-and-dried case. He's going down on charges of assault, attempted homicide, homicide, and god knows what else. It's enough that he'll not see the light of day for a very long time.'

'I should have come forward ages ago. If I'd been braver, none of this would have happened. You wouldn't have been hurt, your men wouldn't have been hurt.'

'Hey, listen, you did what you had to do to survive. You were understandably terrified. That said, I've never been more proud of anyone than I was when you said he kicked like a stuffed mule – his face was a picture. You survived, you kicked ass, and you kept the evidence you had until it was needed. You, Paige Matthews, are exceptionally brave. You got out. And I for one am very glad you did.'

Leaning forward, he gently brushed his lips over hers. Sparks passed between them, and she groaned as his tongue grazed over hers. Her free arm crept up and around his neck, pulling him in even closer, and she kissed him back harder. She squirmed underneath him – the kiss wasn't enough. She felt like it would never be enough. He ignited so much passion in her – passion she'd never known she possessed.

When he drew back, she knew her cheeks were flushed and her eyes were bright – it was the reaction he invoked in her every time. After Al Graham, Paige had never thought she could love again, had definitely sworn off ever feeling that way again, but she couldn't help it with Gabe. There was just something about him that called to her soul.

'Sorry, I know I shouldn't kiss you like that. Not here, hell, not until you're feeling better. And only then if you want me to. Which you might not, I mean, I would totally get it if you didn't. You've been through so much and …'

'Shut up and kiss me again Gabe,' whispered Paige, her hand applying pressure to his neck until he closed in and captured her lips again. 'I'm not going anywhere,' she mumbled against his mouth. 'I don't know how I can be, I'm not sure I understand any of what's happened really, but I do know this: I am in love with you, Gabriel Bland. I have no intention of going anywhere.'

Bland P.I.R office

Gabe took a slow glance round all the people at the table, thankful they were all there, and feeling angry for the people who weren't.

'All right everyone, listen up. I know I said thanks back at the cabin, but you all need to hear what I'm saying. You all did an amazing job yesterday – I have never been so proud to work alongside such a great … family. Cos that's what we are. Each and every one of you came through to help Paige – as you do with every case you work. We will debrief tomorrow. I know you're all prepped for the debrief with Mason and I'Anson right now – any blowback will be on me. Just go in and tell the truth. Like always.

'I do think everyone could use some support at the minute, me included. We all miss Shotgun – what happened to him could easily have been any one of us. But I know one thing – he wouldn't want any one of us sitting around pondering over the what-ifs or let life pass us by. That added to the events of recent days has had us all on edge. Some of you may remember Rachael Stones – she's seen some of us at one point or another. Now she's on the books – everyone will have a sit down with her. It's mandatory. You don't have to tell me or anyone else what you discuss in there, but you will go in and you will open up. We've been closed off as a team since Shotgun died, and I'm including myself in that assessment – it's like none of us are comfortable talking about Shotgun, but he was one of the best. He deserves every word we can say, every thought we can think, and a whole lot more. I know it hurts, but it's time we start dealing with it and not letting it eat us up. Rachael will help with that.'

Gabe half expected groans at the news everyone would be seeing the shrink, but his team nodded slowly. And that made him feel bad for not recognizing earlier that his team might need a friendly ear or shoulder. Contacting Rachael was definitely a good thing.

A knock sounded at the door, and Gabe waited a moment whilst I'Anson and Mason entered.

'We locked the front office door – you shouldn't really leave it open like that when y'all are holed up back here. Doesn't make for good security.' Mason's voice was curt and to the point.

'We watched you pull up in the blue Chevy, straighten your blazer as you stood up, run your hand through your hair, and check your breath by blowing into your left hand before you came in through the door. You stumbled over your feet when you were three feet into the room, mentioned the front door being unlocked to I'Anson, then turned and hit the latch. Still think I have a problem managing the security of *my* office, Mason?'

Mason flushed red. 'You're a jerk, Bland.'

'Yes, I damn well can be. Now, you guys are here to debrief the team, yes? Coffee is brewed in the pot behind you – help yourselves. There are pastries too, if you're hungry. Everyone here will be cooperative and answer any questions you have.'

I'Anson grabbed a cup and immediately poured his coffee – strong and black, just like Gabe took his. Mason poured his and added cream – just as Gabe had known he would.

Sitting back in his chair, Gabe let the debrief begin.

Six days later – Perkinsville General Hospital

'I'm perfectly capable of walking down to the entrance and meeting Gabe there,' Paige huffed at the nurse who was trying her best to coax Paige into the waiting wheelchair.

'I know you are – however, hospital protocol is that until you're handed off to Mr. Bland, then we have a duty of care to ensure you're not at risk. So, the quicker you get in the chair, the sooner I can hand you off to Mr. Bland and you can be on your merry way.' The nurse stared at her pointedly.

Paige sighed, knowing there'd be no other way she'd get out of the hospital room.

'If she's giving you any trouble, ma'am, by all means keep her in longer.' Gabe's drawl from the doorframe had Paige spinning around, her mouth wide open.

'You wouldn't …'

'Try me, darlin'. Do you really think Nurse Constance here can't keep you in here if you're being a pain? Do you think I pull all the strings round here? I managed to spring you out days before the doc wants you to leave on the promise that I'd bring you right back if anything goes wrong. But this here nurse is the boss around here. Everyone knows it's the nurses who keep the hospitals running smoothly. If she says you stay, then you stay.'

Paige glanced at Nurse Constance, a little ashamed she'd never even learned her name in her want to get out of the room quickly.

'I'm sorry. I know I've been … well, let's be honest, I'm a nightmare patient. Please can I go?' Paige dreaded the answer, genuinely a little afraid that Gabe was right and that Constance had some magic way of making her stay. Seven days in hospital was already more than she could bear.

'Sit your ass down in this chair, and I'll happily take you to Mr. Bland's car. He can carry your bags. Last chance, or I'll be contacting the doctor and telling him all about that dizzy spell you're having.'

Paige's mouth had dropped open in shock again. 'I didn't go dizzy … Ohhhh. You mean you'd lie!'

This isn't on – they can't just bully me into getting in the damned wheelchair, can they? She couldn't be sure with the stern look emanating from the nurse in her direction.

'Fine, I'll go down to the entrance in the damned chair. But only because I don't want to be here another minute.'

She knew she sounded like a stroppy teenager. But she'd had enough – enough of being poked and prodded, enough of being woken through the night endless times, enough of the zombie feeling the meds were giving her, and the sooner she could eke herself off those the better. All she wanted was a hot bath, a comfortable bed, and a bit of time to sleep. It wasn't a lot to ask – *well, unless you're Nurse Constance here, apparently. With Gabe supporting her rather than me.*

Scowling, she stuck her tongue out at Gabe, knowing it was churlish but still feeling a tiny bit of satisfaction from the gesture. She gently lowered herself into the wheelchair and waited with as much patience as she could muster, while Nurse Constance instructed Gabe to get the bag with her pajamas in, her medicine bag which was full to the brim, and her purse.

She doesn't even trust me to carry that!

Sulking, she sat silently, refusing to engage even as Nurse Constance pushed her down the corridor, into the elevator, down to the entrance, and waited tolerantly with her whilst Gabe went to get the truck.

Eventually, though, she realized she was being ridiculous.

'I'm sorry for being a bad patient,' she said softly, turning her head toward Nurse Constance who'd stayed at the back of the chair, probably to avoid looking at her patient's grumpy face to be fair.

'You're not a bad patient, you just need to learn that, sometimes, we all need a little help. You make sure you let that man of yours know when you can't manage. Recovery is far easier when you've got someone like him by your side. Did you know he rang every morning, seven a.m. on the dot, always ensuring you were going to be seen by the doc and had had a good night. He's put money in the nurses' saving fund which will get split down and shared at the end of the year. And he's bought us two coffee machines and is supplying the ward refreshments for a while. It's made life a little easier for all of us. He is a really nice guy, and what a catch. You're very lucky, Miss Matthews, he loves you very much.'

Paige tried to swallow the lump in her throat at Nurse Constance's words. She was right – he was a total catch. And all she'd done was make his life harder and gripe at him constantly that she didn't want to be in the hospital.

'I'm really very sorry. I promise if I'm ever in hospital again, I'll do better. You do an amazing job – you deserve better than people like me being a pain.'

'Good enough. Now here's your man. Let's get you loaded and belted in safely. That bubble on your arm needs to stay on – it stops you catching the metal. If you catch it and don't realize, it'll hurt like a mother, so please be careful. Mr. Bland has agreed to bring you back in every few days so we can check your arm and make sure that there's no problems.'

Constance carefully got her comfortable in the passenger seat next to Gabe and, pushing him gently out of the way, she clambered into the driver's side and secured Paige's seat belt, making sure the inflatable arm bubble was secure in the sling and against Paige's stomach. She clambered back out of the car and let Gabe sit in and secure himself with the seat belt.

'Okay, Mr. Bland, she's ready to go. Please be careful with that arm – and make sure she is too. The pins will keep everything in place and allow it to heal, but as you were told, there is a great risk of infection. The only reason the doctor agreed to let her go home was because of your military background – you know what to look out for infection wise. Bring her back in three days – ten a.m. sharp. And make sure she sleeps – the more she can sleep and be relaxed, the faster she will heal. I've plugged my number into her cell. If you have any concerns or questions at all, please just call me. It's always turned on.'

'Thank you, Constance. I'm very grateful for you all taking care of my girl, and my men so well. If there's ever anything you need, please contact me. Okay?'

'Thank you, Mr. Bland.'

Constance patted his hand then closed the door firmly.

Gabe glanced over at Paige once he was out of Perkinsville and on the road leading back to Rhododendron. He had planned to pop to the office first to grab some files, but she'd fallen asleep the minute he'd pulled away from the hospital, and now all he could think of was getting her back to the cabin.

Indicating, he took a turning that was a shortcut home via the back roads. *Home – funny, it was my home for so long and now she's included in that word almost naturally. I can't imagine home without her in it.*

Knowing she was exhausted and wouldn't wake, he used the steering wheel controls to call Dave.

'Hey, Dave, can you do me a favor. Ping me over the files for the Durrant case, as well as the prelim photos for the senator visit next month. I've got Paige in the car, and she's exhausted – she's asleep already. I'll work from home for today. Have we had anything through from Mason yet? I know he was going to keep us updated on his progress.'

'Yeah, he's got the court date set. Graham is remanded without any chance of bail. They've considered him a flight risk, so that's good news for us. Apparently, when I'Anson's men searched his home, they found a pregnant woman handcuffed in the bedroom. She wouldn't say anything at first, but when they told her he's going down for a long time, she's started singing like a canary. From Mason's tone, I think she sounds a bit flaky, but that's his problem not ours. Mason did say they need Paige's written statement as soon as possible. I've put the lawyers on standby as I figured you'd want ours to represent her.'

'I don't know what I'd do without you, brother.'

'You'd flounder and go bust,' said Dave wryly.

Gabe smiled in response even though Dave couldn't see him.

'I'll send the files over – just make sure Paige is okay. Paul is heading to your cabin later with some of his famous stew, said Paige needs a bit of feeding up and that no one can resist the stew. I'll come with him. I'll bring the photos for the senator visit then. I know you're better in paper than on the screen.'

'I know I can't resist the stew – hope he's making plenty for me too,' replied Gabe, his mouth already watering. Paul's stew was legendary. He had yet to find out the recipe, and Paul was very closemouthed about it.

'Double batch already cooking. He knows fine well you can't resist it either. Lou and Becca were on about coming through also – they've both had their first session with Doc Stones, pretty sure they want to talk to you about it. They both seem okay, though. Becca's staying with Lou for a bit. Her lease was up on that poky flat, so Lou's invited her to stay till she finds something else.'

'Great, it'll do them both good to have a bit of female company. I sometimes forget the team isn't all men – they fit in so well as one of the guys that you just kinda forget.'

'Definitely. Right, I've got Kyle walking up to the front door of the office on the cameras, boss. I'll see you tonight.'

Epilogue

Three months later – Oregon Federal Court

Paige stared at Al Graham silently from her seat. He was skinnier than she remembered, the orange jumpsuit doing nothing for his complexion. He also looked afraid – it was as if he knew something in advance of the judge's decision which was coming up. *Maybe he does – he always seemed to be two steps ahead when we were together.* But there was also something about him that was … pathetic. He was a beaten man, sitting there in the dock waiting on the judge.

Gabe's hand tightened slightly on hers, his action asking if she was okay without speaking. She squeezed back gently, telling him she was. Whatever hold Al Graham had once held over her was gone. Now all she felt was disdain – his punishment would be all he deserved and more. The jury had taken all of an hour to make their unanimous decision of guilty. All that was left now was the sentencing. Then she could walk away and forget all about the man who had wanted her dead.

The judge's quiet tone filled the room; everyone was on the edge of their seats as the sentence was read out. 'The guilty verdict was unanimous – never before have I seen a jury come to such a decision so quickly, and that tells me that they see in you what I see, Mr. Graham. You have no remorse for your actions, you fully intended to carry out harm to Miss Robson as you did with Mr. Donnington – you put her in fear of her life. Not to mention your current partner, Kim O'Toole – you had a pregnant woman handcuffed to a bedframe after beating her. You are a very dangerous man, Mr. Graham, and it would be remiss of me not to reflect that when I look at sentencing you. After careful consideration, I hereby sentence you to life in prison – with a minimum sentence served of twenty-three years before you can be considered for parole.'

The room erupted into shouts and claps, but Paige did neither. She was happy with the ruling – if happy was a word one used when considering the misfortune of another – but she also felt numb. As if this was something so long in arriving that it was almost anticlimactic. She watched as Al Graham got to his feet and shuffled forward at the request of the guard. The court deputy had explained before they went in that if found guilty, he'd be taken to the court cells and held there for transport to a maximum security prison.

When a loud crack echoed around the room, there was confusion – people stared around at each other, not sure initially what the noise was.

The confusion lasted less than a couple of seconds. When Al Graham fell forward to the floor, his face now obscured by the damage from a bullet, chaos erupted. People screamed; chairs were kicked out of the way as everyone fled for the court doors.

Gabe gripped her hand tightly and dragged her the opposite way. For just a second, Paige hesitated, panic taking over her.

'No,' said Gabe firmly, 'this way.'

He pulled her hand again, even more firmly, and ushered her toward the doors at the back that led to the judge's chambers. Mason was already there and holding it open, waiting for Gabe.

'Did you see the shooter?' Mason barked. He had his gun drawn, glancing back at the panicked room.

'Came from the back right-hand corner of the room – that's all I can tell you. Back right was where the press were sitting – pretty easy to smuggle a gun in among cameras and hardware if you know what you're doing.'

'Exactly what I thought. My guys are detaining everyone leaving – everyone will be questioned. Including the press.'

'Include the guards in that – the one leading Graham out didn't flinch when the shot went off, didn't even wonder why Graham fell forward. Gut instinct says he knew it was going to happen.'

'I said to I'Anson just this morning that something like this would happen. When you find out Al Graham is but a small cog in a very big wheel, someone out there is going to be afraid he'll open his mouth and say the wrong thing to the right person. I didn't think it would be at the courthouse, though – we both figured the hit would happen once he was behind the prison walls.'

'It would have been easier within the prison, but maybe whoever is responsible couldn't risk Graham getting that far. Have you found anything out about whoever was running his op?'

'No, not yet. The powers that be are sitting with that one. There's obvious links to human and drug trafficking, but you'll know how tenuous those links are without concrete evidence. At the minute, all we have is what was recorded in the journal. Our guys cracked Graham's code, but what's written is vague and makes reference to another document –

possibly another journal of some kind. We're tearing the shipping company offices apart, but I can't see Al Graham being dumb enough to keep a second journal near him.'

'He has a safe-deposit box, you know?' Paige had been doing her best to follow the conversation, as shocking to her as it was. She'd never thought for one second that Al Graham would have been tied to someone even worse than he had been.

'He does?' Both Mason and Gabe turned toward her and spoke at the same time.

'I don't know much about it, it wasn't something he told me about specifically. I remember when Diana …' She paused, taking a deep breath. 'When Diana died, Al mentioned to George something about getting money from the safe-deposit box – it must have been relatively close to home because George went and returned within an hour. I don't remember anything other than that. I'd forgotten about it totally until you were just talking there.'

Mason walked off and started talking into his cell phone.

'Sorry, I feel like somehow I should have known to tell you about that before now.' Paige still had hold of Gabe's hand as she spoke, realizing suddenly she'd been gripping him as tight as if she'd been on a white-knuckle ride. She flexed her fingers, releasing some of the grip.

'No need to apologize – sometimes memories need a trigger. That was a stressful time for you – your mind will have blocked a lot from back then. How you doing anyway? You okay? It's never easy seeing someone die in front of you.'

His thumb drew concentric circles on the palm of her hand – it helped, and her heart rate and breathing slowed.

'I'm okay – I think. I didn't really register what had happened at first. It was all a bit … surreal. I think that after everything he did, to me, to other people, well, I can't say I'm sorry he's dead.'

Paige shuddered, and Gabe pulled her into his chest. She inhaled a deep breath and lay her head on his chest. She'd never felt as safe as she did when she was with Gabe. They'd fallen into the comfortable relationship zone really easily, and it seemed like he'd always been around. He seemed to know instinctively when she needed something from him, whether it was his strength like now, or passion-igniting flames like earlier that morning. She didn't want to imagine life without him by her side.

Mason headed over to them, indicating they follow him back through a door into a corridor.

'You guys can head off, we've got everything covered here. Looks like one of the cameramen had the gun mounted inside his lens – he's been read his rights and is already headed downtown. All seems a little too easy if you ask me, and in no way do I believe for one second it'll be as open and shut as that, but they have him dead to rights, and he's being compliant so far. I'll keep you updated, Bland.'

'Okay, no problem. If you or I'Anson need anything from us, you've got my number.'

Mason nodded then turned and left.

'You up for visiting Mitch at the rehab center or would you like me to drop you off to see Mags?'

'Mags, please. I think I need to tell her about the court case, and also she mentioned she's got a new intake coming in today. I might be able to help out with that. Please give Mitch my best, though, I know how tough he's finding rehab. They really did a number on his leg. It's never easy for anyone getting over injury, but when I saw him last week, he seemed really down and frustrated. Tell him I'll bake and bring him some goodies tomorrow. Won't help the rehab, but a bit of sweet goodness never did anyone any harm.'

'Make sure to save some for me. You know how I love your baking.'

Paige leaned in and brushed his lips with her own. 'I know you like things sweet, Mr. Bland. It's one of the things I love about you.'

Gabe held her even closer and deepened the kiss a little, eliciting a soft moan against his mouth. She loved how her body reacted to his touch. Her eyes fluttered open in confusion as he stepped back, but it was only fleeting. He tucked her into his side with slight pressure of his fingers at her hips and said, 'We need to stop that, otherwise we'll end up at home, and neither of us will be doing the other stuff we need to do today.'

Gabe opened the door to the rehab facility, gave the receptionist a quiet nod, and she waved him through the double doors that led to the rehabilitation rooms. He already knew Mitch would be in the gym – his physiotherapist had spoken to him the day before, expressing concern that Mitch was trying to go too fast and that he might injure himself further.

Gabe frowned. He had a fight on his hands trying to get Mitch to slow down. If he didn't his recovery would take even longer. The knife that had stabbed him in the leg was a hunting knife – serrated on one side and thick in width. When it had been twisted, it had nicked the femoral artery in Mitch's leg and caused a substantial amount of muscular, nerve, and tendon damage. Three surgeries later, including a skin graft, and Mitch was back at the rehabilitation center to do strength exercises and work on getting himself back up to his normal fitness level. The surgeon had said he was lucky to walk again. The knife blade had definitely done its job – a mere two millimeters to the left, and the artery would have been more than nicked. Mitch would likely have bled out in the woods, and they'd have lost another team member.

This was the reason it was so important for Mitch to take it easy and take his time recovering. The team was just starting to come to terms with losing Shotgun – the thought alone of losing Mitch as well had knocked them all. Getting him fit and well would impact on everyone. No one was invincible, but equally they needed the win – they needed to know people came back from such severe injuries.

Opening the double doors into the gym, he paused, and his mouth dropped open a little.

Mitch was leaning heavily on the parallel walking bars; his bad leg was offset backward, as if he'd taken a step then left it there on purpose. And he was all but shouting– a bad sign judging by the red face of this therapist as he aimed the tirade of abuse in his direction.

'… if you'd shut the fuck up and let me do the rounds when I wanted to, I wouldn't still be here. Some fucking therapist you are – barely twenty and trying to tell me how to fucking walk? Get the fuck out of my sight. Where's Walter, he gets that I need to push myself to heal. I want out of this hellhole.'

Gabe marched over at that point. It didn't matter how much pain Mitch was in, or how badly he wanted out of rehab, he wasn't ready to be. And Aiden shouldn't be putting up with crap like that from anyone, let alone one of his team.

'Aiden, go take a break. Leave me here with this stubborn ass of a team member.'

'If you're here to bitch at me that I'm going too fast and I'll end up worse off, you might as well get the hell out as well, Gabe. I'm not in the fucking mood.'

'Yes, you're definitely in a fucking mood, Mitch. I've never seen you like this, brother. Talk to me.'

'Three fucking months, Gabe, three months and I still need the crutch to walk. It's taking too long – I need to be back to full strength. You've already had to cover me for three months – and there's too many fucking walls in this place, man. I need trees, and stars above my head at night. I can't cope with being cooped up in here anymore, everyone always looking at me, talking to me, hell, wanting me to talk to them. I've had e-fucking-nough, Gabe.'

'Mitch, I get that you're finding it tough, you know I do. Hell, the whole team does – not one of us likes being out of action or injured. But cursing at the therapists who're only trying to help you, well, it's downright childish. You're here to get back to full par without doing yourself more harm than good. Three months is nothing – to be where you are after that injury and walking at all is a bloody miracle if you ask me. Yes, it'll take a bit longer, but unless you want to end up on crutches your whole life, and hurting to boot, you'll bloody well do it and stop acting like such a whiny brat.'

Mitch stilled, glaring at Gabe.

'Whiny brat? That's what you think I'm doing? Fuck you, Gabe.'

Mitch tried to spin using the balance bar for support and swung his fist at Gabe's face. Gabe stepped to the side, and Mitch's blow failed to connect, the motion knocking him off balance. He pitched face-first over the balance bar and crashed to the floor with a thump.

Gabe immediately rushed to his side and stuck his hand out to help Mitch up, but Mitch swiped Gabe's hand away.

'I'll do it my-fucking-self. Don't need help from you or anyone else. I'm done. Get the fuck away from me.'

'Mitch, come on. I didn't mean for you to fall – I just meant …'

'I know what you meant, for me to stop acting like a brat, right? Well, how's this for being a brat – fuck you, Gabe. Fuck you and your job. Find another tracker. One who can fucking walk.'

'Resignation not accepted.' Gabe's voice was stern as he spoke. Without saying anything else, he turned on his heel and stormed out of the room. It would be unwise to push Mitch any further at that point, and Gabe knew it.

Once the gym doors closed behind him, he noticed Aiden beside the wall, knowing full well he'd overheard the exchange.

'Leave him on the floor for a bit – don't rush in and help him up. And don't take that shit from him. He swears at you like that again, refuse to engage and walk away. If the point comes when he wants to discharge himself against recommendations, let me know, but don't try and stop him. He's as hard-headed as they come. Sometimes men like him need to be left to figure things out for themselves. He doesn't like accepting help. If he goes off on his own, he'll soon realize just how much he needs it, if that makes sense.'

Aiden nodded. 'That's exactly what Walter says – Walter's ex-army, he pushes Mitch beyond his limits, but then Mitch regresses a little and has to fight again when his muscles tense or seize up. It causes the temper tantrums like today because he's in pain and fighting against it. I totally get what you're saying, though. I'll leave him be for a bit. Walter is due in in ten minutes or so anyway, so when he gets in, I'll have him come help me get Mitch up if he hasn't managed it himself – he'll have cooled down by then, I reckon.'

'Good plan. Keep me updated on his situation.'

'Will do.'

Gabe left the building, wondering momentarily whether speaking to Mitch so candidly was the best option. He had no intention of accepting Mitch's clipped resignation, but it was obvious his friend needed some time to push past what he was going through – and a bit of space was sometimes the best bet.

Hopping into the truck, he sat his hands on the steering wheel for a minute, letting his eyes fill up and not feeling embarrassed as one small tear escaped his eye. His team were the best. He shouldn't feel guilty or responsible when there was an injury – but he did. They were *his* team – he was the boss. They came to work trusting him, and the processes he put in place to protect them. When those processes failed, it was ultimately his responsibility.

Sighing deeply, he rubbed his eyes clear, started the engine, and drove out of the hospital car park.

Home – that was where he needed to be now. Home with Paige.

THE END

Printed in Great Britain
by Amazon